NO MERCY

BLACK OPS MMA BOOK 1

D.M. DAVIS

EVERYDAY
HEROES

NO MERCY
Black Ops MMA Series by D.M. Davis

ISBN: 978-1-7354490-0-5

Published by D.M. Davis

www.dmckdavis.com
Cover Design by D.M. Davis
Cover Photo by DepositPhotos
Editing by Tamara Mataya
Proofreading by Mountains Wanted Publishing & Indie Author Services
Formatting by Champagne Book Design

This book is a work of fiction. Names, characters, places, and incidents are either the product of the author's imagination or are used fictitiously.

The octagonal competition mat and fenced-in design are registered trademarks and/or trade dress of Zuffa, LLC.

This story contains mature themes, strong language, and sexual situations. It is intended for adult readers.

INTRODUCTION

Dear Reader,

Welcome to the Everyday Heroes World!

I'm so excited you've picked up this book! **No Mercy** is a book based on the world I created in my *USA Today* bestselling Everyday Heroes Series. While I may be finished writing this series (*for now*), various authors have signed on to keep them going. They will be bringing you all-new stories in the world you know while allowing you to revisit the characters you love.

This book is entirely the work of the author who wrote it. While I allowed them to use the world I created and may have assisted in some of the plotting, I took no part in the writing or editing of the story. All praise can be directed their way.

I truly hope you enjoy **No Mercy**. If you're interested in finding more authors who have written in the KB Worlds, you can visit www.kb-worlds.com.

Thank you for supporting the writers in this project and me.
Happy Reading,
K. Bromberg

ABOUT THE BOOK

When it comes to protecting his angel, he has *no mercy*.

Gabriel:
The first time I saw her, she made my pulse dance to a rhythm that matched the sway of her hips.
The second time I saw her, she was in the arms of my best friend.
That broken, rusty organ in my chest hasn't beaten since.
Blood doesn't run through these veins. It's pure, unleaded determination.
I've fought my whole life. For safety. For food. For my family.
Five years later, I'm fighting for my position in the MMA world.
No distractions.
Only, my Angel needs me, and that tin can behind my ribs found its beat again.

Francesca:
Gabriel "No Mercy" Stone earned his fight name long before he entered the octagon.
He's been a thorn in my side for years.
He takes pleasure in proving his nickname to me at every turn.
He's relentless. He's heartless.
Until one day he's not.
It took the worst day of my life for Gabriel to show me mercy.
Broken and afraid, I let him piece me back together.
He offers me everything yet promises nothing.

When a man shows he has *no mercy*, you should believe him.

PLAYLIST

So Hott by Kid Rock

Tennessee Whiskey by Chris Stapleton

Bad Guy by Billie Eilish

Way Down We Go by Kaleo

Lovely by Billie Eilish

The Chain by The Highway Women

Ain't No Rest for the Wicked by Cage The Elephant

Falling Like The Stars by James Arthur

My Heart Is Open by Maroon 5 Featuring Gwen Stefani

Mercy by Brett Young

When The Party's Over by Billie Eilish

Find My Way Back by Cody Fry

Can't Go On Without You by Kaleo

Mercy by Dave Mathews Band

Don't Give Up On Me by Andy Grammer

One by Ed Sheeran

Gabriel "No Mercy" Stone's fight entrance songs:

Bawitdaba by Kid Rock

Cowboy by Kid Rock

DEDICATION

May you find someone who shows you NO MERCY
when it comes to loving you.

"Mercy is granted not earned."

GABRIEL "NO MERCY" STONE

NO MERCY

BLACK OPS MMA BOOK 1

CHAPTER 1

GABRIEL "NO MERCY" STONE

THE WORLD SHIFTS WHEN SHE'S NEAR. I CAN'T see her. I can't hear her, but I sure as fuck *feel* her. And I don't mean the blonde pushing her tits into my side, hoping for a ride on my cock.

We've been in Sunnyville for months. I've had my taste of the local pussy. It's good; it's clean and about ten shades of slut lighter than Vegas. But this chick grinding on my thigh has me feeling like I need a sanitizing shower. I've done nothing to encourage her, except maybe breathe and ignore the fact she exists. She's made her rounds with the guys. I'm guessing they've had their fill, and she's set her tits on me. She's feeling brave. My *I've-got-no-fucks-to-give* stare hasn't scared her off. Yet. But she's shit out of luck.

The jukebox in the corner that's been blaring since the band went on break switches tunes. I know without even looking who selected *that* song. Who's dancing in front of that damn box like it can make her deepest desires come true. I swivel in my chair, my dead eyes landing on her like the sway of her hips, the tilt of her chin, and the curve of her ass isn't a siren song to my cock and creates an ache I'll never understand in the middle of my chest.

She's picked *that* fucking song, but all I hear when I look at her is "So Hott" by Kid Rock, pounding out a rhythm, making me want to fuck her like I'll never see her again.

Francesca fucking Angelique—Frankie to her friends—the bane of my existence and my best friend's woman. My best. Fucking. Friend. Yeah, you get the idea. I'm royally screwed and not in the pleasurable *getting-my-rocks-off* kinda way.

Her raven black hair cascades down her back, sweeping across her ass as she sways back and forth, lost in the words of "Tennessee Whiskey." I feel every syllable she whispers to the heavens like a prayer that seems to fall on deaf ears and stream down her hotter-than-hell body to puddle at her feet like used dreams that have been reheated to death. For a woman who's supposed to be in love with my best bud, Austin, she sure as shit looks like heartache and broken promises.

And to stoke the flames of my own personal hell, the words are *mine*. The words I would say to her every fucking day if she were my woman. I would never let her dance alone looking lost and vulnerable in such a public display of despair. If she were mine, I'd grab her ass, pull her close, and tell her with my body and my mouth how adored she is—how perfect she is.

She's my hell on Earth. My temptress. My Angel. It's even in her fucking name *Angel*-ique.

Does she know what she means to me? No. Fuck, no.

She thinks I'm an ass, and I work every day to prove her right.

"How 'bout you and I get out of here, Gabe?" Tits to my left has the nerve to butcher my name while stroking my cock through my jeans. She thinks my hard on is for her. I wish it were.

"It's Gabriel." My eyes dart from Frankie to the guy approaching her. She's oblivious, still dancing to her damn song, and he's ready to pounce. "Austin."

Like the command it is, his head snaps up. His eyes on me, I tersely nod toward the jukebox.

Austin lazily scans the situation and shrugs. "She's fine." He downs his beer.

The fuck? "Man up. Your woman needs you." I stand as the asshat, looking to lose a limb, closes in on Frankie.

Austin rises to his feet slower than molasses, his jaw taut, his teeth clenched. "I said she's fucking fine." He shoulders past me. "Mind your own damn business, Stone."

I don't even bother to see where he's going. All I know is he's not heading toward Frankie. Slipping out of Blonde Tit's hold, my six-and-a-half-foot frame covers the distance from the bar to the jukebox in mere steps.

"Beat it," I growl at the predator seeking a Frankie-meal. I slip my hand around her waist. "She's taken." Just not by me.

I wish death upon his dick, and I swear I can hear it shrivel as he squeaks some excuse and toddles off.

"Gabriel?" My Angel with the wolf-gray eyes frowns up at me.

The pang in my chest deepens. I take a second to revel in the feel of her in my arms against my chest. A moment is all I get, all I deserve, before my asshole ways make a stand. "You can't dance like slut meat and expect not to attract flies, Francesca."

Hurt flashes in her eyes before she covers it with a scowl. "What does that make you?" She pushes me away like she could if I didn't let her. I tower over her by a foot or more, but her backbone makes her deceptively taller. "And don't call me that." Her anger slips. She hates that I don't call her Frankie—at least to her face. It's another wall I've erected to keep her safe from the likes of me.

I ignore the latter. "An asshole."

She laughs. The sound has my cock twitching. I sneer my regret, holding the wall.

"That's for damn sure." She lifts to her tiptoes, leaning in, giving my chest a push. "I can take care of myself."

Her scent fills my nostrils, and I can't help the deep breath I suck in to selfishly capture it all as I step back. "Clearly."

With a brow raise and a quick study of my face, she looks for proof that I'm not the asshole I appear to be.

Keep looking, Angel. You may find it. My heart pounds as I hold my breath, waiting for her to see past my walls to my true feelings. I want her to know as much as I don't.

Thankfully she doesn't. She elbows past me with a brisk, "Goodnight."

I let out the breath—the scent of her—I was holding.

Asshole in full force. *Check.*

I find the blonde occupying my chair at the bar. I give her a once-over, noting my cock is still hard. I might as well use it. "You coming?" I don't even give her a second glance before heading for the door.

"God, I hope so," she pipes up, following me.

"God's got nothing to do with it." I slam through the door and welcome the clean air as it washes Frankie from me.

Now, if I could only fuck Blondie hard enough to knock my Angel from my thoughts…

CHAPTER 2

FRANCESCA "FRANKIE" ANGELIQUE

I PLAY MY SONG, PRAYING IT'LL ENTICE AUSTIN TO come to me. To dance with me like he used to. I can nearly feel his touch. How he used to hold me. How he used to love me.

"It'll be different. Better." Austin's soon-to-be broken promise plays in my head with the vision of him begging me with his brown eyes to believe him. To trust him.

That was two months ago.

I sway a little harder, tip my head back a little farther, and sing the words I wish were his—hot and heavy in my ear—telling me how warm, smooth, and sweet I am compared to the liquors in my song.

My peripherals catch him at the bar, laughing like I haven't heard in a long time with his asshole of a best friend, Gabriel.

The sound rings in my bones, knocking hope free.

We moved to Sunnyville two months ago. It's been two months of long days and lonely nights. Two months of lies, absence, running around smelling of booze and women who aren't me. I squeeze my eyes tighter to stop the traitorous tears burning the back of my them.

I will not cry! I. Don't. Cry.

It wasn't always like this. *He* wasn't always like this. I've been in love with Austin since we were fourteen. He said he fell hard and fast for me, but he couldn't have fallen faster than I did. It only took one heated glance, one mischievous smile, one rough *hey* for me to know my world was about to change. I didn't know if the change would be good or bad, but I knew it would be irreparably life-altering.

I wasn't wrong.

Austin was my first boyfriend, my first love, my first everything. I was *his* first everything too. He promised me the world, and he delivered. It was a fairytale love story for eight years. We were high school sweethearts. Voted most likely to marry and live happily ever after.

I wanted that.

I *needed* that. Austin promised he'd deliver my HEA. We were on track, heading for marriage, a family, our forever after. Until we weren't.

The blonde nearly sitting on Gabriel's lap brings my doubts to the surface. She rubs against him like a cat in heat. I've seen her before but never with him. She's a ring-chaser. I can spot 'em a mile away. His frigid demeanor doesn't seem to cool her down in the least. If he rejects her, I know it's only a matter of time before she moves on to Austin.

He wouldn't, would he? *Has* he?

My dance falls on Austin's deaf ears and blind eyes. The only heat I feel is from the stone-cold stare of Gabriel. I prayed my boyfriend would be the one to notice me, not the resident asshole in my life. Though, I would have to say Austin is nearing the lead in that fateful race.

It all changed a year ago. He injured his back in a car accident, one that sidetracked his training and jeopardized his MMA standing. Luckily, he was in fantastic shape—thanks to said training. He's made a full recovery with the help of his team and physical therapy. All should be good. But it's not.

He's still angry, distant, and absentminded. I can't seem to do anything right. The harder I try, the angrier he becomes. It's like my effort pisses him off, like he wants me to give up, give in, and walk away.

I did. Once.

He came after me. Begged me to come back. The Black Ops MMA team was moving their training to a small town out of the spotlight and the ring-chasers to focus on their goal of taking the championship in every weight class. Austin promised things would be different. Better. If I'd just come with him.

I believed him, for in those pleading brown eyes I spotted the man-boy I fell in love with. The man who knows me like no one else has ever cared to. He's my family. My only family.

Blocking them out, turning back to the jukebox, my hands splay across its cool glass, dancing like it's an attentive dance partner. Its words meant only for me. Its attention focused solely on me.

I flip my hair and bite my lip. This is my song. My dance.

Lost in the words, the fantasy in my head, I barely startle when a warm hand snakes around my waist seconds before I'm pulled into the heat of a hard body. My man came for me. But something's off.

All hope of Austin joining me on the dance floor is ripped away by Gabriel's evil, sexy voice. "She's taken," he growls over my shoulder at some stranger who looks ready to pee his Wranglers.

It's all downhill from there. A toboggan ride to hell, delivered by the devil himself. Terse words from Gabriel "No Mercy" Stone—the king of the mixed martial arts team Austin fights for and I work with as a physical therapist—has me flinching, putting on my big girl panties and buckling up for the rough ride. Mercy is not something I can ever expect from Gabriel. He fights me with words just as fiercely as he fights in the ring with every punch, kick, and chokehold.

He takes me down emotionally in no time flat. It's no surprise. I hide it well, but I'm no match for a man like Gabriel. I can barely hold my own with Austin, and we've had eight glorious years together. I've known Gabriel for five of those years. He was all smiles and sexy glances until he found out I was with Austin. Ever since, it's been a war of words and looks that could kill.

It wouldn't be so bad, if I wasn't shamefully attracted to him. Despite how Gabriel treats me, there's a connection I have a hard time ignoring.

And to top it off, Austin has turned into his mini-me, spawn of the devil, in the last year. I can't escape Gabriel or his influence over my life.

Yeah, I'm an idiot. It's time to throw in the towel. A girl can only take so much. I'm resilient, but I'm not stupid. *So why am I acting like it?* I should just leave, and I don't mean the bar. I mean Sunnyville. I should head home to Vegas, though it doesn't feel like home anymore. Austin was my home, my sanctuary. Wherever he was, I was home.

Now, I feel homeless even in his arms—which I rarely find myself in.

I'm tappin' out.

I elbow my way past Gabriel with a terse "Goodnight." My mind is already moving on from Gabriel's beatdown to plans to end things with Austin.

That is, until the voice of the man my heart bleeds for fills my ears, and his hand slips into mine. "Let's go home." Austin says it like he knows where home is, like I'm as much his home as he used to be mine.

"Don't do me any favors." The bite of my hurt stings my tongue as it leaves my mouth.

"Don't be like that." He squeezes me from behind, wraps me in his arms. "I'm sorry, Ang."

I go weak in the knees at the sound of his love-name for me. *Ang.* I haven't heard it in weeks, maybe months.

He nibbles my ear. "Let me make it up to you."

It's been so long. I don't even know where to begin.

Apparently, he does.

We barely make it through the apartment door before I'm stripped of my clothes, my ass is slapped, and I'm bent over the couch. There are no words of love, only dirty, filthy talk, making me hot and him hard. It's been too long. His attention has been anything but affectionate, loving, or intimate.

His moan as he probes my ass has me clenching with want.

"I want you here, Ang. I need to fill you up. Remind you who you belong to." His alpha talk has my pussy dripping.

I'm not ashamed. We've been together too long to find much taboo in the bedroom. Am I disappointed he didn't lay me down on the bed and make tender love to me? Maybe a little. The girly girl in me wants to be worshipped. The dirty girl wants to be ravaged.

"You want that, don't you, baby?" His fingers find my arousal coating my thighs as proof enough. "Yeah, you do." He enters me a digit at a time, warming me up for his cock. "You're my dirty girl, aren't you?"

My head is fuzzy with need, and my body is begging for the only man I've ever loved. The only man who's ever touched me. Easy or hard. It's only ever been Austin.

At first, it feels like making love as he enters me slowly, tenderly, waiting for me to adjust, to beg for more.

"You're so hot, Ang." He slaps my butt, gripping my hips, sliding his cock in deeper. "God, I've always loved your ass." He covers my back with kisses, pulls my hair aside to kiss my mouth before standing up straight.

He rams into me, hard and deep, his hands gripping my hips like handles. His words feel like love, his touch a soothing balm to my cracked heart and broken promises. I want this. This intensity. I want him to love me like he used to—or love me all new. But love me either way.

Desperate and starving for his attention, I push back, giving as good as I'm getting. His returning groans tingle up my back, making me shudder and my skin prick with goosebumps.

He plays my clit like a man who knows how to get me off. He does. He's perfected it. As if his touch wasn't enough, his command sends me sailing, "Come."

I do. Toes curl, eyes shut, back arches, and a scream on my lips as my release shoots through me hard, fast, and devastating with each tremble, each thrust as he continues to move.

"Fuck, you squeeze me so fucking good," he growls, pounding into me, grabbing my forearms. He lifts me off the couch, using me as leverage as wordless sounds fly out of his mouth in rapid fire.

Captured in his grasp, I'm at his mercy, my body wrung out from my orgasm but building again as the recipient of his rapturous enjoyment of our joining. It's been so long, but it's so good. He's close, and I'm not far behind, his cock hitting me in places that drive me wild.

When I come for the second time, starbursts erupt before my eyes. His cries of pleasure mix with mine as he pounds his release into me. "I've had better pussy, but never better ass. One last time."

Has he been cheating on me? "One last...better...? Austin—"

With one last hard thrust, a loud pop fills my ears, pain rips through my shoulder, bile fills my mouth, and darkness threatens.

"Austin," I gasp through the pain, falling to the floor in a heap before the couch.

He steps back, huffing, looking at me with dead eyes. "I'm out." He wipes the sweat from his face.

The realization of what his words mean take the last of my breath. Tears blur my vision of him walking away, slowly getting darker and darker until I see nothing and feel just as much.

CHAPTER 3

M Y PHONE RINGING STOPS ME MID-THRUST.
"Don't stop, Gabriel," Blonde Tits begs. At least she's
using my full name. I guess I shouldn't complain. I don't
even know hers. Obviously.

I glance at the clock as my phone continues to ring.

I shouldn't answer. *But what if it's important?*

"Fuck. Hold on." I lean over her, slipping my phone out of my jeans
pocket to see Austin's name. "This can't be good." I sink in deep to be sure
she's not going anywhere. I'm gonna need to come after this conversation, I can already tell.

"Tamer," I grunt.

"She's all yours." He's out of breath and angry.

"Who's all mine?" I don't dare go where I think he's heading.

"Frankie."

My hips thrust at the sound of her name and the deceptive hope
filling my chest. Tits moans and asks me to do it again. So I do, contin-
ually, my cock, getting harder and harder as my mind races to Frankie.

"I'm done. I'm out of here." Austin ends the call before I can respond.

I drop my phone and grip Blondie's hips like handles and drill her
until she's screaming my name, and I'm moaning for my Angel in my

head. My release comes hard and devastating. Tits thinks it's all her. She'd be livid if she knew it was for a woman who can never be mine. Bro-code aside, I'm no good for my Angel. She's meant for heaven, and I'm destined for hell.

My cock still at attention, thoughts of Frankie to blame, I switch out the used condom for a new one. "Hang on. This is gonna be a hard ride."

I should feel bad for using Tits, but she knows the score. And it's not like she's not getting something out of it. She's come twice as many times as me, but I'm about to make up for it.

Hours later, the ringing of my phone has me jackknifing in bed, yanked from a dream so sweet with visions of Frankie sucking my cock. I look down to find myself balls deep in Tits' mouth. "Fuck." I fall back on the bed, my phone forgotten, close my eyes, and recreate the vision in my dream as my body fucks Blondie's mouth like my next MMA fight depends on it.

Tits has just come all over my hand as my godforsaken phone rings again at two in the morning. "Jesus Christ, did somebody die?" I bark. "Hello!"

"Man, chill the fuck out." Grant's voice has me sitting up straight. Not good.

I stand and search for my clothes as panic breaches my post-sex haze. "What's wrong?" It can't be good if Detective Grant Malone, son of the former Sunnyville Chief of Police, is calling me at this time of day… Morning.

"You need to get to the hospital." He's calm. Too calm. He's using his detective voice. Not the *I'm-your-friend-and-beer-buddy* voice I usually hear.

"What happened?"

"It's Frankie."

I fall to the bed as the blood drains from my head. *Austin, what the fuck did you do?* "What. Happened?" I am not calm. I'm in savage mode. Fighting mode.

"Your boy put her in the ER."

My special forces training—the ability to think through the panic, the need to reach my target to save them—kicks in.

"Ten minutes." I hang up, pull on the rest of my clothes, and say to Tits over my shoulder, "Be gone by the time I get back."

Asshole in full force. *Check.*

Grant stops me outside the sliding doors of the ER. His hand on my chest halts my progress. "I need you to hear me." He pushes, forcing me back a step.

I'm bigger, stronger, but damn he's been a good friend the last few months. And not only because he's a cop and it's his job to get to know the new fighters in town. He and Emerson have become family. His brothers are a pain in the ass and funny as fuck. His dad… Well, he's the retired chief of police—enough said. And his mom, she's a saint for having put up with them all. And Emerson and her skydiving crew have a special place in my heart—burned and calloused as it is. Once she heard I was an ex-Army Special Forces Combat Medic with parachuting training, she was a force to be reckoned with until she got me jumping with her every few weeks.

For him, I squelch my bulldozing tendencies with clenched fists and flared nostrils. "I'm listening." I'm thankful he called. He knows I'm protective of Frankie. I'm an ass to her face, but behind her back, I'd never let anyone treat her like I do. Grant knows it too. The intuitive SOB.

"She's going to be fine." His stare is intense, burrowing into mine. I nod and take a breath, which seems to be the answer he was looking for before continuing. "She's got a dislocated shoulder."

My step falters, and I lean against the brick pillar to keep me on my feet. "How the fuck did he dislocate her shoulder?" Austin called me, and I was too busy getting my rocks off to pay him any mind, other than to use his words to fuel thoughts of Frankie now free to be mine.

Jesus, fuck, my asshole mode was in full force. I die a little thinking of our last interaction, the cruelty of my words. I called her *slut meat.* Jesus.

Grant clears his throat, looking over my shoulder. "Jimmy." He nods.

I don't have to look to know the Jimmy he's referring to. Captain Jimmy Durant, the Black Ops MMA gym owner, my boss and head asshole. I give him a chin nod. He pats my shoulder before grunting, letting me know he'll be inside.

I return my attention to Grant, waiting for him to tell me how Austin managed to dislocate her shoulder.

He puts his hands up. "She'll have to tell you that."

"Fuck." It can't be good if he's not saying. I scrub my face with my hand. "Did he beat her up? Can you at least tell me that?" My heart races, and my anger threatens to tear this place apart to get to her.

"If you're asking if he hit her, then, no. He didn't hit her." He looks through the doors and back at me. "You want to see her?"

"You're seriously asking?" Like he could keep me from her.

The asshole laughs and claps a hand on my back as we step through the parting doors. "Yeah, I am. She's scared and won't let anyone see her." He stops at the front desk. The lady behind the glassed-in counter buzzes us in with hardly a glance. "You're not her favorite person, you know. She may not want to see you."

"Like she has a choice," I scoff.

He scans the hall as we walk past the curtained-off beds of the emergency room, coming to a stop before a closed door. His eyes finally land on me. "Be nice."

A smart-ass remark on the tip of my tongue, I simply nod, reach for the door handle and pause. "You sticking around?"

"Yeah, I'll be here."

"And Austin?" The knob squeaks as I strangle it in my grip, my murderous stare on the door in front of me as I picture my Angel lying in the hospital bed on the other side, banged up by the man who supposedly loves her.

"He called 9-1-1 and then disappeared. We're looking for him."

"You'd better pray you find him before we do." Grant doesn't have to ask who the *we* I'm referring to is. He knows. I put the word out to the team on my way here, woke up some grumpy-asses, but it had to be done. We take care of our own. Though Austin is one of us, he went rogue on Frankie, who's also one of us, and a woman. We don't disrespect women. We may fuck 'em hard with barely a thank you, and we may fight for a living, but the two don't mix. Austin forgot that. We'll be happy to remind him. *I'll* be happy to remind him.

I hear Grant's silent struggle. He's a cop, but he's also a friend.

"You do what you do. We'll do what we do." I meet his gaze over my shoulder. "And hopefully we end up on the same side."

I turn the knob and step inside.

CHAPTER 4

I HEARD VOICES IN THE HALL, BUT WHEN GABRIEL steps into the room, he freezes when our eyes lock. I want to run away from him nearly as much as I want to run to him. His blue eyes, normally cold and intense, flash with heat, threatening to burn the flesh from my bones. His clenched jaw could crack diamonds, and his hands fist at his sides. His black hair is a mess, like he just got out of bed. Given the hour, I'm sure that's exactly where he came from.

"Angel." His rasp is so quiet I hardly hear his shocking endearment. He's never, I mean *never* called me anything other than Francesca. He's made it painstakingly clear he views me with little regard. Yet when he moves closer, each step silent and agile as he takes in my pale blue hospital gown, the scorn I've come to expect from him is absent.

Leery of this change in demeanor, using my good arm, I pull the blanket higher, feeling all too naked around a man who exudes testosterone like he drinks it for breakfast, wears it like a suit of armor topped off by a cleft chin to reinforce his masculine genes.

I sink back as he steps closer. Raw and scared is not the right frame of mind to deal with the larger-than-life presence Gabriel exudes like breathing. His shockingly tender eyes, which deeply contrast the coolness I found in Austin's as he left me broken on our living room floor, take me in. I gasp when Gabriel runs the back of his hand down my tearstained cheek.

I tried to be brave, holding in my screams when they popped my shoulder back into place, but I failed horribly. The doctor wanted to sedate me, but I refused. I need to keep my wits about me, especially if Austin comes for me. I've never been afraid of him, but I saw a different side of him tonight. If I ever doubted his love, his faithfulness, he shattered everything the moment he fucked me hard enough to tear my arm out of its socket and left me broken, naked, and passed out, only coming to when the EMTs rolled me onto the backboard to place me on the stretcher.

"I'll kill him." Gabriel's intensity has never scared me, not even his asshole ways, but I flinch at his murderous tone. I don't doubt him.

"Don't. He's not worth your future." I'm done with Austin. I don't know the logistics of how I'll untangle my life from his, given I work for the company he fights for, but I'm determined to do it—even if it means I'll lose everything.

"What happened?" Gabriel shakes with rage, trying to keep it in check. I nearly feel sorry for him. Nearly. I'm sure his asshole—his natural state—is gonna show up at any second to taunt me, call me a slut, stupid for putting up with Austin's philandering.

There's nothing he can say I'm not already saying to myself. Even his words of hate can't hurt me today.

I roll to my side—away from him—as best I can, ignoring the pain that has my eyes watering. I'm not going to cry in front of him of all people. "Like I'd tell you." I close my eyes, praying for sleep, for peace, a way out of this situation that doesn't include more humiliation at the hands of Austin or Gabriel.

"Why aren't you asleep?" The heat of Gabriel's attention sends a chill across my skin, making me tremble, setting off a new wave of pain in my shoulder. "Why the fuck aren't you medicated?" He presses the call button before I can stop him.

"Don't," I grit through the pain. "Why are you even here?" Grant already told me Austin is gone, but finding Gabriel rushing to my side is unexpected. But surprisingly not unwelcomed. As much of an asshole as he can be, I know if Austin did show up, Gabriel wouldn't let him touch me. I've seen Gabriel with his mom and sister. He doesn't stand for men disrespecting women, unless, of course, it's him doing it to me.

"I needed to check on you, be sure you're okay." He walks to the other side of the bed so I'm facing him again.

I close my eyes to avoid the concern in his. *He doesn't mean it. He doesn't give a shit about you.*

When the nurse's voice comes over the intercom, he insists they give me meds even though I tell him I won't take them. He growls his discontent. The patter of his lighter-than-air steps as he moves around and the scrape of a chair on the linoleum floor fill the silent room. A whoosh of air hits me a second before his large, deadly weapon of a hand encompasses mine.

I frown, determined not to look at him. *It doesn't mean anything.*

"Frown at me all you want, Angel. You're taking whatever painkiller the nurse brings."

My eyes fly open at the sound of his gruff voice using that endearment again. *Angel.* WTF? Austin went rogue, and the biggest pain in my ass just went soft. It must be the apocalypse.

"I won't watch you suffer any more than you already have." He reconfirms his intentions with a tender gleam in his blue eyes sparkling with stardust.

Stardust? I must be delirious from the pain. "Then leave."

He chuckles. "Feisty as ever." He brushes his hand across my forehead and down my cheek. "That's a good sign."

I've never seen him so affectionate or tender. "What's wrong with you?"

"That list is too fucking long to get into now."

"I mean, why are you being nice to me?"

"I have no reason to be mean to you."

"You had reason before?" What the hell is he talking about?

He nods.

I scrutinize him, looking for some secret I know I'll never find the key to. "You need to leave."

His lips touch our joined hands. "I'm not going anywhere." He nods to the door. "Take your meds, Frankie. I'll be here watching over you, keeping you safe."

The tenderness in his voice and the fact he knows why I wouldn't take any painkillers has my damn eyes leaking again. For fuck's sake!

The nurse shoots something into my IV, telling me to rest, and I should be released in a few hours.

Gabriel touches my cheek. His thumb slowly swipes across my brow over and over again. His touch is calming. But even more surprising, his touch makes me feel cherished. "Sleep now, Angel. You're safe."

When her breathing evens out barely five minutes after the drugs were introduced into her IV, I take my first easy breath since getting the call from Grant. Reluctantly, I remove my hand from hers and sit back in the hospital chair that's made for children or lesser men than me. But I'll sit here all goddamned day or night if it means she feels safe enough to sleep. It only took a second to see the fear in her eyes to understand why she remained in the hell of her pain instead of sleeping blissfully unaware of her surroundings.

I didn't know what I'd do or say when I stepped into her room, but the second I saw her wrecked and so fucking vulnerable, instincts kicked in. The instinct to kill to protect what's mine.

I will protect her. I'll hunt down anyone who wants to cause her harm and end them before they can touch a single strand of her silky raven hair or bring another tear to her eyes. When it comes to protecting my Angel, I'll have no mercy.

My phone is blowing up with texts from the guys. There's no sign of Austin, which I choose to take as good news. Sunnyville is not big enough to hide in. We're too well known to go unnoticed for long, especially once word gets out about what he did. The details don't have to be known. The fact he hurt his woman is enough to get him turned in by anyone who spots him in this wholesome community. He knows he's in deep shit and skipped town.

I'm not fool enough to believe he won't regret his decisions, that he won't come back for her. I'll be ready and waiting. In the meantime, I need to get my Angel out of that uncomfortable, thin-ass emergency room bed and into something much more comfortable. My bed. It'll hug her curves and ease the pressure on her damaged shoulder.

I know the pain she's feeling. I've had my shoulder dislocated twice: once on tour in Afghanistan, and again during one of my first MMA fights. It hurts like hell coming out of the socket and even worse going back in, and then it's a grumpy bitch for weeks. She's not going to like being laid up. Frankie's never been one to sit on her ass—as delicious as it is. She's the physical therapist for our Black Ops MMA Team. Captain Jimmy adores her. He won't have a problem giving her the time she needs to heal. No, the problem will be Frankie.

I might have to be an asshole to get her to stay put and give her body the time it needs to heal. Though, me being an asshole is probably the last thing she needs right now.

My Angel not only has wolf-like gray eyes, but she has a tendency to chew off her own foot to make a point.

She won't take kindly to feeling weak or vulnerable.

CHAPTER 5

THE ROOM IS DARK WHEN I OPEN MY EYES. Trying to blink my fogginess away, I look around. I can't see much, but I know I'm no longer in the ER. The bed is entirely too comfortable to be a hospital bed, and last I looked, I was hooked up to an IV with blinking lights. I have a vague recollection of trying to sign papers and a bumpy car ride, but not much else. I reach for my right arm to feel for an IV and instantly regret it. Pain shoots from my left shoulder, making me moan my distress.

Movement in the shadows has me jumping back, nearly tumbling to the floor before strong arms catch me.

"Fuck, Angel. Where you going?" Gabriel's gargled-with-shards-of-glass voice eases my panic as my shoulder protests my quick movements.

I nearly puke from the pain. Going limp in his hold, relieved it's him and not Austin, I close my eyes and wait until the nausea and discomfort subside.

Gentler than a man his size should be capable of, he situates me back in bed. "I'm sorry I scared you."

"It's okay." I dare a glance. His face looms over me as he sits on the edge of the bed, his arms bracketing my body. He brushes my hair off my shoulder, eyeing the damage beneath the sling I can feel strapped around my body. I stifle the urge to fight the confinement. "Where am I?"

"Home." He smiles at my frown, his thumb sweeping across my brow in that oddly soothing way. "My home," he clarifies.

"How long have I been out?"

He glances at his watch. "Four hours, give or take. Here." He holds up a glass that magically appeared in his hand. "You need to hydrate."

"I need a shower." And a toothbrush. I take a sip of water as he carefully holds the glass to my lips.

"You need to eat. It's time for your pain pill." His eyes remain on my mouth as I take another long drink. "Slow down. Need to be sure you can keep it down."

Easy for him to say. The Sahara hasn't taken up residence in *his* mouth.

He sets the glass on the nightstand. "Do you think you can stand? Not sure I trust you won't pass out if you take a shower."

"We won't know until we try."

Grumbling his dissent, he helps me sit, maneuvering me until my feet hang off the side of the bed. Besides my shoulder pain, I ache from head to toe. "Did you kick me out of that monster you drive?" *Or run me over?*

He chuckles. "Hardly."

No, I imagine he very carefully placed me in his baby—his tricked out Hummer, his pride and joy he won in one of his early maybe-not-so-legal MMA fights—before carefully carrying me inside to his bed, where he's been watching over me from the chair, sitting close by while I slept.

As much as I never thought I'd experience this side of Gabriel "No Mercy" Stone, I knew he was capable of it. I've seen him with his mom and sister. He's gentle and caring with them in ways I've never seen him be with anyone else.

Until now.

In some strange twist of events, my heartbreak and physical condition brought out the nurturer in him, I suppose.

"Do you have something I can put on after?" I'm relieved I'm still wearing my hospital gown but also a little ooged out I'm *still wearing my hospital gown.*

"Yeah." He heads to his closet.

I stand, thankful he's not there to witness me sway on my feet. Maybe a bath would be a safer choice.

He steps out of the closet with clothes clutched in one hand, his other gripping the doorframe. His eyes land on my hand holding on to the chair for dear life. "Why didn't you have any clothes or belongings at the hospital?"

As he stalks closer, I take pity on my aching body and sit in the chair with tender regard for my condition. I almost forgot why I'm here—the events leading up to me being naked under a hospital gown at the mercy of one Gabriel Stone and wincing from the pain in my shoulder and my sore ass. A bath would be good.

"Frankie?" The brick wall of a man kneels before me. "Where are your clothes?"

I can't bring myself to say the words he wants to hear. The answer to the question he's been asking since he walked into the emergency room: *What happened?*

"Do you think I can take a bath instead?" I give him the only words I can muster.

His fingers rub the fabric of the gown covering my knee as he plaintively searches my face. "Sure." His fingers trail up my arm as he stands and turns to the bathroom. "Let me get it started."

He walks with the weight of the world on his shoulders. The burden impacts each step as he forges forward. The air is thicker around him—visceral and textured. I can nearly make out the waves of glimmering atmosphere as he pushes through the debris of his past, our tortured connection, and the knowledge that his best friend betrayed me in the worst way possible.

I let out a breath and relax into the chair, closing my eyes. I thought for sure he'd push for answers, but for now, he seems content to let me be. This side of Gabriel is hard to comprehend. He's always been a bit of a paradox. He's gruff, but friendly and loyal to his friends. He served his country in the army as a Special Forces medic—a healer, a caretaker, a first responder. He's highly trained and as tough as they come. Now he's an MMA fighter who inflicts pain for a living, for sport. His asshole flag flies high, especially when I'm around.

I'm thankful for the white flag that seems to be flying currently. I doubt the reprieve will last.

Though willpower and self-deprivation are my strong suits, it took everything I had to leave Frankie standing in my bathroom, looking soft and vulnerable. She needs help bathing. I know it. She knows it. But it's not a line I'm willing to cross or push, especially without knowing what happened with Austin.

Did he force himself on her? Was she left naked and hurt, and *that's* why she doesn't have any clothes? The hospital said she didn't have any personal effects. They didn't elaborate, and I was too focused on getting her home before her pain meds wore off to question them.

My mind reels with darker and darker thoughts of all the possibilities of how she ended up at the ER. I leave the food warming on the stove, grab my phone and pace the entryway leading to the stairs, listening for any signs she's in distress. I left the bedroom door open, hoping I could hear her call if she needs me.

Grant picks up on the first ring. "Did you get any sleep?"

"No." I run my fingers through my hair, noting I need a shower too. It's early, not even seven yet. We've only been home a few hours. I knew he'd be up, even though it's Saturday and he's off work.

Behind his sigh I hear the leather of his couch give as he settles in. "I figured as much. How is she?"

"Hurting. I'm making food so she can take her meds."

"Awful nice of you."

"Not nice. Necessary."

"If you say so." He's trying to goad me. Get me to admit things I have no intention of admitting to myself, much less him.

"Why doesn't she have any clothes?" My eyes draw up to the top of the stairs. I'd rather she not overhear our conversation, but I choose to stay where I am instead of seeking privacy.

"She hasn't told you what happened, then?"

"No. She ignores my questions. I don't want to push. She's been through enough." The idea of not knowing doesn't sit well with me. I have to wait for her to be ready, though.

"Be patient. She needs you right now. That should be all you need to know."

"Should it?" The edge of my frustration clips my words. But he's right. She doesn't have any family. She only has Austin, and, well, he's proved he's not to be trusted. Cap and the guys love her like family, but none of them would dare think to cross me on being the one to see to her now, especially after what Austin pulled.

"Would you want to hurt Austin any more than you do now if you knew the worst happened?"

"No."

"Would you want to hurt him any less if you knew nothing happened, and it was an accident?"

"No. Fuck. She's his girl. He *let* this happen to her. He left when he should be the one by her side. Whether he meant to hurt her or not, he did when he didn't protect her."

"Exactly. The details you're seeking aren't pertinent to how you feel about Austin. Or your feelings for Frankie, I imagine."

"I need to know so I can help her." So I don't hurt her in the same way.

"You'd care for her differently if you knew he didn't mean to hurt her?"

"Fuck. Okay, I get your point, *Doctor* Malone."

He chuckles. "Then my job is done."

"Ass."

"Takes one to know one." He ends the call.

Grant's laugh still echoes in my ears as I make a tray of food and head to the bedroom.

CHAPTER 6

THE RATTLING OF DISHES HAS ME GLANCING through the open bathroom door to the adjoining bedroom where Gabriel sets a tray of food on the bed. Before I can look away, his eyes meet mine. "Feeling better?"

"Mm-hmm." He's still wearing his black jeans and t-shirt from last night at Davenport's where he said I was dancing like *slut meat*. I cringe at the memory. He's probably right. I was desperate to get Austin's attention. I got Gabriel's instead.

He stalks like a jaguar on the prowl, stopping inches from me, his eyes perusing me wearing his t-shirt and boxer briefs. "My turn." He tugs his t-shirt off by the neck and tosses it to land on the hamper on the other side of the bathroom. His body is on full display, a body I've ingrained every sinewy dip, angle, and curve of into my brain so thoroughly, I could probably recognize it by touch alone, though I've never touched him—at least not in the way my mind is racing to do now. The breadth of his shoulders is as impressive as the definition of his abs and obliques. If there were an ideal MMA heavyweight fighter's body, it's standing before me now on glorious display.

He touches my wet hair as I try to brush the tangles free with one hand. "Eat while I shower. I'll brush and dry your hair when I get out."

My gawking—not only at his body but his comment—doesn't go unnoticed. His brows arch as a laugh escapes his expansive chest. He grips my hair in one hand at the base of my neck and twists it, holding it in place with a clip he found in a vanity drawer.

"Eat." He gently urges me out the door as he turns and starts to remove his jeans. I stand frozen in shock, only looking back at the sound of the shower door opening, and catch sight of his naked ass stepping inside.

Holy hell. He's one fine man—asshole or not. I swallow my lust and close the bathroom door. He apparently doesn't need privacy, but I sure as heck do. A girl can only take so much Gabriel at one time. A much larger dose, and I might explode from exposure… Or embarrassment.

I've barely settled on the bed and taken my second bite of the bacon and egg sandwich when he emerges from the bathroom. He finds me immediately, taking in my stance and the sandwich in my hand, my chewing paused as my attention is drawn to him. A towel wrapped around his waist is the only layer protecting me from his utter nakedness. Water still glistens on his tanned skin as if he couldn't bother to dry off before checking on me. His black hair, cut to spikey perfection, drips in ignored chaos, and his hands flex at his sides, fingers twitching to touch.

Jesus. What's wrong with me? I'm ogling my ex's best friend only hours after said friend trampled all over our relationship and my heart… And my body.

Shame floods me, and heat warms my cheeks. I look away, setting the food aside. I'm a horrible person.

"Hey." Rough fingers lift my chin till I meet his blue gaze. "Whatever you're thinking, stop."

I grimace over the emotions building. *Do not cry. You cannot break down in front of Gabriel!* He's being all sweet, but it doesn't erase the past five years. Between Austin's confession of infidelity and abandoning me after injuring me, and Gabriel's personality transplant, my head is swimming. I can't decipher what's real and what's a lie.

I shake off his touch. "I'm fine."

He scowls, knowing it's a total lie. "Let me get dressed, and I'll help with your sling. Then medicine. Then hair." He disappears into the closet while I stare at my hands, absorbing his list of to-dos, and try to come to terms with my broken body responding to him the way it is. I have no self-preservation. I'm obviously high on drugs to be considering any of the things my mind keeps throwing out in random blips that are far too dirty and delicious.

"Eat, Frankie," he barks from his mancave of a closet, causing me to jump and then gasp from the pain. His hawk ears must have heard as he sticks his head out. "Sorry."

"For barking at me or causing me pain?" I glower, knowing the latter is not his fault.

"Both," he simply replies, pulling a white t-shirt over his head, further mussing his towel-dried hair. Barefoot and in workout shorts, he stops next to the bed, reaching over to nab one of the other three sandwiches he made.

"You have to stop that," I protest.

"Stop what?" He sits on the edge of the bed, lopping off a sizable bite of his breakfast. I try to scoot over to give him room and me space, but he stops me with a hand on my thigh.

"Being so nice." My eyes remain on his hand as he squeezes, his thumb slowly moving back and forth.

"You need to heal." He stands, taking his sandwich with him and talks around another bite, "We can go back to hating each other when you can move without groaning in pain."

He says it like our hating each other was a game. It wasn't a game to me. His words hurt. He's dead-stare unraveled me more times than I care to admit. At times, it was a barrier between Austin and me, yet Austin seemed to tolerate it better than I did. I avoided Gabriel. Gabriel avoided me. But given our working relationship, it wasn't always possible.

So, why is he taking care of me? Out of pity?

He finishes his sandwich as I watch him collect stuff to do my hair.

"I don't hate you," I whisper my confession. I may not always like him, or how he makes me feel, but I never hated him.

He turns, his eyes intense and masked. "I don't hate you either." He swipes a pill bottle from the nightstand, opens it, and hands me a pill. "Never have."

Could have fooled me. I swallow my reply along with my pill. I don't want to fight. He's being nice. Anything I say will be caustic and detrimental to our truce. I'm worn out, tired, and in pain. Not the best condition to question motives and changes of hearts.

Gabriel, situated behind me on the bed with me between his massive legs, sprays detangler in my hair before gently combing it out. Then he turns on the hair dryer with the concentrator attachment and blows it out, clipping up sections to keep it out of the way as he goes. It's a skill he says he learned from doing his sister's hair when she was younger. He keeps this stuff on hand for when she visits.

The next twenty-ish minutes might be the most enjoyable of my life. The warmth of the hot air, his hand on my back, neck, and hair has me more relaxed than I ever remember feeling.

My head nods a few times as I start to doze off. He only chuckles and says, "Just a few more minutes, Angel. Then you can sleep."

Finally clean, hair dry, food in my tummy, and drugs coursing through my system, I fall asleep with Gabriel watching over me.

Hot and squished, I open my eyes to find myself wrapped in strong arms I immediately recognize are not Austin's. It takes a second before the visions of last night come flooding back in a stream of cringey memories. Austin used me, admitted he's cheated with his lewd remark comparing my pussy and ass to others he's had. I'm an idiot. A fool. I believed in us or maybe the fantasy of the us I'd hoped we could be. It's not easy giving up on nine years of my life. As much of an ass as he was in the end, he was my savior in the beginning.

With that thought, no matter how natural it feels to be in Gabriel's arms, using his chest as a pillow, I just can't. I need distance. I need space to breathe. I move.

"Don't." His gruff timbre and tight embrace stop my retreat. "You were whimpering in your sleep until I held you. Then you finally quieted down and rested."

Yeah, that's not embarrassing. "Sorry."

"Don't be. I slept like a rock." He presses a kiss to my forehead.

I try not to read too much into his statement or the kiss. "I need to move." I roll out of his arms and onto my back, regretting it the moment my shoulder gives its painful protest. "Shit! Will it ever stop hurting?"

A chuckle from my right has me looking at him, his hair a riotous mess, his chiseled face softened by the tenderness in his eyes. "It will. I promise." He helps me sit. "But it's going to hurt like a bitch for a few more days." He checks his watch. "Time for more meds."

I know all of this. I'm a physical therapist. But my training falls to the wayside when I'm the patient. For now, I'll blame the meds and the emotional stress of my life falling apart.

"I'd like to get out of this bed, maybe sit on the couch, not feel like such a bum." *Or a burden.* I need to make a plan. Do I dare go home? Maybe Grant and Emmy would lend me their guest room until I'm back on my feet. Could I stand to be in their lovey-dovey faces right now? Meh, beggars can't be choosers. I don't have anywhere else to go. I'm not sure Cap and his revolving door of women would want me in his space, no matter how much he cares for me like a daughter. I can't go back to my apartment. Austin could show up. Though Grant says he's gone, I don't have any desire to be in any space shared with Austin. Gabriel's seems like the safest bet at the moment.

"We can do that."

We? He's entirely too agreeable. "Don't you need to train?" I need some distance from Black Ops MMA Gym's golden boy playing Mother Teresa.

"Tomorrow," is his only response as he lifts me from the bed.

"I can walk," I half-heartedly protest. Being in his arms isn't all that bad. I'm a little needy at the moment after being thrown away by Austin. Maybe it's not wrong to let Gabriel take care of me. For the moment.

"I know." He traipses out of the room, down the stairs, and into the den, placing me gently on the couch with the recliner option. "Here." He hands me the remote. "Find a movie or something. I'll make lunch." He throws a blanket over my lap and is gone without so much as a look back.

As much as I can't trust this gentler side of Gabriel "No Mercy" Stone, I have to say, I don't hate it. His mother and sister have to feel like queens if he dotes on them half this much. I'll accept it as payback for every dirty look and hurtful word he spit in my direction. Frenemies. Maybe that's what we are.

"College football? That's what you want to watch?" Gabriel returns, setting up tv trays and propping me up with pillows.

"It's Saturday." Don't most guys watch football on the weekends? My dad did. It's probably the only trait I got from him I don't despise. Austin used to tease me, saying I loved football more than him. I couldn't admit—even in all the years we were together—I love football because it was the only thing my dad liked about me.

"So, that means college ball?" He heads back to the kitchen.

"Yep," I respond loud enough for him to hear.

"I can get behind that." He places a bowl of what looks to be beef vegetable soup on each of our trays, disappears, and comes back with a plate piled high with grilled cheese, napkins, and drinks.

"I'm impressed." He's got all the bases covered.

"Don't be." He sits next to me, his own tray close enough to touch mine.

I take a tentative spoonful, blowing till I'm sure I won't scald my tongue. My first taste will definitely not be my last as the warm, rich goodness coats my mouth. "This tastes homemade." Some chick must have made this for him.

"It is." He places a napkin in my lap. "I couldn't sleep when we got home from the hospital. I was sure you'd sleep soundly for at least a few hours, so I made beef stew. Hearty, and doesn't require two hands to eat."

When was the last time anyone cooked me a meal? Damn. This man's thoughtfulness brings tears to my eyes. I nod and sniffle into my bowl. "Thank you."

"No thanks needed, but you're welcome."

Gabriel's attention to detail, his ability to know what I need before I need it highlights how far Austin and I have—*had*—fallen. He used to be the one to know what I needed when I needed it. But that was a long time ago. The man he is now is not the boy I fell in love with. I doubt I'll ever see him again.

I drown my feelings in food and football until I'm too drowsy to keep my eyes open. Gabriel pulls me into his chest like it's a normal occurrence. I go willingly. I'll figure out my plan tomorrow. Where to go. What to do. "Tomorrow," I murmur, my eyes already closed, sleep teasing my consciousness.

His chest ripples with a laugh as he softly rubs my back. "Sleep, Frankie. No more worrying tonight."

CHAPTER 7

BLARING MUSIC JOLTS ME AWAKE. "WHAT THE—?" I scramble from bed as only a one-armed woman with a lame shoulder could—gracefully and without cursing. Hardly.

I stumble down the stairs, my heart beating nearly as loud as the music rocking the house.

"Gabriel, what the hell—?" My rant dies when I step into the den and take in a frantic Emmy trying to silence the music as her daughter, Gwen, sits on the floor, screaming with her hands pressed to her ears and tears streaming down her face. "I know how you feel, honey," I say to Gwen, knowing neither of them can hear me.

I pluck Emmy's phone from the dock, and the music falls to an acceptable volume, continuing to play "Cowboy" by Kid Rock on her phone. "What the fuck, Emerson?"

She scoops up her daughter. "It's okay, Gwen. Mommy is so sorry." She silently apologizes to me with a quick glance as she soothes her whimpering daughter, who's buried her face in her mother's sizable chest—motherhood has been good to her.

I stop the song, my ears still ringing, and look up to find Emmy on the couch with Gwen attached to her breast, peacefully nursing. "Well, I wish all upsets could be calmed so easily."

Emmy smirks. "Believe me, I've soothed Grant many times this way."

"Uh, yeah, I didn't need to know that." I hand Emmy her phone, not even missing mine one bit. I'm happy to be ignorant of any text or phone calls I might have received from Austin. Or worse, the knowledge he hasn't even reached out at all. "What are you doing here, and what's up with the musical-rock-the-house wake-up call?"

"Sorry. I was trying to find a new entrance song for Gabriel. His next fight is in a few weeks, and you know he's a big Kid Rock fan. So, I thought..." she trails off, rubbing the tears from Gwen's sleeping face.

My heart pangs at the sight. That could have been me. That *should* have been me with Austin's baby. We've been together for nine years. We should have been married with babies by now. Granted, we were busy growing up. But still, nine years is a long time to find myself in the situation I'm in now. Husbandless and my arms barren of children. This is not the life I imagined for myself. It's not the life Austin promised me.

Anger and regret try to fight their way to the surface. I can't deal with this now. I stand and cringe from the pain. Meds. I need my pill. "Want something to eat? Drink?" I round the couch and head to the kitchen.

"Gabriel left breakfast in the oven."

I stop in my tracks. "He cooked?" Again?

She slowly nods, surprised by my surprise. "He was finishing up as we got here." She unhooks Gwen, patting her lightly on her back. "He wanted me to tell you he'll be training most of the day, but he'll pick up your *things* on his way home."

"Things?" I shrug and continue to the kitchen, knowing Gwen still has another side to drain. And she will, sleep be damned. That girl can *eat.*

As I set everything on the kitchen table, Emmy steps into the kitchen. "Have you never had Gabriel's breakfast?"

I scoff, "No. He'd rather kill me than cook for me." I regret those words the second I say them. He has been cooking for me. But I was referencing the man he was two days ago, before Austin went psycho on my ass and then AWOL.

"I wouldn't count on it." Emmy sits, loading her plate with egg casserole, bacon, and biscuits. "Damn, that man can cook."

"He makes a mean beef stew too… And an egg sandwich."

"He'd rather kill you, huh?"

I point to my shoulder. "Before this? Yes."

She sets down her fork, tenderness filling her eyes as she takes in my sling. "How are you? I'm sorry I didn't come sooner. Grant convinced me you didn't want any visitors, but when Gabriel called last night, I was all over coming over today to keep you company."

"I'm fine."

She shakes her head. "You're a horrible liar."

"I'm not a horrible liar." I am. Unlike Austin, I've never been good at it. When I do, I feel guilty, and it must show on my face. It's one trait I did *not* get from my father.

"Yeah, you are. You're not even good at lying to yourself, saying Gabriel would rather hurt you than feed you. I take this spread here and the food he made you yesterday as evidence to the contrary. Not to mention the fact he's brought you into his home to care for you." She takes a bite, then adds, "He even missed a day of training, and you know that man is hardcore when it comes to his training."

He's hardcore about everything. Gabriel is an all-in kind of guy. He's black or white. There is no gray in the world he inhabits. "He feels bad, that's all."

"Why, because his best friend beat you up?"

Damn, sometimes I forget how painful it can be to have Emmy's truthfulness thrown in your face. "He didn't beat me up." To demonstrate how okay I am, I force a bite of food I don't want.

"I point out your shoulder as evidence to the contrary."

"What, are you studying to be a lawyer or something? Evidence shmevidence. I give you the past five years as evidence of Gabriel's disdain for me."

"I give it as evidence that he has the hots for you. Always has. His assholiness is a defense against the power of your pussy."

If I had food in my mouth, I'd choke on it. "Power of my pussy? Sounds like a great fight entrance song."

She laughs, "God, it would be an epic entrance song!" She butters a biscuit and hands it to me. "Gabriel made me promise you'd eat. So, eat."

Thankfully, we don't talk about Gabriel succumbing to my so-called *all-powerful pussy*. Instead she fills me in on their occasional Sunday ritual where Gabriel cooks breakfast for the entire Malone clan—Grant's parents, two brothers, their significant others, and their kids. She lights up talking about how well he fits in like the tougher, bigger, and scarier Malone brother.

I, on the other hand, have never felt so alone and isolated. Austin and I have no family—we've been each other's family for the past nine years. Well, maybe eight. The last year felt like we were distant relatives who can barely tolerate each other's presence.

After cleaning up, taking meds, and finding my home for the day on the couch, Emmy asks what I hoped she wouldn't, "Do you want to talk about what happened?"

"I imagine you already know." Grant tells her everything, even stuff I'd rather he didn't—and probably shouldn't.

When my tears start to fall, she's at my side, gently holding me to her chest. I never knew my mom, and though Emmy is only a few years older than me, I imagine this right here is what it feels like to be loved and comforted by your mother.

"How could he hurt me and then leave me alone on the floor like that? Like he didn't care what happened to me. Maybe he didn't." He had been cheating on me for who knows how long. "Why do men cheat? And why do I feel like it's my fault?" I blubber as quietly as I can, not wanting to wake Gwen, but unable to keep it together any longer.

"One—he's a jerk. Two—because men are assholes." She smooths my hair. "Not all men, but the ones who cheat and hurt women are."

I can't disagree, but it doesn't relieve the ache in my chest or stop my tears.

"It'll get easier. I promise." She should know. She's overcome abuse at the hands of her father.

I thought my father was bad, but he never touched me. He just never did anything for me either. He acted like I wasn't there, like I wasn't worth the air he breathed or the ground he walked on until the day he walked out.

It dawns on me then: Austin turned into my father, and he left me just as easily, never looking back.

There's no need to look when there's no one there you care about.

CHAPTER 8

MY MIND'S NOT IN IT TODAY. I'M WORRIED ABOUT my Angel. How's her pain today? Was she upset when she woke to find me gone? I should have left her a note so she didn't think I pawned her off on Emerson. I needed to train. I've only got a few weeks before my next big fight. But mostly, I needed space. I carried a sleeping Frankie to bed again last night and held her while she slept. That wasn't my intention, but when I started to pull away, she grabbed my hand and said, "Stay." So, I did.

I don't doubt it's the pain meds making her sleep so soundly in my arms like I'm her safe place. Fuck if I don't want to be just that.

"Your timing's for shit today, Gabriel." Jonah lets the weights slam down on the press.

Tell me something I don't know.

He waits until he's standing in my view before he asks, "How is she today?"

"I don't know." I still the speed bag before catching his eye. "She was asleep when I left."

Arms crossed, he nods. "You're worried?"

"Yeah." I start up again, hitting with my right three times, then my left three times, right, then left. Right. Left. Right. Left.

"Call her."

"Emerson is with her."

"So you can't call her?"

"She doesn't have her phone." *She doesn't have anything.* A cold reminder that spurs my frustration and reinforces my ire toward Austin. *I'm going to kill him.*

"Call Emerson." Jonah doesn't know her well enough to call her Emmy.

I call her Emerson out of respect for Grant. She's Grant's Emmy. She's Emerson to me no matter how much I like her as a friend. No matter how many times I jump with her at her Wings Out Skydiving School. It's her baby, her passion, but she's still Emerson. Never Emmy. There's a bro code you don't cross, and the line, for me, begins with her nickname.

It's a distinction I kept solid with Frankie too by only calling her Francesca, until a few days ago. Now, I can't seem to stop calling her *Angel* and *Frankie*, even to her face—especially to her face. Her gray eyes fill my vision, and it fucks up my rhythm. Again.

Jonah laughs. "You're gonna have a shit day if you don't call and check up on her."

I grunt in response, giving up on the bag. Weights will be a better distraction.

Three hours later, I'm pouring sweat and steaming with frustration. It was a shit show of a training session, and everyone knows it. They were kind enough not to razz me about it too much. No one mentions Austin or what he did to Frankie other than to ask how she's doing. I gave vague, half-grunted answers since I don't know *how the fuck she is today.*

When I arrive at her apartment, I use the key Austin gave me. We've always had keys to each other's places. Today, I feel like a creeper using it without her okay. I'd never invade their privacy, but today it seems necessary in order to get her some clothes and any personal items she may need.

I enter on high alert, expecting Austin to be hiding out, but there's no one. It's eerily quiet when I shut the door behind me. They don't have any pets, so the place is still with no echo of life having been here in days. My sight immediately goes to the clothes strewn on the floor from the front door to the couch. Though I hate the thought, it's obvious they didn't waste any time getting naked on Friday night. If they were in the mood for sex, what the hell happened to turn things south where Austin ended up hurting her? The thought has my anger simmering.

I kick the clothes into a pile. Her panties and bra looking like they were ripped from her body only fuel the fire. It's then I notice the blood-stain on the floor by the couch. It's not huge, but it's not small either. She didn't have a busted lip or any open wounds I could see. She could possibly have some I can't see. My darker thoughts take over, and my anger boils into rage. "What the fuck did you do, Austin?"

Maybe it's his. I don't entertain the thought for long. He's been an ass lately, and that's saying a lot coming from me, King Asshole. No, I doubt it's his blood.

He made my Angel bleed, a fact I can hardly swallow. I kept my distance, purposely keeping Frankie at arm's length because he loved her, and she loved him. I knew he'd been off with her since his accident. He's a tightlipped motherfucker. I assumed he'd come around, and time was what they needed. I was wrong. Now she's hurt. I can't help but blame myself for not seeing it sooner. I was so busy focusing on building the wall between us to keep her safe from the likes of me, I didn't ensure she was safe from Austin. I never thought he'd harm a hair on her head.

I can't wait to get my hands on him. I won't let him hurt her again. Ever.

Texting Grant to confirm I can clean up the blood and dispose of her ripped clothes, I make use of my time and throw a week's worth of clothes and what I assume are her toiletries in a duffle bag I found in the closet. I find her purse, cell, iPad, laptop, and all cables, and add them to the bag. When I get the okay from Grant, I place her stuff by the door and look for cleaning supplies. Hydrogen peroxide is the best choice to get the blood out. It may lighten the carpet, but it's better than leaving a dark stain. After I find some in the bathroom, it's a quick cleanup.

I throw her ripped clothes away and put the others in the laundry. I'm relieved when the evidence of what happened here is gone. I don't want Frankie walking in and feeling like it's a crime scene. Though, I guess it is. Maybe. What did he do? Is she pressing charges?

The thoughts tumble around in my head as I make my way home, anger my only companion.

Slamming cabinets jar me from sleep. What is it with this house and rude awakenings? *It's a sign you need to find other accommodations.*

Was Gabriel trying to wake me as a hint he wants me out? Emmy left sometime after lunch and my second nap. Yeah, I'm a joy to be around, but between the meds and my emotional breakdown, I was worn out.

I trudge into the kitchen to find Gabriel at the stove. "Hey."

He whips around, scanning me from head to toe, lingering on my face, which I'm sure is puffy from my emotional collapse. Obviously finding me annoying, he resumes his tasks, ignoring my greeting.

"Training go okay today?" I don't want to jump to conclusions. It's not all about me. Maybe he had a bad day. Got bad news. Or is simply in a bad mood. It happens, especially to Mr. Asshole.

"Fine," he grumbles. "Dinner will be ready in ten." He covers the pot and stomps out of the kitchen.

"Okay, then…"

Dinner's not much better. I make small talk as we sit at the kitchen table. I thank him for breakfast and for letting me stay here. When all I get are one-word responses and no eye-contact, I take my bowl to the sink, dumping my uneaten food in the disposal before rinsing it out as best I can and placing it in the dishwasher.

Anger, shame, and disappointment have my pulse pounding and words forming in my throat. "I'll find another place to say." I make for the stairs. "I'll be out of your hair tomorrow."

"Angel." His chair scrapes across the floor as he stands.

I pause, my back to him, unwilling to show what his new pet name does to me. For the last thirty minutes he's made me feel like less than the dirt on his shoes, and that one word—Angel—has tears threatening and hope blooming that I'm not nothing to him too. That he's not discarding me like my father and Austin so easily did.

He stops behind me, so close I can feel his heat. I brace for his touch on my back, my shoulder, my hair. But nothing comes. He takes a filling breath and lets it out slowly. His voice is like razors on my skin when he speaks, "Did he rape you?"

I grip the counter with my one usable hand as my knees try to give way. A sob attempts an escape, but I clamp down, unwilling to give it air. With my eyes pinched shut, I shake my head.

Sex with Austin may have ended badly, but I was a willing participant.

But the fact it's a question at all shows how fucked up things with Austin have become.

Gabriel grips my hip, stepping into me, offering his hard body as support. "Did he hurt you?"

Obviously. "My arm." How do I even begin to talk about this? It feels like a bad dream that happened to someone else…only I've got the battle scars to remind me it really happened.

Gently, Gabriel touches my bad shoulder. "Not what I meant."

I feared as much.

"There was blood on the floor near the couch." He offers proof I didn't need to hear.

"You went to my apartment?" Panic laces my words. I can't imagine what he found. I know our clothes—Austin's and mine—were everywhere in our urgency to breach the distance that had grown exponentially over the last few months, or longer if I'm being honest. "There was blood?"

Shame floods every part of me. I step out of Gabriel's hold and back away. I don't deserve his touch. His support. His pity.

"You needed clothes. Your phone. Your purse." Now he sounds flustered, trying to justify his actions. "It's all on the bed, by the way."

"I wish you hadn't." I step back as he moves toward me. The idea of him seeing where I lay unconscious and naked—bare to the EMTs who came to help—makes me sick.

"You didn't answer. Did he *hurt* you? Before this?"

A tear breaks free. He'll never understand. Gabriel is a black and white guy. He sees no gray, and there was a lot of gray that night. I wanted Austin to want me like he used to. I needed to feel loved, cherished. Instead, his unfaithful admission killed all hope, then he pulverized it into dust when he compared my body parts to his other women—before he… "Did you know?" My tears fall freely, uncontrollably.

"Know what?"

"About the other women? That he was cheating on me?" I'm shaking with anger as my voice remains deceptively calm. Gabriel reaches for me, but I can't stand his touch and move away. "You knew!"

"No!" His vehemence matches mine. "I suspected." On a second attempt, he manages to capture my hand. "He wasn't talking, and he sure as shit knew better than to flaunt his cheating around me." Moving closer, he adds, "You're not the only one he pulled away from. He did it to me too."

"Oh?" I lock on to him. The idea that he thinks his Austin relationship woes are comparable to mine has venom building, ready to spew. "He fucked your ass hard enough to make you bleed, dislocated your arm, then left you unconscious, naked and bleeding on the floor too?"

Oh, God!

Horrified, I dart up the stairs, ignoring the pain that throbs with each step. I didn't mean to say that. Well, I meant to say it. But I shouldn't have.

My revealing outburst must have slowed his response as I manage to make it to the guest room and lock the door before he reaches me.

Gabriel tests the handle. "Frankie, let me in."

I brace with my back against the door. "I'll be gone tomorrow. Just... Give me tonight." Where am I even going to go?

"You're not going anywhere." He bangs on the door; the vibration radiates in my shoulder. When I cry out, he stops. "God, Angel, I didn't mean to hurt you." His voice softly seeps through the crack under the door. Even when he can't see me, he knows when I'm hurting. Maybe he didn't know Austin was cheating. "Please, let me in. Let me take care of you."

"I can't. I need time. Space." I sink to the bed. If he chooses to break down the door, I can't stop him, and I certainly don't want to be standing on the other side of it.

I swear I can hear him breathing, contemplating on the other side of the door. "Okay. Rest now. I'll check on you later."

I lie down, not bothering with the covers. I need a quick nap.

Hours later I'm roused from sleep by Gabriel slipping me under the covers. So much for the locked door. The bed dips behind me, and he pulls me into his chest. "I'm sorry for upsetting you." He kisses my head, squeezes my hip. "So sorry for what he did." He buries his head in my neck. "You're not alone. I'm here."

"I don't trust you." It's a sleepy confession, rife with truth. "I want to..."

"You trust me. You're just afraid to."

"Austin hurt me in the worst way, but you've hurt me too. You were awful to me for years, but...you're not like that lately. I don't know what to think anymore."

He stiffens, the lazy circles he's been fingering on my hip still. He chews on his response so long I start to doze off. "It was a necessary evil. I'll tell you all about it, someday. But know this, I've always had your back. And I always will."

The lazy circles resume.

He's right. I am afraid to trust him. Mr. Asshole made an appearance tonight, crushing my vulnerable sprit that was starting to heal. *He's always had my back?* I don't understand how making me feel like shit was *having my back.*

As confused as ever, I drift off to sleep.

CHAPTER 9

I'VE LEFT HER ALONE FOR A WEEK. I'M IRRITABLE as hell. Everyone's keeping me at a distance, even her. I haven't slept in her bed since the night I went to their apartment and found out what really happened. Austin took her hard, dislocated her arm and left her bleeding on the floor. Naked.

And that asshole's been cheating on her.

He broke her heart, broke her body, and I don't think I'll ever get the image of that out of my head—or stop wanting to kill him.

I don't know what the fuck happened to Austin. The guy I met five years ago would move heaven and earth for his girl. He would never physically hurt her, and he sure as shit wouldn't cheat, except for the random blowjob he regretted for years. This new Austin surpasses even my level of assholiness. I've never physically hurt a woman, and I've never been in a relationship requiring faithfulness, but I know I would be faithful.

If I were with Frankie, she would never doubt my commitment to her. Ever.

But I'm not with Frankie. She's still broken and healing from the effects of another man's hands on her body. I am guaranteed to fuck this up, and I can't have any part of making this harder on her. The strength it's taking to stay away from her is nearly killing me.

King Asshole is back. Not because I'm being a dick to *her*, but because the distance she needs is ripping a hole in my chest I can't seem to breathe around. I want to protect her. Keep her safe. But every time I look at her, I see Austin hurting her. I see the effects of his dismissal of her pain. I see a broken angel I want to scoop up in my arms and heal with my words, my body, and promises that I'll never hurt her like he did. But the truth is, the promises of forever after she wants, deserves, I can't give. I don't want a wife and kids. My father made sure of that. So, I'm giving her space, which is making me act like a temperamental ass to everyone else around me. It's necessary to keep her at arm's length while she heals, and I focus on winning my next fight.

If I ever do win her heart, I want it to be because it's me she wants, and not because I'm the rebound guy, the one looking after her, a convenience.

I don't want to want her. But I do. And everyone around me is paying for my terrible mood.

The guys haven't found Austin. I've been too preoccupied with training and keeping her safe to go looking myself. I'm Army-trained special ops, but I'm a medic—a first responder—not a spy or a tracker. I fix those injured while on the hunt, not doing the hunting myself. If I could heal Frankie's heart with my med-kit, I would. But time is the healer she needs. Not an overprotective asshole who wants her in his bed for the foreseeable future.

So, I train. I cook. I watch after Frankie as much as she'll let me. I sneak into her room at night to be sure she's safe. I don't climb under the covers and hold her like I want—like her restless sleep calls to me to do. I sit in the chair, or if I'm bold, at the foot of the bed. I don't stay long, only long enough to ease the knot in my gut and soothe the beast who never believes she's safe unless she's in my arms or in my sights. Sometimes, when she wakes from a bad dream, she holds my hand or urges me to rub her back until she falls back to sleep. It's not nearly enough, but it's what she needs. And I'll move mountains to give her that.

That makes for long-ass days, and even longer nights. It's not conducive to training, to my focus, or my commitment to the team. They depend on me. Captain depends on me to set an example, to forge the path the others can follow. I will win every fight this year, even if it means I do it without my Angel by my side. I've had my blinders on for the past five years. It should be a piece of cake, but I've seen the promised land. I've held it in my arms. I've cared for those fields. I've stood as sentry, protecting it. Now I want to dwell in it. I want to take up residence and never leave.

Every day is a test of my willpower. And today, it's starting early.

Frankie had a follow up with the doctor this morning. She's hoping the doctor will give the okay for her to begin physical therapy. She and I both know it's too early for that. I doubt the doctor will even let her out of the sling.

Emerson is taking her. I offered, but Frankie shut me down. I didn't fight her on it. I have a sparring match I didn't want to miss or have to reschedule. Alex Young is only in town for few days. He's a former heavyweight champ and here as a favor to Coach, who's friends with Alex's father. If I don't take the opportunity, Sloan or Walker will, and I'll be damned if I'm going to give them a leg up on me. We're all heavyweights. I'm set to get the matches, the big invites this year. It's my time. My title to take. And as much as Sloan and Walker are brothers in arms, they are nipping at my heels. We're on the same team, but MMA fighting is a solo sport. When I step in the octagon, ring, or cage, it's me against the other guy. My team is there to support me leading up to and after the fight—during, it's all on me.

The air is thick in the Black Ops MMA Gym this morning. I can hear the planes taking off and landing at the old Miner's Airfield where we've taken up residence in an old hangar. It's ideal, really. We don't get walk-ins or curious spectators, which is the point of Captain setting up shop here. It's not for casuals. I'm not sure if this an experiment to keep our focus on training and not fighting off ring-chasers and the multitudes of distractions in Vegas, or if Cap is thinking of making this a permanent move. The Vegas gym is still in full swing, but the big contenders—like me—made the move here with strong prodding from Captain Jimmy.

I'm warming up, getting ready to step in the practice ring, when a commotion at the door gets my attention.

Frankie.

My Angel.

My demon from my own personal hell.

Emerson dropped me off at my apartment to get my car. She thought she was coming with me to the doctor, but I had other plans. I don't need an escort or anyone telling me what I can't or shouldn't do. That's why I didn't take Gabriel up on his half-hearted offer to take me. He never would have agreed to let me get my car, much less drive it to the doctor alone. Though, he didn't put up a fight when I turned him down.

Ever since Gabriel found out what happened with Austin, he's been distant and angry. I don't believe he's only upset with Austin. If that was the case, he wouldn't be giving me the cold shoulder too. I'm tainted, and he can barely stand the sight of me. Except at night. I've woken up more than a few times to find him watching over me. He makes me feel safe, but my gut twists at the idea of wanting more from him. I'm not sure I can trust another fighter, another man—especially one who runs through ring-chasers like it's a sport.

I don't have time for men who don't see my potential. I know I'm a diamond in the rough, my edges worn down by the last year of living in Austin's shadow. Perhaps even longer than that.

Captain never would have given me a chance as a physical therapist for his MMA Team if it weren't for Austin. I'm thankful, but it's my hard work and dedication that keep me in Cap's good graces. He hired me while I was still in school, paying me while I interned for his sports medicine doctor and physical therapist. While they covered other facilities, I was dedicated to Black Ops MMA Gym, and I've never regretted my decision.

I got into physical therapy as a way to stay relevant in Austin's life. I didn't want to be the outsider when it came to the world of professional MMA fighting as so many girlfriends are. I wanted to be right there in the middle of it, as close as possible, in a key role other than arm candy. I succeeded. But my success is not because of favors, but because of hard work and a true love of what I do. The human form is a spectacular thing—especially highly trained athletes at the peak of their game—a beautiful sight to behold. And when hurt, I want to be the one to help them get back to top form.

My profession is no longer due to a desire to stay close to Austin, but to pursue a job I love in a field that excites and challenges me. Never short of testosterone, it's a daily test to prove myself to the guys, ensure I'm needed and respected by guys strong enough to snap me like a twig.

Before leaving the doctor's office, I called Cap to let him know I'd be coming in. Checking in. I'm not fool enough to believe I can return to full duty. But I need to let him know I take my job seriously, and I will be back—sooner than later.

He must have told some of the guys I was coming, as I'm greeted by gentle hugs and gruff, "I'll kick his ass," comments the moment I walk in the door.

"I know you've missed her, gentlemen. But give her room to breathe," Captain Jimmy Durant's command parts the way as he approaches. "It's good to see you, Frankie." His hug lingers, like a father who's not convinced his kid is okay. "Let's go to my office." His large hand on my back and his impressive scowl ensure we make it with no further interruptions.

"Sit." He rounds his desk as I take a seat across from him. "How are you?"

"I'm good." I lean forward, ignoring the discomfort the effort produces. "I'm ready to come back to work."

He shakes his head, leaning back. "Frankie."

"At least part-time. I can assess injuries. Stock supplies. Light therapy—"

"No."

I take a breath to reply when I notice Cap's eyes are on the door and not me. It's then I realize the *no* didn't come from Captain but Gabriel.

Cap points to the chair next to me. "Join us, Gabriel."

"No." I stand and step to the window. "This is none of your business," I say to Gabriel. "This is between Cap and me. *He's* my employer. Not you."

Gabriel stands, legs wide, arms crossed. "Cap?"

"He's right, Frankie." Cap draws my attention. "You're in no condition to return to work. Give it two weeks. Then, with a doctor's note, you can return to work with limited duties."

"Two weeks?! Limited duties?" I thought for sure he'd let me hang out and slowly get back to full swing.

"You heard the man," Gabriel smugly replies. "Let's go."

"Go?" I look between the two of them who share a conspiratorial look. "I'm not going anywhere with you."

"Oh, yes you are." Mr. Asshole stomps toward me.

"No." I hold my hand out, which only manages to press against his chest as he pushes me backward. "I have my car. I don't need you to drive me."

"You drove!" The sing-song effect of their joined voices has me smiling despite myself.

"Yes. I drove." I stand a few inches taller, hoping it'll make them back down.

"What the fuck, Angel?" His hand covers mine, holding it against his chest. His heart is beating rapidly, and his eyes soften as if he's truly concerned. "I know the doctor didn't approve you to come back to work, much less drive."

I open my mouth to reply, but he cuts me off. "Don't lie."

A shrug is the only answer I give.

"That's what I thought." He holds out his hand. "Keys."

I narrow my eyes at him and then Cap, who simply shakes his head, his eyes dancing with amusement. "Fine." I dig them out of my purse and smack them in Gabriel's palm.

Gabriel tosses the keys to Cap and grabs my hand. "Will you see that the guys drop her car off at my house later?" He doesn't wait for a reply as he drags me out of Cap's office.

"I hate you," I mutter, trying to dislodge my hand from his.

"No, you don't." He picks me up with gentle ease as if I weigh nothing, kissing my forehead and whispering against my skin, "You only wish you did."

CHAPTER 10

L AST WEEK, WHEN I BROUGHT MY ANGEL HOME FROM
the gym, it took everything I had not to kiss the hurt off her face. In
her eyes, I'm unreasonable. I'm a traitor. I said I'd have her back, and
I do. But it doesn't mean I supported her plan to hurt herself by returning
to work and driving too soon.

"What if you had an accident?" I glanced at her beautiful, pouty face
as she tried to ignore me from the passenger seat. "What if a kid ran out in
the road? Could you have slammed on the brakes and turned the wheel fast
enough—with only one arm—to avoid hitting him?"

Color drained from her face as she grasped the reality of what could
have happened. "I didn't—"

"I know you didn't. But you could have killed someone, or yourself." I'd
been exaggerating. I doubted anything would have happened, but it could
have. And then where would I have been?

That was last week. Things haven't been much better since, though
she's still staying with me.

The memory of that day has my fingers twitching with the need to touch
her, to see her. I've got two days until my next fight. It's a big one, an important one that will guarantee me an invite to the biggest match of my career.

I've fought my whole life, for food, for shelter, to keep my mom and sister safe. I've been fighting for so long, I don't know any other way. I set my sights on a goal, and plan, fight, and kick my way till I've decimated all in my path, making my dream a reality—in life and in the octagon. I can't drop it all to become Frankie's personal bodyguard. That's important short-term, but I need to focus on the big picture. The Big Picture will allow me to take care of her the way she deserves, even though we can't really be together.

I have to hold out, focus. She can't distract me. I must behave as though she isn't my world.

"You're chopping those veggies like they have it out for you." My Angel's sultry voice has my cock stirring and my knife nearly slicing off my finger.

"They're devious vegetables, particularly the onions." I don't glance her way. Two days. Then I'll regroup and see about this thing between us.

She settles on a stool at the breakfast bar, facing me—too fucking close. Her vanilla scent washes over me. I shove a carrot in my mouth to keep from nibbling her.

"Can I get one?" She snags a carrot from the cutting board.

"Doesn't seem I can stop you." The coolness of my tone is all an act. Fuck if she doesn't affect me on some deep level I don't understand. It's always been this way, and it always fucking confuses me.

"You could stop me at any time, and you know it." She doesn't try to hide her hurt.

I ignore it.

Two. Days.

I can do this.

Sliding the veggies into the wok, I toss and stir till cooked to crisp perfection, adding the mix of cooked chicken, steak, and shrimp back in to be coated in the sauce and let the flavors mingle. Behind me, she sets the table, fetches drinks, and sits. Waiting.

It feels like she's waiting for more than dinner.

I fill her plate with more food than she can eat. My desire to provide for her is too strong to ignore. A smile cracks my cool façade when she digs in like she's starving.

"Man, this is good. I'll miss your cooking."

The satisfied warmth that filled my chest at her praise dies on her last words. "I'll only be gone a few days. Besides, I left you some meals in the fridge."

"Thank you, but that's not what I meant."

I lock eyes with her. "What *did* you mean, Angel?"

A wisp of a smile touches her perfect lips. She likes my pet name for her nearly as much as I do. She shrugs her good shoulder, breaking eye contact. "I mean, when I leave."

I suppress the roar threatening to break free and bend my fork in half before her small hand touches mine. Instantly, I release the utensil. She hops up and grabs a new fork out of the drawer, replacing the mangled one.

"I thought you'd be happy to have me out of your hair, not cramping your style." Her tentative words have my heart pounding. She has no idea how much I like having her here. *Knowing* she's here even when I'm not.

That's because you're King Asshole, asshole. "That's what you think?"

She shrugs her damn shoulder again, her eyes on her plate. "Doesn't matter."

Like hell it doesn't.

"I need to find my own place. Stand on my own two feet."

You don't have to leave me to be strong, Angel.

"I've been with Austin since I was fourteen. I moved out of my father's house and in with Austin. I've never been on my own."

Being alone is overrated.

Her gray eyes find mine, and the hopeful uncertainty I see in them twists my gut. Her next words escape like a plea, "I need to know I can do it."

Fuck. She needs room to bloom.

I scrape the contents of my plate into the trash and set it in the sink. "I leave tomorrow." I trudge down the hall, my feet like lead weights, making the journey away from her that much harder.

"Good luck." Her whisper barely reaches me.

You too, Angel.

Apartment hunting totally sucked. Emmy accompanied me, and though she tried to be upbeat, she was as disappointed as I was by what my budget would allow.

As soon as the door to Gabriel's closes behind us, she tries to cheer me up. "Maybe you should stay here, or your current apartment. You said it's paid up for two more months. It would give you time to save more money, and maybe something better will come along by then." She's selling, but I'm not buying.

"I can't stay there, not with how things ended. Plus, what if Austin comes back?" No one's heard from him. Grant says he's fallen off the face of the earth. He withdrew some money from our joint account a few days after he left. He was in Vegas at the time. Luckily, he didn't wipe me out. I opened a new account and moved half of the balance. It seems fair. He can have the rest. After all, we both earned it.

"You should have taken all the money." Emmy's a mind reader too, apparently.

"Just because he's an ass doesn't mean I have to act like one too."

"But you could afford a better place."

Nope. "I'd feel dirty. I'd rather live in shit than be a shit." I learned that lesson from my dad, except he'd rather be a shit, treat me like shit, and amazingly enough—we still lived in shit.

"God, that'd make a great t-shirt." She makes a note on her phone.

I know what I'm getting for my birthday. I shake my head as we make our way to the kitchen. "Hungry?"

"Always."

Our snack of cheese and apples devoured, I sit on the couch staring at the blank TV while Emmy talks to Grant in the other room. This is my first full day out of the sling. My shoulder aches, but nothing me and a few Advil can't handle. It's a good sign. Hopefully, I'll be able to return to work in a light load capacity. I'll have to leave the massages and manipulations to the contractor Cap brought in, but I can assess and oversee.

Now, if I can only convince Captain and Gabriel of that fact. I have a follow-up on Monday, and I don't plan to leave the doctor's office until I have a note saying I can return to work. I'm going stir crazy, and, though Cap is paying me while I'm off, something about medical paid leave, I can't help feeling guilty.

"You can stay with us." Emmy frowns, scanning the room, the black TV, and then back to me. "Are you going to watch the fight?"

Gabriel has the TV all set to stream most fights that are only viewable from the internet. "I hadn't decided." I rarely watched Austin fight. It's hard to watch the guy you love get beat up or hit someone with such anger and bad intent on their face. I know it's part of the package I signed up for, and I don't have a problem watching other MMA matches. It's Austin's I can't stomach. Maybe it was a clue to the man he eventually became as I've seen his anger and intent to inflict harm this past year, and he wasn't in the ring—he was fighting with me.

She grabs her purse. "I'm going to head home to watch with Grant, but I wanted to tell you, you can stay with us. We have our guest room. It sits empty most of the time. You're welcome to use it for however long you need it."

I have no doubt she talked Grant into agreeing. They like their alone time, and with a baby, those times are few and far between. "I don't want to cramp your style."

Her laughter is genuine and warm. "Oh, we'll still fuck at every opportunity. You being there won't stop us. Trust me." She squeezes my arm as I walk her to the door. "Think about it?"

"Yeah, okay." A quick hug and she's down the driveway. "Thank you for going with me today."

"Welcome. I wish we'd had better luck."

"Me too."

"Call if you need anything." Her eyes roam Gabriel's large home.

It's larger than any place I've ever been before. He's come a long way. I know he grew up with nothing, like Austin and me. We all had tough upbringings. I had Austin to rely on. Gabriel, well, I don't think he relied on anyone—he had his sister and mom he looked after—but I doubt he relied *on* them.

"If it's worth anything, I think you should stay here. See this thing through with Gabriel. You're good for each other." She points to the house. "And he obviously has plenty of space."

"I think he's ready to see me gone."

"Really?"

I nod, the knot in my throat betraying my calm.

"He told you as much?"

"No. But he's an ass—or was an ass. I don't know. He's been a dick to me for years, then incredible after... After. Lately, he's been distant. I told him I was looking for a place. He didn't say anything." Literally. Not. A. Word. "I'm sure he's ready to get his life back." I scan the house. "I'll only cramp his style."

She laughs again, tossing her purse in the car. "He's always been an ass, particularly to you. I think that says something right there. You're his kryptonite. Even Superman has his Lois Lane."

"But she wasn't his kryptonite. Kryptonite was his kryptonite."

"Whatever, you know what I mean. Maybe Superman was a shit analogy, but you're Gabriel's Achilles heel. Without you, he walks for shit."

It's my turn to laugh. "You're really bad at this."

"But you got my drift?"

"Yeah, I feel ya. I just don't agree. He couldn't care less. He's barely even talking to me."

"That's because he's too busy fucking you in his head."

"God," I groan. The ideas she puts in my head. It's too soon to even consider moving on with someone. I need to find my own footing. Besides, I don't think I can trust my feelings when it comes to Gabriel. He swooped in to save me, but that's not his norm—at least not when it comes to me. Mr. Asshole will come out. I have no doubt. He makes me feel safe, even in his home when he's not here. Which is why I need to move out. I need to feel safe on my own.

"Truth, babes. It sucks sometimes." She hops in her car, turning it on and rolling down the window. "Think about my offer, but think about staying here even more." She drives off with a, "Wings out, bitches!"

Emmy is as crazy and bold as they come, but she's got it bad for Grant. I'm happy for them. I kinda wish I knew her in her single days. She was a wild one, I'm sure. But Married Mommy Emerson is a rock star.

Something to aspire to.

I head inside and turn on the TV, setting it up to watch Gabriel's fight when it starts. The knot in my stomach I used to have before Austin's fights is present, but I don't fear the face of Gabriel when he fights. He is—was—Mr. Asshole all the time. There's no hidden monster with him. He's as alpha as they come, and he wears it proudly. Gabriel is who he is with no apology, no pretenses. Though, he's shown me his gentle side, something I never thought I'd see directed at me. It's been amazing… And confusing.

With an hour before it starts, I take a shower, donning yoga pants and an oversized shirt, sans bra, and set off for the kitchen. I think Gabriel made another batch of beef stew. I squeal when I find it—thank God I'm alone. My elation over Gabriel's cooking would be an endless tease-fest if anyone else were here. Setting the pot to warm on the stove, I check the time and the TV, confirming I'm all set.

The fights start, one right after the other, but it's the heavyweight match I'm waiting for. My nerves kick into high gear when "Bawitdaba" by Kid Rock blares through the arena—it's Gabriel's entrance song. It's not the one Emmy was listening to a few weeks ago, but it's good. Effective. The crowd goes crazy, their roar nearly overpowering the heavy beat of the song.

Gabriel's menacing mug comes on the screen. His blue eyes—electrified from the strobing lights—flash to the screen for a split second. In that second, I feel his gaze on me like he knew I'd be watching. A smirk slips free before he banishes it with a clenched jaw and a punch in the air. He mouths something, kisses his wrapped fingers before raising his hand to the heavens. I've watched Gabriel fight, and I've never seen him do that.

Over his shoulder, I spot Coach, flanked by Jonah and Walker. They look ready to spit fire, demons escorting the devil to hell. They're all ex-military, including Coach. This is nothing compared to what they endured while fighting for our freedom. The MMA universe may be tough as nails, but these guys know they're the powerful nail-gun who will spit out the competition like the hunks of metal they are. These men know fear and death—and beat both, tirelessly. An MMA match is like a church social for them.

Gabriel tops the steps at the octagon entrance. Arms raised as if he's already won, he turns, giving the camera a full view of his impressively muscled back, but it's not the muscles that has them clamoring, it's his tattoo. It's Gabriel, the avenging angel whose dark shadowy wings span the breadth of his back. The figure is dark yet glows with inner light, a spear in one hand and a shield in the other. Gabriel may liken himself more to the devil, but his back says otherwise. He's Gabriel the archangel.

With a quick look to his corner, he enters the cage.

Music for his competitor begins to play. The main camera pans to the entering fighter, but a picture-in-picture display on the bottom right of the screen stays on Gabriel. My eyes don't leave him. I step closer to the TV as if my motion could make the camera zoom in. He bounces, light on his feet, too light for a man his size and weight:

6'6" and 240 pounds. All muscle. All man. Dipped in testosterone and rubbed to glistening perfection.

"You never looked at me like that."

I scream, pivoting to find an angry-faced Austin taking up space in the arch between the entryway and the living room, hands fisted at his sides, his fight face, his intent to cause harm radiating off him—focused on me. "Austin."

He steps forward, pointing at the TV. "You never fucking looked at me like that!"

CHAPTER 11

THE TRIP TO LA WAS UNEVENTFUL. THE GUYS tried to get me to go out last night, but I wasn't interested. They were out to get laid. There's only one woman I want, and she's home—at my house—waiting for me. At least, I hope she is. Grant said Frankie and Emerson were going apartment hunting today. I prayed she didn't find anything. It's a shitty prayer, but I'm King Asshole. Whaddya expect?

The Russian dude I'm fighting tonight tried to intimidate me at the weigh-in. I all but laughed in his face. Now, if he had a rocket launcher in his hand or was disemboweled by an IED, and I was expected to put him back together, then I'd be sweating. But as it stands, he's got nothing on me. He's no threat. It's only a fight. An important one for the key invite I need, but still, it's not life or death.

I texted my Angel right before my entrance. It was stupid. Who the hell let me have my phone? She didn't answer. Of course. I kept glancing at the screen.

"Jesus, you're Gabriel—*No Mercy*—Stone." Walker punches my arm. "What the fuck do you care about a text message?"

"Hand it over." Jonah offers his palm. "I'll keep it safe." I know he means he'll keep checking for me. He knows I'm worried about her, being away, unable to see her, confirm she's safe.

I should have called earlier. I was trying to be good, give her what she says she needs. Space. But fuck if that space isn't strangling me. It's just a fight, but anything can happen. No one's died in the cage yet, but people have been seriously, irreparably fucked up. What if something happens, and I never took the chance to tell her how I really feel because I gave her the bullshit space she asked for?

Relinquishing my phone, I bounce and shadow box in the corner, my air pods blaring. My guys surround me, keeping me focused. But they don't know she's gotten in my head, under my skin, and dug in deep. Focus? How can I focus on anything but her?

Damn! What the fuck was I thinking? I knew she was a distraction. *Why do you think you've been an ass her to all these years? For fun?* I punch Walker in the shoulder.

"Bitch! What's your problem?" He turns, facing me.

I nod to his hands, and he sticks 'em up, palms out. I punch into them, fast, hard, but not hard enough to hurt his pansy-ass.

Coach pulls out one of my air pods. "Who are you?"

"Gabriel."

"Gabriel who?"

"Gabriel No Mercy Stone!"

"Who are you?!" Coach, Walker, and Jonah all ask as one voice.

"Gabriel."

"Gabriel who?!" they ask.

"Gabriel *No Fucking Mercy* Stone!" I roar.

"What are you doing here?" Heart racing, but still in control, I glance around the room, planning my escape—looking for a weapon.

"I had to see for myself, Ang." The pain is evident in Austin's voice, but his eyes are wild, and his skin is beading with sweat like he's on something.

"You need to leave. Grant and Emmy will be here any second to watch the fight."

He steps closer, backing me to the fireplace below the TV. "Now, that's a lie. I saw Emmy leave. Even heard your conversation."

He's been here that long? "Austin." I push his chest, but I'm no match. "You need to leave. The police are looking for you."

His hand is around my neck before I can dodge it. He forces me against the mantel. "Why would that be? Did you tell them I raped you? Did you lie to get in Gabriel's bed? Did he pity fuck you?"

"No!" I screech, losing my calm. I would never lie about being raped, but I did feel violated by his words, his assault on my arm, his cheating, and the way he left me injured on the floor like a discarded, broken toy instead of a person he cared about. "I didn't tell them that. I told them the truth." I try to push him off. "You hurt me."

"Not as bad as I wanted to, Frankie." His hold on my neck tightens. Austin has never laid a hand on me. He may have cheated on me, lied to me and broken my heart. But he never hurt me physically before the night he dislocated my shoulder. Now, he's crazed. I don't even know who this is standing before me.

"He hates you, you know," he spits out.

I know. *No, Gabriel is different now.* God, I wish he were here. Austin never would've made it two feet into his house if he'd been here. Austin must have had a key. Is nowhere safe?

I can't squelch my rising panic. I can breathe, but my hammering heart might make me pass out anyway.

"I can't stand the look of you. The smell of you." He holds me at arm's length as he steps back, sneering down at me. His eyes lock on my breasts. I whimper under his scrutiny, regretting not wearing a bra.

He leans in, whispering in my ear, "Has he fucked all your holes? Does he fuck your mouth till you gag?" He squeezes.

I claw at his arm, clamoring for air.

He cuts it off.

The pressure pounds behind my eyes. I have seconds. My thoughts race to Gabriel. *What if I never see him again?* The thought has me pleading with the man I used to love, "Please," I mouth.

He releases me.

I fall, choking, to the floor, shaking my head. "No," my voice is raspy and tight.

"Does he make you come, Ang?" He squats before me, tipping my chin till my eyes meet his. I'm shocked to find tears streaming down his face. "Are you his now?"

"What do you care? We're done. You can't hurt me like you did and expect to come back like nothing happened." I slap his hand away and scramble far enough to stand, placing the couch between us. "You think I want to be with a cheater? Someone who hurts me?"

He moves toward me but catches himself, tugging at his hair in frustration. "I couldn't stand the look in your eyes. Your love. Your expectations. Your loyalty. So damn fucking loyal, Ang. I've fucked around for years, even before the car accident. And still, you were loyal to a fault."

Jesus. "Get out." I reach around the corner to the house phone on the other side of the kitchen wall, the verbal knife he just speared me with fanning my determination.

"I loved you, Frankie—"

"You have a fucked-up way of showing it!" Holding the wireless handset out of sight, I punch in 9-1-1 and hit what I hope is the *talk* button. I'm pelted with relief when I hear the soft ringing.

He shakes his head, defeat written all over his demeanor. "I couldn't stand up to the weight of your expectations."

"I had no expectations of you, Austin, other than the promises you made." I point at him with the phone in my hand as the operator answers. "You promised to love and protect me!" I step forward, the knowledge that help is coming emboldening my resolve. "I would have loved you to the end of days, Austin. I would have given you everything!"

He backs up, shoulders sagging. "I know. I know you would've. But I couldn't."

A muffed woman's voice says something about police being on their way. I bring the phone to my ear. "Call Grant Malone. Tell him Austin is at Gabriel's house. Now." I drop it on the couch, leaving the line open. If I keep the phone in my hand, he'll see how badly I'm shaking. I can't let him see my fear. "It's time for you to go, Austin."

"I know." He moves to the door. "I really just came to apologize."

"Well, that was a shit-ass apology." I cross my arms, moving toward him, acting braver than I feel.

"I didn't mean to hurt you." He opens the door and steps out and down the stairs.

He didn't mean to hurt me?! "You acted like you were the one saving me from my childhood, but you always needed me more than I needed you." Grabbing the door handle, I start to close it, but stop when I hear sirens in the distance. "You hurt me worse than my father ever did—ever could."

"Frankie," his voice quavers. His anger dissipates, completely replaced by a sorrowful man I nearly recognize.

"You're a lying, cheating sack of shit. I don't know what happened to you, Austin, but you aren't the boy I fell in love with or the man I'd hoped to marry. I'm ashamed I invested so much of myself in you. For what? To be cheated on, lied to, and physically abused? I don't think so. Go fuck yourself. I'm done."

With that, I slam the door, locking it for safe measure, and sink to the floor in a pile of useless tears and shattered dreams. What the hell happened to us? When did he change into a stranger? Was he always such a monster, and I was too blind to see it? I feared I might want to take him back if I saw him again. But the second his anger sparked, I knew I could never love him again. I can't love someone I can't trust—someone who would treat me like that.

He broke us. He smashed what we had into irreparable pieces— even if I could, I wouldn't want to put us back together.

CHAPTER 12

I T'S THE LAST ROUND, AND THE RUSSIAN IS putting up a better fight than I thought he would. He slipped in a few hits and kicks I never would've allowed had I not been distracted.

Jonah greases the cut above my left eye. "Your concentration is for shit, Gabriel."

"Tell me something I don't know." I breathe out, taking a swig of water.

He glances over my shoulder to Coach. "They don't want me to tell you, but—"

"What?" I look between them, a new wave of adrenaline hitting my veins.

"It's Frankie. She called the cops from your house. Austin showed up," Jonah rapid fires.

"Motherfucker!" I stand, ready to blow this fight. "She's alright?"

"Yeah, she's with Grant." Jonah gives my shoulder a squeeze. "She's good."

Coach pushes me back to my stool. "Finish this. Then go get your girl."

He's right. If I win this, I'm guaranteed an invite to the next tournament—the one I want, the one I've been training for.

"Make sure I'm on the next flight available. I don't care if it's an hour from now. I'm on it. Fuck the press conference." I stand. The Russian has no idea what he's up against. "I'm done playing with this asswipe."

The bell rings. The Russian starts mumbling in his native tongue. I have no doubt it's slurs about my manhood, my mother, or my girl. It's all wasted on me. I don't see him. I don't hear him. The only face I see is Austin's, and he's a dead man.

I'm known for my power punches, my takedowns. But I'm not taking him to the floor. I don't have time for that. I've played around with this guy long enough. It's time he felt the full force of Gabriel *No Mercy* Stone.

I let the Russian have one hit. It barely grazes my jaw. I let its force turn my body as if it's packs a wallop. But really, I'm using the momentum to fuel my pivot, coming back at him with a left jab to the jaw, wiping the smugness off his face. He doesn't even recover before I follow with a straight right to the other side of his jaw. The jerk of his head, the blood gushing from his mouth, the roll of his eyes are confirmation enough he's on his way down, but to be sure, I finish him with a left hook.

I back away, bouncing, waiting as he crumples to the mat with a heavy whomp. The shrill of the crowd is deafening.

I'm declared the winner by KO.

It's a blur of activity from there: out of the cage, up the ramp, a two-minute shower, dressed in street clothes, orders given to the team, and I'm on my way to the airport.

"Do you want more tea?" Emmy circles like a mother hen.

"No, I'm good. Thank you."

"Want something stronger?" Grant offers, checking his phone for the hundredth time.

"No. Thanks." I gave my statement at the house before Grant brought me home to his, where a waiting Emmy paced at the door. She squished me in a hug, only letting go at Grant's urging.

Their house is a buzz of activity. Gwen is with her grandparents, so there's no reason to shush the noisy cops milling around like they're waiting for something. They weren't at Gabriel's so I'm assuming they were here watching the fight before Grant got pulled away.

They caught Austin before he could leave Gabriel's neighborhood. He didn't put up a fight. He went peacefully. Seems his fight was all for me.

It's hours later. I'm tired. I'd like to lie down, but I don't want to be alone. I know I'm safe. It's just—

"Angel."

I whip around so fast I lose my balance. Gabriel catches me before I cause myself any harm. "You're here."

He straightens me in his arms. "I wouldn't be anywhere else." He touches my cheek, scanning my face.

But he was somewhere else. "You won. You should be celebrating in LA." I notice the cut above his eye and then the busted lip. My fingers itch to touch, to investigate his injuries. I take in his chest, his arms, as if I can see through his clothes. "You okay?"

"Fuck, Angel. I'm not the one who was attacked." He pulls me into a hug. "Are *you* okay?"

"Yeah." My voice cracks as I nod into his chest. The emotions that left me the moment the police arrived to find me huddled on the entry floor come back full force. I was so scared, but more than anything, I feared I'd never see Gabriel again. Austin took so much from me. Would he take Gabriel from me too? Austin said Gabriel hated me, but he's here. He rushed home to my side. That matters. I grip him tighter.

He sinks his fingers into my hair, lifting my face to his. "No, you're not." He swipes at my tears.

"I am," I sob.

He chuckles. "My Angel, always so strong and brave." He holds me against his chest as I cry.

The noisy room behind us quiets. I hope they've left instead of standing there staring at the spectacle I'm sure I am.

"It's alright. I've got you." He rubs circles on my back. "You're safe."

I didn't realize *he* was what I was waiting for. Emmy offered me the guestroom bed, but I couldn't. I didn't want to be alone, but more importantly, I was hoping he'd come for me and take me home. "I was afraid if I fell asleep, you wouldn't come. You wouldn't wake me up. You wouldn't take me home."

"I would have. I would've crawled in bed with you and held you all night." His lips graze my forehead. "But I'm glad you're awake and dressed so I can take you home."

We find Grant and Emmy in the kitchen. He's holding her close. She's clearly shaken by what's happened. Maybe it hit too close to home, brought up skeletons from her past.

I try to apologize for upsetting her, but she and Grant quickly shut me down.

With a brief exchange and borrowed keys, Gabriel walks me to Grant's car.

I didn't even know I'd fallen asleep until he's carrying me up his stairs. "You've got to be sore after your fight. I can walk."

"Shh, no more protesting. No more acting brave. Let me take care of you." He sets me on his bed. A soft smile curves his lips as his thumb grazes mine. He pulls his shirt off, toes off his shoes, and undoes his jeans before kneeling before me. "I need a shower." He takes off my shoes. "You're coming with me."

"You smell freshly showered." I touch his shoulder, cupping his face. "You need arnica on your cuts, your muscles."

He stands, pulling my shirt over my head. I'm thankful I was clearheaded enough to put on a bra before leaving with Grant. His gaze falls to my chest and moves up to my neck. His fingers gently follow. "I'm sorry I wasn't here."

"It's not your fault." I capture his hand before he notices the marks left by Austin's grip on my neck.

Gabriel scoops me in his arms. Stepping into the bathroom, he doesn't turn on the lights. He sets me on the counter, squeezing my hips before moving away to turn on the shower. When he faces me again, he moves slower, shrugging off his jeans as he nears. "Let me wash away the pain he caused."

I want that. But I stop his hands as he reaches for the clasp of my bra. "He said you hated me." I don't want to believe anything Austin said, but this needs to be addressed. I can't be with Gabriel believing he hates me.

His hand grips the back of my neck, tilting my head back. "He lied." His blue eyes are pools of languid truth. "I hated the way you made me feel."

Leaning into his touch, I ask what I'm afraid to, "How did I make you feel?"

"Like I was losing my mind. You loved him, but I wanted you."

"I can't be one of the many." I'm not asking for forever. I just can't feel like I mean nothing to him.

He leans forward, in my face. "You've never been one of anything. You've always been the one and only." His lips touch mine, reverently and all too briefly.

I unclasp my bra, sliding it slowly down my arms.

His hands and eyes trail my every movement. "I might have been angry with you for loving him instead of me. But I never hated you, Angel." He pulls me to my feet, sliding my yoga pants and panties off. "I never could." He kisses up my stomach, between my breasts, working his way to my neck, then ear as he stands.

Lit with need and shaking from exhaustion, I manage to stay on my feet when he removes his boxer briefs. I suck in a breath at the sight of him naked, his bruised ribs, his face and lip, cut. His strong legs supporting his impressive form, and at his center, a raging-hard cock.

Cupping my ass, he pulls me flush against him, his hands kneading my flesh. "Let me take care of you. Let me worship you."

The naughty girl in me screams *yes, please!* The good girl in me screams *it's about time!*

I nod my acquiescence, and two seconds later he's devouring my mouth. It's a slow and sensual kiss, backed by urgency and suppressed lust. We're breathless when he pulls back. "I've waited five years to do that." He leads me into the shower, my hand in his.

I only get a few seconds of water wetting my hair before he backs me to the wall. "And I've waited just as long to do this." He lowers to his knees, slinging my leg over his shoulder as he holds me steady with a splayed hand across my stomach, his eyes on mine. "I'm sorry if you're tired, Angel. It might be a while before I get my fill."

I gasp when he buries his nose in my pussy, separating my folds with his tongue. "A long fucking while," he murmurs against my skin, sending goosebumps rippling across my body.

"God, Gabriel." I grip his head and shoulder. He's so dirty and delicious.

"God's not here, Frankie. It's only you and me."

CHAPTER 13

MY ANGEL TASTES LIKE HEAVEN AND MOANS like a siren from hell sent to torture me, test my willpower. I delve in deep, my tongue missing no crevice, having no mercy.

"Oh, God."

"Gabriel." I open my eyes, taking in her flushed skin, tight as hell nips, and undulating body trying to fuck the air, and smile. I've fantasized about this. I've jerked off to this. "When it's my mouth tasting you, when it's my cock fucking you, it's *my* name on your lips."

She holds my face in her hands. The mix of tenderness and want in her eyes has me wanting to spout words I've never said before. I've never *felt* before. But the next words out of her mouth save me from such fairy-tales, "Then fuck me already."

I'd planned on making her come a couple of times before taking her to bed—to *take her*. I stand, exploring my way to her breasts, feeling them for the first time. *God, these breasts.* "Angel, I'm not fucking you for the first time in the shower." I hardly recognize my voice, full of lust and a need to conquer. I've always been possessive of Frankie. Whenever Austin got handsy, I avoided them like they had the plague. My time in the service was a reprieve from their love. This is my chance, and I'm not screwing it up by fucking her for the first time in the shower like a ring-chaser I picked up at a bar.

My Angel deserves better.

Grabbing the shampoo, I guide her under the spray to wet her hair before losing myself in her dark locks. "I've always loved your hair." It's black as night and matches mine like we were forged from the same slab of marble.

When I finish, she washes mine as I explore her with my hands, my fingers, my mouth with the pretense of getting her clean, like she wasn't already pure. Austin may have hurt her. He may have touched her, but he could never make her dirty.

By the time she's washed me and grips my cock, I'm on sensory overload, ready to plunder, ready to blow. I rinse us off, pull her from the shower, towel us off, and carry her to bed.

If my Angel had any sense of shyness, I've washed it away. She lies on the bed, her legs open enough to see the glory land, bare and ready. I rip open a condom, hating the idea of any layer between us. We will be discussing going bareback, but for now, I sheath my beast and crawl between her legs.

Her hands ignite chills as I come in reach. Her legs wrap around mine, urging me forward as I settle over her. "Slow, Angel." It's not a command but a plea more for myself than her. "The first time I saw you, I knew." I press between her folds, letting my cock do the investigating. She arches, drawing me closer to where she needs me, where I've been destined to be since the day I was born, my fucked-up life bringing me to this point.

The head of my cock slides into her warmth. My groan silences hers, the feel of her so perfect. "I acted like I didn't care." I surge forward, sinking in deep and stilling.

"Gabriel," she cries against my lips.

Cupping her face, I hold her gaze. "I cared, Angel." I pull out and pause at her entrance. Her eyes water, and I thrust in again. "I care so fucking much, it scares me."

"I thought you hated me." Her hand brushes my cheek as tears run down the corners of her eyes, and that damaged organ in my chest breaks.

"I never have." I kiss her tears. "I never could."

I thrust into her over and over until she arches, coming off the bed as she squeezes my cock and falls over the edge.

"So fucking beautiful." Holding her to me, I rise up, sitting back on my haunches, pulling her into my lap, her legs straddling my hips, circling my back—my dick fully seated inside my Angel… My heaven.

With my arm supporting her back and my hand cradling her neck, I gently guide her as I swivel my hips, gliding slowly in and out. "You're mine now, Angel." *Not fucking his.* "You've always been mine."

She gasps, clenching me in a vise grip as her body responds to my declaration. Biting my lip, she whispers words I want to hear over and over again, "You're gonna make me come."

I surge deep, circling, pressing her ass, getting maximum pelvis to clit contact. "When you do," I swipe my tongue across her mouth, dive in deep and claim what's mine, "I'm coming with you."

"Yes." Her exultation on writhing hips has my orgasm tingling in my balls.

"Fuck, Angel. Ride me. Just like that."

Her moans grow as her movements become demanding, needy, and sexy as hell. I squeeze the back of her neck to get her attention. She locks on me. "I want your eyes, baby."

She grabs the back of my neck. Nose to nose, she rides my cock in rolling movements as I thrust into her. Her fingers press into my scalp, and I wish I had longer hair for her to hold on to.

When she falters, I swallow her cries as she comes, my mouth feasting with a hunger I've never known. I bark my own release into her mouth as she hungrily feeds on me, her grip so tight, I fear she'll hurt her shoulder. But there's no letting up for either of us. We continue to ride until the wave of pleasure ebbs, and we're panting in exhaustion.

"Holy hell," she whispers across my mouth.

I kiss her soundly, surging in one more time, and relish her soft sigh in response. "Holy fucking hell is right."

"I never knew…" I fall to the bed, worn out, in shock, and buzzing from two remarkable orgasms.

He collapses beside me after disposing of the condom, pulling me into his body. "Never knew what?"

"That sex could be like that." I peek up at him, feeling shy all of a sudden. Sex with Austin was good, but it was different. Never like this.

"Because it wasn't just sex." He tips my chin, pressing his mouth to mine. "That was the universe coming together."

I can't stop my laugh. Mr. Asshole has become rather deep and share-y.

He pins me to the mattress, his eyes alight with humor. "You don't believe me?"

"I think it was a fluke," I tease. Fluke or not, it was incredible.

"Really?" He presses his impressive, already hard again cock against me. "Maybe I should prove my point."

"You couldn't possibly," I taunt. He's not one to pass up a challenge.

"Angel." He tenderly caresses my cheek. "You have no idea what I'm capable of, especially when I have you as inspiration." He pulls my leg up over his hip and pushes inside me, groaning, "Fuck. Tell me we don't need a condom."

"I'm on the pill. I'm clean." I don't think this is the right time to tell him Austin hasn't entered my pussy in months. He preferred my ass, which he made abundantly clear the last time we were together. Plus, he always used a condom with ass play.

"Hey." Gabriel kisses my neck. "Don't think about him. He has no place here between us."

I nod, unable to find my voice.

"I'm clean. We get tested every month, but you know that."

I do. Testing is required for all of Black Ops' fighters.

"I've never *not* used a condom, Frankie." His sincerity touches me in a way that's surprising—he's surprising.

"Then prove your point." I move under him, loving the weight of his body on mine, his strength and power, all focused on me.

He chuckles. "Remember you said that." He drills in deep. "Fuuuck, you feel good." He sits back, pulling my legs over his thighs, my ass and lower back off the bed, gripping my hips, and sinks in again and again. His head falls back. "So fucking good," he groans to the heavens like a prayer.

His pleasure sends tingles through my body, and I clench around him.

"You like that?" He brings his thumbs closer, separating my folds, edging my clit, watching the whole time.

"Yes," I hiss, wanting more, but too lost in his enjoyment to demand it.

He thrusts, then grinds. One thumb rubs my clit as the other hand squeezes and teases my breasts. "I've neglected these." He pinches my nipple, and I cry out. "Yeah, I'm gonna have to play with these more next time."

Next time. I love that he plans on there being one.

I grip his arms for leverage, trying to keep up with his thrusts, and lose myself in his movements, his touch, his dirty words of praise. I feel like a goddess in his hands. Like I could do no wrong. Like I could have no better body. Like I couldn't be a better lover. All of which I know are not true, but for the moment, in his eyes, I am all of those things.

We come like rolling thunder, our ecstasy reverberating off the walls, our bodies mere vessels for the bounty of our joining—like the universe becoming one.

He was right.

And I'll gladly let him prove it anytime.

CHAPTER 14

SOMEWHERE BETWEEN ROUND THREE AND THE SUN rising, I get her to talk to me. Tell me what Austin said, what he did. The intimacy of our bodies broke the emotional barrier we've spent years erecting between us.

Perched on my elbow, hovering over her, I rub the spot on her neck where his thumb left a bruise. "I'm sorry, Angel." I want to suck on it until my mark covers his, but that's a selfish move. She's not a toy to be claimed. She's a woman to be worshipped.

She traces the tattoo on my right bicep. It was my first and why *no mercy* was my call sign and now part of my MMA name.

"Mercy is granted not earned," she reads. Her thoughtful eyes meet mine. "Do you still believe that?"

"Yeah." Now more than ever.

She nods her acceptance. "And this one?" She rolls to her side, pulling my hand that's supporting my head to read the other bicep. *"Loyal. Brave. True."*

I watch as she studies it, not asking, but pondering all the same. "It's so you." She smiles as I run my fingers through her hair.

"You think so?" I'm honored she sees it. It's what I strive to be, and what I expect from others if they care to have any place in my life.

"Yep." She pops the *p*. "Totally you."

Pressing a kiss to her mouth, I lean back on the headboard, bringing her with me. "I think it's you too."

"Austin said I'm loyal to a fault."

I prop her on my lap, covering us with the blanket. "He's falling off the deep end. Don't let his craziness change who you are." I cradle her against my chest. "You love him. Loyalty is part of the package. Or, at least, it should be."

Her eyes, full of sadness, meet mine. "I *loved* him."

"Loved?" My heart pounds, wishing it were true, but it seems too soon for her heart to be open for me.

"I may always love him." She sits up, her eyes watering. "He saved me, Gabriel. Without him, I wouldn't have survived my father." Her chin wobbles, and I want to take away her pain and kick the ass of every man who hurt my girl.

I cup her cheek, holding her face and kiss away the tears. "It's okay."

She nods, her eyes pleading. "I thought he was it. I thought he was the one."

My gut twists for her, for me. He should have been. That's what I had accepted—what she was expecting.

Burying her head in my neck, she cries. I comfort her as best I can, trying to be a friend and not the guy who wants her all for himself.

"He broke something in me. He took what I gave him and shit all over it. He's so angry. I don't even know what I did that was so wrong. Why did he turn on me? Why did he cheat? Was I old news—the ball and chain?" Her stream of questions kills me. Questions only *he* can answer.

"I don't know, Angel. It's like he's become a different person since his injury. We're not the only ones to notice."

"He said he cheated before the accident." Shame lines her words as if it's her fault. Her admission proves he was spiraling before the accident.

Fuckwad. "He's an idiot for not holding on to you, Frankie." I kiss her swollen lips and pull back to capture her glassy eyes. "I won't make the same mistake."

She simply blinks in response. I'm not sure she heard me over the thoughts in her head and the exhaustion in her bones.

Quietly, I lay us down, holding her until she falls asleep.

I hope Grant has some answers for me in the morning. I'll call him, but first I need sleep. My body is getting sorer by the minute. I didn't do any of the post-fight care I normally would. I'm going to regret it tomorrow, but my Angel is worth the sacrifice.

Any sacrifice.

The night comes rushing back to me the moment I slip from sleep. The delicious soreness of my underused sexual parts brings a smile to my lips and a flush of heat to my cheeks. But the discomfort around my neck serves as a reminder of where the night started and the state of my life.

"You're thinking too much for having just opened your eyes." The morning edge to Gabriel's voice has me digging deeper into his embrace and breathing him in. He chuckles, his hand pressed to my back. "Did you just scent me?"

I squirm and glance at his smiling face. "Maybe." I pull away, needing the bathroom and a toothbrush.

He tightens his hold on me. "Maybe, huh?" He's enjoying this entirely too much. With the ease of a seasoned wrestler, he rolls us so I'm on my back. On automatic, my legs open for him and wrap around him. When his impressive manhood rubs against my core, he moans, "Fuck, Angel." Closing his eyes, he circles his hips and buries his nose in my neck. His deep intake of air and his exploring mouth have me rocking under him. He kisses up my jaw and pecks my lips, his eyes burning with want. "Good morning."

A smile teases my lips. "Morning."

He grinds his hips and stills. "Food."

What? Who wants food when there's a sexy beast between my legs?

He brushes my cheek and lips with his fingertips. "If we don't get out of this bed, I'm going to fuck you all damn day."

"And that's a problem… Because…?"

A tender smile softens his rugged features. He presses a kiss to the tip of my nose. "Because you'll be too sore to walk, much less take me tonight." He rolls off me and the bed in one fell swoop. "I'm gonna shower and make breakfast."

Any disappointment I feel is squashed as I watch his fine backside lumber to the bathroom. He looks back and smiles when he catches me. "I'd ask you to join me, but we both know where that would lead."

I sit up, letting the sheet pool at my waist. His eyes fall to my breasts, and I can feel my nipples pucker under his stare. He turns around, arms bracketing the doorframe, his body filling the space as he takes me in.

Slipping out of bed, his heated gaze fueling my bravado, I walk to him, stopping when my nipples brush his chest and his hard cock bobs between us.

"Angel," he warns.

"Gabriel." My tone rasps with want. He thinks I'm trying to seduce him, and maybe a part of me wants to. Actually, a very large part of me wants to. But what I do next isn't about sex or fulfilling long suppressed carnal desires for the man who's been a running stream of negativity in my life for the past five years.

I wrap my arms around his waist and press the side of my face against his chest and hug him.

His muscles flex, and his breath catches. "Frankie?" he asks seconds before hugging me back. I sink into his warmth and let out a sigh of contentment. He curls around me, his head resting on mine, his entire body encapsulating me in his hard planes and tattooed art. "Angel." It's a prayer whispered into my hair and wraps around my broken heart. It's power threatening to heal and mend what I never thought possible.

"Thank you," I breathe into his neck. I don't want to make it weird, but I don't think he'll ever know how much last night meant to me. How much I owe him for the past few weeks. He may be Mr. Asshole much of the time, but he's given me a soft place to land by offering up his home, by taking care of me even when he was the last person I thought I wanted, by showing me I'm not nothing to him.

As if he heard all of that, he kisses my neck and squeezes me tighter. "Anything for you."

...and for the first time in a long time, I believe in a man who's giving me more than he's taking.

CHAPTER 15

I WANDER THROUGH THE HOUSE. IT'S NOT THAT big of a place, but my Angel disappeared a half hour ago, and I haven't seen her since. The ache in my chest warns me I need to ensure she's safe. After checking all the usual places, I stop in the laundry room doorway, finding her folding clothes.

"I have a woman who comes and does that for me." Granted, I haven't had her come since Frankie has been staying with me. I didn't want even Mable invading our space.

Frankie jumps and squeaks out her surprise, clutching a towel to her chest. "Jesus, Gabriel, for a man your size, you're entirely too quiet."

"I've been told." I come up behind her, gripping her hips, and kiss her behind the ear. "Why are you doing laundry?"

"Because I needed clean clothes." She continues to fold the stack in front of her.

"But these aren't yours." By the stacks of clean clothes, towels, and sheets, she's been at this for a while. "When did all of these get washed?"

"I've been doing it on and off all day."

WTF? How did I not notice? "You don't need to do my laundry."

"I don't mind." She places the folded towel in her hand on the tower of towels.

"Where are your clothes?" All I see are mine.

"In the dryer." She points to the rack in the corner. "Except for those." What seems to be every shirt she has with her is hanging up, air drying.

"Mable wouldn't mind doing yours too."

"I wouldn't feel right about that. Plus, this way I'm assured my tops don't get dried."

"Hmm." She's wearing one of my black V-neck t-shirts. My hands travel up her waist and then down to investigate her bare thighs. When I don't find what I'm looking for, I have to ask, "Where are your panties?"

"Drying." She leans into me, her head resting in the crook of my shoulder, her butt shimmying against me as she rubs her thighs together.

My girl needs me.

I turn her away from the folding table, keeping her back to my front. "Place your hands on the washing machine, Angel."

Stepping back to take in the visual of her leaning forward enough for her ass to stick out, barely covered by my t-shirt, I pull mine over my head and discard it on the floor. She'll be wearing it later.

I slough off my workout pants, boxer briefs, and cozy up behind her, clasping her hips and grinding against her. Her sigh of appreciation isn't lost on me, but I force myself to go slow. The last time she had a man saddled up behind her, he hurt her. That won't be happening here.

I slide one hand around her front and between her legs, running my fingers through her folds—testing the waters. She must have been thinking of me to already be this wet. I trail my hands up her stomach to her bare tits under my shirt. God, I'd nearly forgotten what real breasts feel like, how they respond, how much I love their supple peaks in my mouth, against my tongue. My Angel has great tits, round and full with dark rosy nipples and sensitive as fuck.

"I've thought of this all day, Frankie." I flex against her ass as my fingers knead her breasts and tease her nipples.

She's trembling. I need to be sure it's in anticipation and not fear.

Kissing up her neck, thankful she's got her hair in a messy bun, I still at her ear. "You okay, Frankie Angel?"

She curls her head into me, rubbing it back and forth. "I'm good."

"Good." I pinch her nipples. She whimpers and bucks. I bite her neck and lick away the sting. My cock aches to bury itself deep inside her heaven. "You trust me?" I explore her ass to her pussy and back.

"Yeah." Her response is quick but questioning. She doesn't know what I'm asking of her.

"I'm only touching, Angel. No penetration." I round her tight bud with my thumb. "When you give me your ass, we'll have talked about it first. Okay? No surprises here."

The sigh of relief she releases has me massaging my hand up her back as she curls forward, resting her head on her hands. I don't want to push her further than she can take. I want to work through her discomfort, remind her ass-play can be enjoyable, and just because I want to take her from behind doesn't mean I want to dominate, control, or hurt her.

In fact, at this point, I'd rather carry her to bed and make love to her face to face. But we're here. She's hot and ready.

"Let's take this off." I push my t-shirt up her back and off over her head. Now I really wish we were face to face so I could suck her tits as she rides my cock.

Next time.

With me nearly a foot taller than her, taking her standing up has its challenges, but my girl anticipates and rises to her tippy-toes, giving me a better angle, with my spread legs and bent knees.

"Please, Gabriel," she begs when I run my cock along her folds.

Her neediness is going to end this before I'm ready if I lose my head. "Patience." I lean over her, flexing my cock over her opening a few times. "So wet, baby."

"Yes," she groans as I push in.

I grip her hips to pull her down on me as I thrust into her. Her gasping moans have me ramping up my pace and nearly lifting her off her feet with each forward drive.

"Fuck, Angel." I about lose my mind when she leans her weight on her arms and hooks her legs around my hips, curling at the knee so her feet are pressed against my ass pulling me to her, like a standing reverse cowgirl. She rides me, pushing down as I push up, our joining on full display as the sound of slapping flesh echoes in the small room.

Without having to worry about her touching the floor, I stand taller, supporting her weight with a hand on her abdomen, and slam into her over and over again. My balls buzz with my impending release each time they make contact with her pussy.

Her head thrown back in complete abandon has me galloping over the edge the second she screams my name and her hot walls contract around me.

"JesusfuckingchristI'mcoming." I grip her hips as I release into her, so fucking happy to not be wearing a condom. I pump into her until I'm spent, and we're both folded over the washing machine, panting as we catch our breath.

"Who knew doing laundry could be so fun?" my Angel puffs out between sucking in air.

My laughter takes us to the floor, where I collapse on my back with her lying on top of me. "I don't think doing laundry with Mable will be as enjoyable as it is with you, Angel."

She turns, curling into me. "I'm happy to hear that."

I kiss her head, throw a noodle-arm over her back. "No more doing laundry without me."

"Deal."

"Deal." I bury my nose in her neck. Her scent fills my lungs. And my tin-heart grows a new layer of flesh that vibrates and threatens to beat—only for her.

CHAPTER 16

MY HEART IS HAMMERING AGAINST MY CHEST. It's not nerves. It's excitement. I'm excited to be back at work. And, okay, maybe a little nervous. I step out of my car and stare up at the Black Ops MMA insignia on the front of the old hangar. It doesn't look like much from out here, but inside is a state-of-the-art training facility. I'd even dare say it's better than the gym back in Vegas. Everything is new and shiny with all the equipment the guys love, and the office space and rehab space I've only dreamt of. But as much as I love the space, it's the people I've missed.

I've been hanging out with guys since I was fourteen. Austin rarely went anywhere without me—his choice, not one I pushed on him, but I was happy to oblige. And being the football and wrestling star he was, being surrounded by other guys was status quo. Once he got connected to Captain Jimmy and his MMA gym and his crew, it felt like I found my family. If I'm being honest, Austin wasn't the only reason I became interested in physical therapy. When the guys got hurt, I wanted to take care of them, and learning about the human body, how it works, and how it heals was an excellent way to do it. Enter Gabriel, stage left, he took Austin under his wing, treated him like a brother and me—well, you know how that went.

"You ready?" Gabriel slides his hand along mine, linking our fingers. He follows my gaze to the building and back to me, frowning. "He's not in there."

"What? No—"

"He's in rehab. Court-ordered. He can't hurt you."

I tug on his arm when he starts to move forward, dragging me with him. "Gabriel." I wait until he steps back to me, his hand resting on my hip and his eyes on mine. "I wasn't hesitating out of fear."

"No?" He cups my cheek, resting his forehead against mine.

When I place my hands on his chest, his racing heart lets me know he's a little anxious too. "No. I was reminiscing in my head about the guys and how Austin and I became a part of Cap's family. I'm happy to be back. I've missed them."

"Them? Not Austin?"

"*Them*." I push on his chest and laugh when he doesn't even budge. "God, you're like a brick house."

He corrals me till my back hits my car, his hands resting on the hood on either side of my body, pinning me with his stare, tight-jawed, and no humor to be found.

"What's going on, big man?" I tug on the front of his shirt. "You don't want people to know about us?" *Us?* Is there even an us?

"Fuck, Frankie." He bends till his breath is teasing my neck, his eyes still slanted on me. "I want to fuck you in the center ring, so they all know you belong to me." *Not Austin* is what I hear at the end of his statement.

On tiptoe, I press my mouth to his—not sensual but a thank you, a promise, a whisper of a truth he just offered up. "As much as I'd like that, Big Man, I don't think Cap would approve it as a sanctioned MMA technique."

His chiseled façade cracks. "No, Angel, I don't imagine Cap would like to watch me fuck you." His thumb teases my cheek. "Especially since he sees you like a daughter."

My blush doesn't escape his notice. He runs his lips across my heated skin. "I talk about fucking you in public, but it's hearing Cap thinks of you as his own that makes you blush?"

He hugs me to his chest when I groan in embarrassment.

"Are you two gonna come inside or dick around in the parking lot all day?"

Speak of the devil. We turn to see Cap holding the door open, waving us in.

"Give us a minute." Gabriel speaks to him, but keeps me locked in his arms. When we're alone, but probably still under the gaze of prying eyes, he captures my face between his powerful hands. "Don't think for a minute I'm not proud to have you on my arm. I'm only worried how being back here without Austin is making you feel. I'm not going to pretend you don't have nine years of history with him." His forehead is back on mine. "Trust me, I was painfully aware of every one of the last five. I've wanted you before I knew you were his. I don't plan on letting him get in the way of having you now."

"God, Gabriel." I'm melting for him. "What was it you said about fucking? Can we do that now?"

His head falls back on a full-belly laugh. The sound eases my nerves, and I take a few cleansing breaths as he composes himself.

"Come on, Angel." Taking my hand, he leads me to the door. "Our family is waiting for us."

The warmth his words produce in my belly blooms again on my cheeks. He eyes my face and smiles his panty-dropping smile.

It's only been a few hours, but the door to my office has been on a revolving hinge since Gabriel and I arrived. We separated ways after the guys came out to greet us. He headed for the locker room and then to train. I followed Cap to my office, which doubles as the medical facility. I'd barely dropped my purse in my bottom desk drawer when the visitors started coming in, one by one.

First it was Jonah "The Whale" Tate, ex-heavyweight champ, trainer, and sometimes coach. He complained of deltoid discomfort. I examined him, not finding anything obviously wrong, but treated it like a pulled muscle with manual manipulation and ice. He left smiling, swearing he felt better. "It's good to have you back, Frankie."

"It's good to be back."

He swung his arm, free of pain. "You've got the touch." Then he ducked out my door.

My second visitor was Sloan "Killer" Michaels, up and coming heavyweight contender like Gabriel. Though he's big and strong, Gabriel has him beat, hands down. Sloan complained of a hamstring pull. Once on the examining table, he proceeded to talk my ear off, filling me in on all the happenings since I've been gone: who was pissed off at whom, who he had the hots for, and whose ass he was going to kick in his next match. I was done treating him long before he ran out of things to say.

The next knock at the door ushered out Sloan and in Patrick "Dirty Irish" O'Malley. With his reddish-brown hair and ivory skin, he looked the part of good ole Irish boy, except he's from Tennessee and has a twang to match. He's the lightweight of the bunch, but he's scrappy and strong as a miniature ox. He didn't have any injury. He was nice enough to bring me a cup of coffee, a banana nut muffin, and stories of his visit home last weekend.

I'd forgotten how much these boys could talk. Get them together, and they're gruff, trash-talking macho men. But get them alone, and they're sweet momma's boys who miss having a female to talk to—one they *aren't* trying to sleep with. That's me, by the way. In all the years I've known them, no matter how much of a player they are, they've never hit on me. Sure, I get playful looks and compliments up the wazoo, but they respect me. Or, maybe they respected Austin.

A cleared throat has me looking into the mesmerizing blue eyes of Gabriel, standing in my open doorway. His arms are crossed over his chest, stance wide and powerful. "Why the scowl, Angel?"

I frown and release it as fast, not even realizing my consternation showed. "How come the guys never hit on me?"

He stops mid-sit in the chair before my desk. "What?"

"I mean, they tease me, but none of them have ever seriously hit on me." I motion to myself. "I know I'm no ring-chaser, but you'd think out of all the fighters who have come and gone through Cap's doors, one of them would have tried at least once."

The air rushes out of the cushion as it bears the weight of his fine ass when he finally sits. "Are you for real?"

I study his expressionless face, the tick of his jaw, the glare in his eyes. "Never mind." I wave it off. "What's up?"

"What's up?" He leans forward, his hand clasped between his wide legs. "Angel, am I not giving you enough attention? You need more that you're wanting the guys to hit on you?"

"What?!" I squeal and then clear my throat, trying to find my calm. "No." I stand and cross the room, eyeing the poster of this year's Black Ops Team, my back to him. "It's not about you and me." Though, admittedly, I don't even know what we are.

I turn and face him. "It's just, with everything that's happened with Austin—I had no idea he was doing drugs, doing steroids. I didn't even know he was a lying, cheating, piece of shit for years. What else have I missed? What else have I been blind to?"

He closes the door on his way to me. "First off, don't let me hear you comparing yourself to ring-chasers ever again." He points at me. "You hear me? You and them aren't even in the same universe of hot."

"I know. I'm not an idiot. But thanks for pointing that out." *Sheesh.* Way to make a girl feel special.

He pinches my chin between his thumb and forefinger. "Angel, you're not gettin' me." A quick press of his mouth to mine, and his fiery eyes are on me again. "*They're* not in the same universe of hot as *you*. Feel me?"

A smile ticks my lips. "Really? You think I'm hotter?" My ego apparently needs petting.

"Yeah, Angel. Way. Fucking. Hotter." He releases my chin and comes to his full height. "As for the guys not hitting on you." He fingers my ponytail. "That *is* about you and me."

"What?" My brows shoot up, and he rubs them down with his thumbs.

"*I* wouldn't let them hit on you. I made it clear you weren't a toy to be played with." He presses forward. "I'm the reason they leave you alone, but you're the reason they treat you like family." He runs a finger down my cheek. "Because you are."

"But I was with Austin."

"I'm well aware."

"Then why did you protect me instead of Austin?"

He leans in, closing the distance, tipping my head back so his lips brush mine as he speaks, "Because you were *mine* even before I knew you were his."

I swallow around the lump in my throat. "And now?"

"And now, I'm claiming what's always been mine." His voice is so soft, belying the intensity of his words.

"I'm yours?"

"Every delicious inch of you."

"And you?"

"You want me?" He grinds his hardon against me.

"Every delicious inch of you." I give him back his words, meaning them and also hoping he literally gives me *every delicious inch* of him.

"Then I'm yours." He tugs on my ponytail, keeping my eyes on him. "Make no mistake, Angel. I'm playing for keeps."

All thoughts leave my sex-laden brain. "Okay."

He smirks. "Okay?"

I nod.

His lips press to mine, his tongue teasing my seam before diving in. I fist his shirt at his waist, begging for more. But he breaks our kiss, leaving me breathless with only a taste of what I want.

"I gotta go kick some ass now." He steps back, hands on my hips until I'm steady. "You got visions of guys hitting on you taunting me." He cracks his neck. "I need to reinforce my claim."

Leaving me slumped against the wall, he walks out. The taste of him on my tongue. The smell of him in my nose. The touch of him still on my skin. His words ringing in my ears, and his promise of *playing for keeps* have hope knocking free. Again.

Maybe this time it'll live free and blossom into dreams that come true.

CHAPTER 17

"**G**ABRIEL," MY GIRL MOANS, STIRRING FROM sleep.

"Yeah, Angel?" I resume eating my breakfast, relishing her squirms and pleas long before she joined the world of the waking.

"Oh, God." She fists my hair.

I pull back, looking up the length of her writhing body, ignoring her hands trying to pull me back down to finish what I started. "Who's between your thighs, Frankie?"

"At the moment? No one." She lifts up on her elbows, spying down at me. "Finish me before I get pissed."

A chuckle leaves my chest before I can stop it. My Angel is not a morning person. "Call my name. Not His." I hide my smirk in her pussy lips.

"Gladly—"

Her words fade off when I fill her with two fingers and suck her clit, wrestling her legs to the mattress to keep her wide open for me.

I think she might have missed her calling. She could be a killer MMA fighter. She has strong leg muscles and a knack for slipping free of my hold—not to mention knocking me flat on my ass with a single wanton look. The idea of her rolling around on the floor with another woman has me nearly blowing all over the bed.

Fuck. I'm not sharing my Angel even if it is with an imaginary MMA female fighter.

She's almost there, but before she can trip the wire, I flip her on her belly and fill her to the brim. Her hands clasped in mine, my body covers hers, rocking into her slowly. I swallow her cries for more, swiveling my hips, grinding her into the mattress, chasing her orgasm, knowing she'll pull mine from me in equal measure.

Before she can voice what her body is pleading for, I slip my hand between her and the bed, giving her clit the extra friction she needs. She calls my name, and I growl my approval of her tone and word choice, and encourage her to say it again. She does. Over and over until she's mute on a silent scream as her orgasm racks her body in thunderous waves, leaving her shaking from head to toe.

"Fuck. Angel." I slow my pace, wanting it to last, wanting her to feel every morsel of pleasure her release has to offer.

When she stills, I pull out, turn her over and suck on her tits until she's writhing for me again. Then and only then do I take her, face to face, hard and with the lust-induced frenzy she unleashes in me.

The lion marking his lioness.

The beast claiming his beauty.

The devil loving his angel.

The past month has been good. Great, even. Austin is in rehab. Out of sight. Out of mind. Out of my heart, my life, at last. I didn't press charges: the man I knew had been taken over by Anabolic Steroid-induced Mania according to his doctors. But his cheating ass was due to lack of character or balls to tell me he wanted to sleep around long before his car accident. That's all on him. The steroid freak out, I can forgive. The lying and cheating—I'm still working on.

Forgiving myself for putting up with it for so long is a work in progress. I fell in love with a boy-man at fourteen. I loved him into manhood. But somewhere my love turned to loyalty and only hung by a thread that Austin so easily ripped free. He felt trapped by me, and I never want another man to feel trapped by me.

I never want *Gabriel* to feel trapped. He's loyal to a fault. Like me.

We don't talk about Austin. There's not really much to say. Gabriel was there for the last five years. He witnessed our breakdown with clearer vision than I. He knows where I stand. I'm with him and not Austin. Even if Austin returns to the Black Ops Team and was the old Austin I used to love, too much has happened to pretend he didn't break something precious. Something that can never be fixed.

We can maybe mend it enough to be civil, but never more than that.

Never will I be vulnerable to Austin again. That ship has sailed. That door has closed.

Where does that leave Gabriel and me? I have no idea. I wake up every day in his arms and fall asleep every night in those same arms, against his hard chest and heated parts that fit so perfectly with mine. He worships my body at every opportunity. He fills my belly with food. He provides a roof over my head. And he fills an emptiness I didn't even know was there until Austin's absence ripped open a void his love masked but never truly filled. Remarkably, Mr. Asshole fills it, and fills it, and fills it. His tender ways and beastly claim over me are the magic touch I was missing.

Who knew?

I think he did.

But he's not saying.

He's heads-down on training for his next match that's only a few months away.

He's not distant. He hasn't turned into Mr. Asshole. He's just not saying what we are. What I am to him. And I'm afraid to ask. Afraid to scare him off by asking for more—or the possibility of more.

I've heard him often enough claiming marriage and kids are not in the cards for him. I don't believe he's changed his mind—that he'd want that with me.

But I do want it. Someday.

I ache when I see Grant and Emmy with Gwen. Or a random couple on the street walking hand in hand with their children in tow.

I. Want. That.

But what do I know about being a mother? I never had one. I had a shit for a father. Maybe parenthood isn't in my deck of cards either.

The longest relationships I've had were with my father and Austin. Both of those turned to shit—or always were shit. I don't have a good track record. Nothing to fall back on and no one to rely on.

My desk phone rings, bringing me out of my thoughts. *Dark much?*

Cap's voice fills the line when I answer, "Come to my office." Not a question.

"Be right there."

I walk past the guys training, slipping by unnoticed, even by Gabriel. But I don't miss the flex of his chest as he bench-presses an ungodly amount of weight. I squelch my smile as I knock on Cap's door.

"Come in," he barks.

Stepping inside, I note the disarray of his desk. The mess extends to the conference table. "Where's Margaret?"

"She… Uh… Quit." He flips folders, looking for something.

"Jesus, Cap. Did you try to sleep with her too?" I love Captain, but he runs through personal assistants like they're going out of style, all because he can't keep his libido in check.

"Try? No."

Which means he slept with her.

"You know you can't keep sleeping with your PAs, right?"

Ignoring me, he finds what he's looking for and hands a folder to me. "Here. I need you to read up on these guys."

I open the folder. "Why?" I spot a name I'm familiar with. "Oh, are these the guys you're looking to bring onboard?"

"Yep." He picks up the phone, tucking it under his ear and dialing. "We leave tomorrow. Early."

"I'm sorry, what? Was there a question in there?"

He sighs, clearly exasperated and not happy with having to deal with me. But I won't let him push me around. I'm done being walked over by alpha males. He hangs up and sits back in his chair. "Frankie, I need you to come with me to check out these guys. I need your trained eye and medical expertise to see if they have medical issues they're hiding or downplaying."

I glance around the room. "You mean you need an assistant, and I'm the only woman smart enough not to sleep with you?"

His lips tilt on one side. "That too."

Crossing my arms over my chest, I spear him with my glare. "How long? Where are we staying? I'm not sleeping in roach motels, Cap."

"Three days. No roach-coach. Got it." He leans forward. "You in?"

I smile, loving the next words out of my mouth as I leave his office: "You get to tell Gabriel."

"Fuck," he curses as I head back to my office to pack up for the day.

I've got girls' night out plans to make.

CHAPTER 18

"**G**ABRIEL," CAP CALLS FROM THE MEN'S locker room door.

"Yeah, Cap?" I've showered and slung on my jeans, hoping to catch Frankie before she leaves for her night out with the girls. I'm trying to be adult about this and not begrudge her her girl-time. She's coming home to me, and that's what's important.

Cap looks at the guys as he shuffles in looking uncharacteristically chagrined, maybe a little annoyed I made him come to me instead of jumping to attention the second he called for me. We're not in the fucking military anymore.

"I... Ugh—"

"Spit it out, Cap." I finish tying my shoes and stand, pulling my shirt on. "I'm trying to catch Frankie before she leaves."

"She's already left."

"Oh?" I cross my arms. Waiting.

"Yeah." He inspects the wall behind me.

WTF? When he doesn't say any more, I grab my bag, pocket my phone and keys. Give him a nod and a "Good talk" on my way past him.

"Wait."

I stop. "Cap, you're a man of few words. You don't beat around the bush. Tell me what's on your mind."

"Frankie. Tomorrow. She's coming with me." He lets out a bunch of air as if he's been holding it this whole time.

I step closer. "Going where?"

"Scouting."

"The fuck you say?" I close in, and to my surprise, he actually steps back. I look down on him. I've got a few inches and about fifty pounds on the guy—not to mention twenty years or so.

He holds up his hands. "Look, I know you and she have a thing now. But this is business. I need her with me."

I narrow my eyes at him. "Why isn't Margaret going?"

"This has nothing to do with Margaret. Frankie has gone with me before. She's got a good eye and her medical knowledge is invaluable in assessing injuries."

"She's gone before?" How did I not know this?

"You know you avoided her most of the time when she was with Austin. You don't know everything about her, especially when it comes to my business."

"Wow, Cap. I think that's the most you've ever said to me."

"Fuck, Gabriel. She's coming. I don't need your permission. Neither does she."

Fuck, I know, but I can't help the need to protect her. "Then why you telling me?"

He scratches the back of his head and smiles. "She said I had to."

I chuckle and pat him on the back. "If I didn't know you love her like a daughter, I'd say you're pussy-whipped."

"Don't talk about her like that." He nearly cuts my head off with the grit in those words.

If he only knew the things I've said and done to her pussy, he would not be a happy camper. "Yes, sir."

My mood plummets as I walk to my car. I'm disappointed she still went out with the girls instead of coming home to spend her last evening with me, knowing it would be the last night together for four days. She has every right to hang with her girls. Only, it would be nice to be considered a priority when she's leaving town. Four days isn't long, but given I've spent five years without her, I'm not in the sharing mood.

Jess pulls up beside me. "We're heading out for some beers. You in?"

Why the fuck not? "Sure."

I could use some guy-time. *They'll* understand she should have come home to me instead of going out.

Now who's pussy-whipped?

Emmy, Desi, Sidney, Dylan, and myself squeeze into a booth in the back of Davenport's. There's a new wine bar we wanted to check out, but it turns out it's not open for another month. So, here we are at the normal hang-out. It's turning out to not be much of a girls' night out. The Malone brothers—Emmy, Sidney, and Dylan's other halves—are holding up the bar. It's more like a middle school party where the girls giggle on one side of the room, while the guys check out the girls from the other side.

"Your men are checking y'all out." I nod in their direction, finishing my first beer and kinda regretting not canceling and going home to spend the evening with Gabriel, since I'm leaving town in the morning. But then I remember, I need to stand on my own two feet and not rely on Gabriel, no matter how much I want to.

I'm guessing Grant and Grayson left their kids with Betsy, their mom, since their women, Emmy and Sidney, are here. Dylan and Grady, Grant's youngest brother, don't have any kids yet. But by the looks of it, Grady's about to steal Dylan away to go try to remedy that in the bathroom. The giggles Dylan is emitting prove I'm not far from the mark. She excuses herself, and she and Grady disappear around the corner.

"They're totally gonna have sex," Emmy whispers, following my line of sight.

"Yep." I pop the *p*, a little exasperated it's not me.

Emmy nudges my shoulder. "What's up?"

"Nothing. Just thinking about my trip."

"Three days isn't a long time." She edges the plate of appetizers my way, but I decline. "You might even get some phone sex out of it."

"Oh, did I hear phone sex?" Desi, Emmy's longtime friend, chimes in.

I wave off the idea. "No one is having phone sex." I lean forward. "Unless you have details to share from your date last night."

"Nope. No deets." Desi zips her lips. "The only action I've seen lately is expressing a rottweiler's anal gland."

"Eww! No. If you think that's action, then we need to have a talk." Emmy swats at Desi's arm.

The four of us break into a fit of giggles, leaving me breathless and looking into the blue eyes of the man who's been on my mind nonstop since I left work.

"Ladies," Gabriel greets the table. My earlier stance of standing on my own falls to the wayside as thoughts of climbing the sexy brick wall of a man standing before me take precedence.

"Let me guess." Emmy motions to me. "You're here for your better half?"

He nods, barely giving her a smile, and reaches for me. "It's time to go."

"What if I don't want to go?" I object as I scoot out of the booth, not really wanting to put up a fight but feeling like I should make a show of it.

"Then I promise to make it worth your while." He all but starts to drag me away. "Say goodnight, Angel."

I turn to the girls. No reason to fake disappointment, because I'm not. He came after me because he misses me. "Thanks, ladies. I'll see y'all when I get back."

Gabriel growls, tightening his hold on my hand.

"Obviously Cap told you about my trip."

"The question isn't did he tell me? The question is why didn't you?"

"I was punishing him for sleeping with his assistant and for dragging me along at the last minute." I pull from his grip, standing my ground only a few feet from the exit. "That's why. I don't like being an afterthought."

"Angel, you have one of two choices." He leans in, his lips grazing my ear, ensuring I hear him over the hum of the bar. "One: you *walk* to the car." He fingers toy with my waist, skating along the edge of my jeans. "Two: I *carry* you to the car." He stands, raising his voice, "You have five seconds to decide."

As much as I love his alpha ways, I have to give him a hard time. I can't help it. It's in my nature to push back as much as it's in his nature to want me to surrender. He'll have to work for it. "Why are you upset?"

"Four."

"Because I'm going?"

"Three."

"Or because you don't control if I go?"

"Two."

"Gabriel."

"One."

"Gabriel!" I squeak when he lifts me in his arms. At least he didn't throw me over his shoulder fireman style.

"Time's up, Angel." He barrels through the double doors and heads for his monster.

"What about my car?"

"You didn't drive."

"Oh, right." The girls picked me up at Gabriel's so I wouldn't have to drive and could have a few drinks. Totally forgot we rock-paper-scissored to see who was the designated driver. Desi lost—or won the honor.

He sets me in the passenger seat, buckling my seatbelt like I can't do it for myself. "I still don't see why you're so upset, Big Man." His lips twitch. "I saw that smile!"

He kisses my forehead. "There's no smile." He shuts my door and crosses in front to the driver's side.

"What if I was going out of town tomorrow and instead of coming straight to you as soon as I found out, I asked Jonah to tell you—as an *afterthought*." He pulls out of the parking lot. "And instead of coming home to spend my last night with you, I went out drinking with the guys? How would that make you feel?"

"Like shit. I wouldn't like it." *I wouldn't like it at all.*

"Welcome to my night."

"I'm sorry," I whisper to the dark and receive no response other than a grunt. He's right. I was only thinking of myself. I'd be hurt and disappointed if the guy I love spent his last night drinking with the guys instead of quality time with me.

Wait? What? Love?! No. No. No. It's too soon for love. I can't possibly love Gabriel. He's been Mr. Asshole to me for the past five years. We've only been together for a minute. I can't love him already.

Oh, God. But I do.

CHAPTER 19

S TILL REELING FROM MY REALIZATION, I FOLLOW
Gabriel into the house and up the stairs. I stop inside his
bedroom, watching the show as he strips off his clothes. He
pauses on his jeans and eyes me, noticing I'm not advancing into the
room. "Get naked, Frankie."

Frankie. Not Angel.

I suppose he's too upset to use his love name for me. *Love* name?
Does he? Could he possibly?

I should be happy he didn't revert to calling me Francesca.

"I'm so sorry you felt de-prioritized, Gabriel. I wasn't thinking." I
need him to know I didn't intend to hurt him.

A grunt is his only response as he continues stripping.

"Are you not speaking to me?"

"I don't feel like talking." Completely naked and his impressive cock
in hand, he strokes his length a few times as he advances. "Naked. Now,
Frankie."

"Frankie? Not Angel?"

He stops and frowns, his eyes scanning me like I'm a potential IED.
"Same difference."

I nearly tumble back from the blow of his verbal dagger. "It's not the *same difference* to me." Yes, I sound like a petulant child, but he's hiding behind sex instead of telling me how he really feels.

He shrugs. "Not my concern."

Wow. I knew it was too much to believe Mr. Asshole wouldn't make another appearance. He snuck in on me after my defenses were down. After I believed I could possibly be more to him than just a hole to fuck.

After I fell in love with him.

I turn and head down the stairs before the first tear falls. I need a drink, and I don't mean water. I make it to the kitchen before he catches up with me.

"Where are you going?" He managed to throw on his jeans. Though they're still unfastened, I guess I should be thankful I'm not staring at a gorgeous naked asshole.

"I'm getting a drink." I pour a shot of something dark from his liquor cabinet. I'm not a hard liquor kind of girl. It's either beer, wine, or something cold and fruity for me. Though, even then, I don't drink often. I doubt he has the fixings for margaritas. He doesn't look like a margarita kind of guy. He looks like a whiskey guy.

I throw back the shot and gasp. "Fuck." Was that whiskey? It sure as hell burns like whiskey. I pour another one.

"Angel, what are you doing?" He steps closer, but I hold my arm out.

"Oh, now I'm *Angel*?" I pick up the shot and face him. "Make up your mind, Gabriel. Am I *Angel*—the girl you care about? Or am I *Frankie*—the girl you fuck?" I swallow the shot and welcome the burn this time as it warms my insides. "Or better yet, am I *Francesca*—the girl you hate—the girl you demoralize at every turn?"

"I never hated you." He steps closer. Worry riddles his face and softens his eyes.

"Yeah, well, you could have fucking fooled me!" I'm slipping. I should shut up, but I can't seem to make myself stop.

"You're upset."

No shit.

He takes the shot glass from my hand, cautious and slow like he's dealing with a rabid dog.

I swipe at the tears that defiantly fall. "What are we doing, Gabriel? What am I to you? You want me naked? You want to fuck? That's all you want?" I rip at my shirt, trying to get it over my head and failing miserably, with it stuck half on and half off.

His powerful hands stop my struggle. "I wanted to spend the evening with you." He pulls my shirt down, smoothing it into place.

"But why? Why do you want me here? Am I only a convenient fuck? What about what *I* want?" I push at his chest. He doesn't budge. "Why are you upset I'm leaving?"

His silence is deafening. His hands in his pockets, he just stares at me. The clock on the wall clicks the seconds away.

"*Are* you even upset I'm leaving?"

"Yes." He breaks his silence. Finally.

"Why?"

Nothing.

Nothing.

Nothing.

With acceptance of what, I don't know, I turn, climbing the stairs. I can't humiliate myself like this anymore.

"Because I want you here," he calls from the entryway.

I turn, gripping the railing. "Why, Gabriel?"

He shakes his head. He clearly has something to say, but he's holding back.

Realization dawns. My heart sinks. My will to fight flees. "Sex." It's only one word, but it's the only word needing to be said. "You only want me here for sex."

Of course he only wants me for sex. He said he wanted me from the first time he saw me over five years ago. Five fucking years, he's wanted to fuck me. And here I am, living under his roof, in his bed, at his beck and call. He wanted to fuck me at the gym, in front of the guys, to show he could—that I was *his*, for the taking. Whenever. Wherever. However.

I'm a fool.

I believed we could be more.

I could be more.

It turns out, I'm nothing.

When a guy shows he's an asshole—you should believe him.

Gabriel's asshole flag is flying high.

"Congratulations, Gabriel. You've managed to join the ranks of my father and Austin." I top the stairs and stop, not looking back, but I feel his eyes burning holes into my back. "I'll be gone in the morning."

Asshole in full force. *Check.*

I nearly swallow my tongue to keep from calling after her. What have I done? I made her feel like a piece of ass. I wanted to fuck her, true. But that's not all I want from her. I want her here. Under my roof, in my bed, under my body as I pound into her all night long. So, sue me if I'm attracted to her. If I can't get enough of her body, her face, her mouth.

But is that all I want?

I grab the whiskey off the counter on my way to the back deck. Maybe she had the right idea. Drown my sorrows and deal with it in the morning. She's not listening to anything I have to say tonight.

But you didn't say anything.

Fuck! I'm so out of my league here. What do I know about being a boyfriend, a husband, a father? Isn't that want she wants? Isn't that what she was asking me? Can I give her more than my body and a safe place to live?

My Angel is destined for heaven, and I'm destined for hell.

That's what life would be like without her—hell. I've never been in a relationship. The only women in my life are my mom and sister. I won't lie to her. I can't promise what I don't have to give. I'm fucked up. My dad saw to that. I always knew Frankie was too good for me, but I thought she could be happy with what I have to offer. She was happy, until she wasn't. Her tears were bad enough. I'd never forgive myself if I hurt her more. If I took and took without giving her what she deserves. A forever after, and I'm clean out.

I look for answers in the bottom of the whiskey bottle. By the time I finish it, I don't even know what the question was.

The phone buzzing in my pocket pulls me from sleep. Laid out on the deck lounger, my mouth tastes like death. My head pounds like there's a jack hammer trying to break through, and my stomach threatens to make me relive it all.

"Yeah." I spew the sawdust from my mouth.

"What the fuck did you do?" Jonah's bark has more bite than mine. Impressive—and unusual.

"Specify," I groan and roll to my side, managing to sit up without puking.

"Cap says Frankie is red-eyed and not talking. But by the looks of it, she spent the night at the gym and was waiting outside for him at the ass-crack of dawn. That *specific* enough for you, Mr. No Mercy?"

"Fuck."

"Yeah, you managed to fuck up the best thing you've had going."

"Tell me something I don't know."

"Her shit is packed into her office. She moved out on your ass. Fix it. Fix it now." Though cell phones don't click, I swear I can hear the anger of his hang-up ringing in my ear all damn day.

After brushing my hand across my face, I stumble inside and upstairs, confirming my Angel did, in fact, move all her shit out. There's not a speck of her left in the guest room, my room, closet, or bathroom. It's like she was never here. She never existed in my space. She never shared the same air I'm having trouble breathing now.

A snap of her fingers, and poof, she's gone.

The tightening in my chest takes me to the bed. I've fucked up.

Asshole in full force. *Check.*

CHAPTER 20

I'M NOT SURE IF MY HEAD'S POUNDING FROM ALL the crying or the beer and two shots of liquor I had last night, but either way, I'm paying for it today, dearly. Cap's been nice enough to leave me be, only talking about business. He's a man of few words. I greatly appreciate that trait today.

I had to ask him to pull over a few miles back. My stomach churned as much as it could before insisting on a mass exodus. Finding my head in a toilet, again, at the nearest rest stop, proves me and alcohol don't mix. I've never been a huge fan. Another gift from my father.

When I exit the restroom, Cap hands me a new toothbrush and travel-sized toothpaste. "You okay?" He pulls me in for a hug. Cap's a good man. He's younger than my father, but he's been more a father to me than any man's bothered to be. He's gruff and rough around the edges, but his green eyes hold the knowledge of the world, and they have a soft spot for me. Plus, not many men would pull a woman reeking of puke into their arms.

"Too much to drink." I leave out the broken heart part I think is contributing to my current state more than last night's alcohol. I think it was whiskey. It could have been Drano for all I know, but I'm sure it wasn't. You can't swallow Drano and survive, right?

"We're ahead of schedule. I got to the gym early, thinking I'd work a couple of hours before you sauntered in around nine or so. Go brush your teeth. We'll stop for some breakfast and let you rest a while." He turns me toward the bathroom door, patting me on my way. "See you in the car."

A few minutes later, I slip in the car, feeling a little better, and thank Cap for the toothbrush and toothpaste he bought from the vending machine. Who knew they had that kind of stuff in vending machines nowadays? It's a smart idea. Wish I'd thought of it.

"Gabriel called," he mentions casually as he pulls onto the highway. When I don't respond, he continues, "He said your phone must be off as it's going straight to voicemail."

It is off.

"He wanted to be sure you were okay since you weren't answering. He asked that you call him."

"Mmm." My eyes remain on the road, but I let him know I heard him. I'm not open to discussing Gabriel with Cap. The last thing he'd want to know is Gabriel only wants me for my holes. Cap may be a bit of a manwhore, but as far as he's concerned, I don't have sex.

As for Gabriel, it'll be a big fat day in hell before I'll be calling him. Let him stew in his sex juices, since that's all he cares to share with me.

We've got a few more hours before we reach our first prospect. I pull out the folder Cap gave me yesterday and study the fighters we'll be checking out over the next three days. Usually the guys come to us, but a few times a year, Cap will hit the road to woo the ones who haven't made it to us yet. The ones who caught his eye, who haven't made it big, and probably are underdogs. He tends to like the broken souls. He says they have more fire and more to lose once they get a taste for the life they could have—once they see the kind of family they could be a part of. Cap takes good care of his fighters, really anyone he deems worthy of his attention, his family.

I was lucky enough to get on his radar. He made sure I knew it wasn't because of Austin. He gave me a chance because he saw the same fire in me. I think he saw a broken soul that needed a place to belong. He was right. He made me feel welcome and integral to the team's success. Besides Austin, I'd never felt anyone cared if I lived or died, or if I even existed in the first place.

Because of Cap, I know I'll be okay no matter how many Austins or Gabriels dump me for greener pastures. Cap would never let me dwell in this world alone, and whether I stay or move on, he'll always welcome me back with open arms.

That's Captain Jimmy Durant for you. I reach over and slip my hand in his. I may never find a man who will fall in love with me, but I know this man loves me as a daughter, and maybe that'll be enough.

He's quick to give it a squeeze. "It'll be okay, Frankie. He'll come around. And if he doesn't, it's his fucking loss." He squeezes and shakes my hand. "And it'll still be fucking okay. *You* will be okay."

I nod my assent. The hole in my chest feels the furthest it can be from okay, but I can't dwell on it now. We've got work to do. Fighters to impress. And air to breathe that's not tainted by the man who stole my heart and trampled on it like it was just another hole to be fucked.

I stand in Frankie's office. The belongings she didn't take with her on the scouting trip with Cap are stuffed in a corner behind her desk—in fucking trash bags. I rub at the ache in my chest. What the fuck has she done to me? The sight of her stuff sitting here like discarded trash has rage bubbling to the surface. I did that. I didn't leave her better than I found her. I left her worse off.

We moved her and Austin out of their apartment a few weeks ago. I was shocked to see how little stuff she had, how few clothes she possessed. I always thought she and Austin were doing good. I believed they had enough to do more than just survive. I was wrong. I know Frankie makes a good living. Cap pays her well. But you'd never know it by the contents of their closet or the scarceness of their furniture. The living room looked normal with two couches and a kitchen table with four chairs. It was a one-bedroom apartment. There's not much space. But it was the bedroom that only had a bed in it. I didn't notice the day I went to collect her things a few days after Austin hurt her. The vision of its starkness is burned into my brain. No suitcases, only a single duffle bag I'd used that day to grab essentials she needed. Everything they had went in a handful of boxes. It turned out the place came furnished with the couches and dining table, and what was in the kitchen wasn't theirs either. Not even a coffee cup belonged to them—to her.

Now, as I look at her trash bags of belongings, guilt eats at the lining of my stomach. I told her I was playing for keeps. I didn't know what that meant. I still don't. I'm not husband material. And fatherhood? Who the fuck would want me as a father? How I feel about my Angel can't be labeled. It's not tied to some pretty picture of a husband and wife with two point five children. I never saw much beyond today.

I said *for keeps*. I may not know what that is. But it sure as fuck doesn't end with her crap stuffed in trash bags and discarded like yesterday's garbage.

She may not be returning my calls, but her stuff is returning to my home. She'll have to see me eventually. I'll make her see reason then. Make her see we don't need labels. We don't need visions for the future that go beyond having her in my life, in my house, and in my bed.

It's enough.

It has to be.

I'm not capable of more.

CHAPTER 21

THE SUNSHINE IS PISSING ME OFF. WE'VE BEEN going nonstop, and my mood calls for dreary skies and thunderstorms, but all we've gotten are beautiful days, mild temps, and a coastline calling to me to run away with a carefree surfer and forget about these MMA boys.

"Darlin', you're far too pretty to be out here scowling at the sun." Rowdy, a fighter on Cap's list closes the door behind him, coming to stand by me as I hold up the wall, needing a break from the testosterone inside Max's Gym. "What'd it do to you?"

"What'd what do to me?"

"The sun."

"It dared to be bright when I'm feeling dark." I shield my eyes from the sun as I look up at his tall, well-sculpted form. I'm regretting leaving my sunglasses in the car.

He chuckles, releasing his sandy-brown hair from the man bun he's rocking quite successfully. "If it's darkness you seek, I know the perfect place." His dimpled grin has me smiling while he squints down at me. The sun is too bright for his light blue eyes too.

"Are you trouble, Rowdy?"

Pushing off the wall, he comes to stand before me, blocking the sun, one hand resting against the wall beside me. "No, ma'am. I'm far less trouble than the one who's tainted your ability to enjoy a beautiful California day."

"Ma'am?" I can't be older than his Texas ass.

He tips his invisible hat. "It's out of respect, Frankie. My momma would have my hide if I gave you less."

I believe him. He's not full of piss and vinegar like most of the fighters I've run across. But he's got a dark streak I can spot a mile away. So does Cap, or he wouldn't be on our list. I mean, his nickname is Rowdy... "Give it to me in feet. This dark place of yours. How far we talking?"

"Frankie." He leans in. "I'd rather give it to you in inches." His eyes bore into mine. "But I sense that's not attention you'd welcome." He steps back. "And since I'm tryin' to make a good impression, I'll give you this..." He rubs his chin, narrowing his eyes down the road. "I'd say about fifty feet, give or take a mile or two."

He's funny. I'll give him that. He's got good ole boy mixed with devilish charm down to a science. And though he's virtually a stranger, he doesn't feel like one. His touch should bother me, but it doesn't. There something about him that seems familiar—safe. Right now, I could use all the familiar and safe I can find. "Lead the way, Darkboy. Show me what you got."

Rubbing his hands together, he motions to the left with his head. "A woman who lives on the edge. I like that." He swings his arm around my shoulder, I don't stop him as I text Cap to let him know I'll meet him later for dinner.

I'm on a mission to forget Gabriel, at least for the next fifty feet, give or take a mile... Or two.

"She fucking what?!" I couldn't have heard him right.

"She's out with one of the prospective fighters. He seems nice enough. I'm sure she's fine," Cap rambles, entirely too laidback.

"I know what you're doing, old man. Even if she is out with a guy—which I doubt—you wouldn't let her step two feet away from you without believing she's one hundred percent safe."

"I'll let her know you called. Though, I'm sure you've left her a message or two."

Try twenty. She's a stubborn one.

I end the call with Cap and storm into the training room. "I need to get fucked up. Who's in?"

My girl's out having fun. I might not be having fun, but I'm sure as fuck not going home to an empty house. A stark reminder of what the rest of my life will be like if I can't convince my girl I'm enough. Just me. Nothing more. Nothing else.

Rowdy is full of surprises. I thought he might be taking me to a dive bar or worse. Thankfully I was wrong. He brought me to an aquarium. It's small and locally run. There are no whales or dolphins here. But there's a wall in the back. It's dark, secluded, and glows from the light coming from the wall-to-wall jellyfish tank. I can't take my eyes off the hundreds, maybe thousands of jellyfish as they swim, bob, and glow, tentacles gliding behind them in a smoke-like trails. They sway in a silent dance to the current and rotate like colored lights in their very own personal disco.

"It's amazing," I murmur, moving in to study one particularly weird-shaped one.

"He's wrong-side-out," Darkboy offers.

"What?" I glance at Rowdy before looking back to inspect it closer.

He points to the one in question. "He was born wrong-side-out. But somehow, he survived."

I reach out as if I can touch it. "I can relate. I've always felt a little wrong-side-out myself," I say to the jellyfish, not him.

"You look perfectly right-side-out to me."

I look over and find him already watching me. "You always so charming?"

He shrugs. "I try to be, but no. Not always."

"Good. We'll get along better if you're not always roses and sunshine."

"You want to get along with me?" He seems genuinely surprised.

I turn, giving him my full attention. "I think I do."

That earns me a dimpled grin.

I shake my head and hold up my hand. "Don't get any ideas. I don't need your *inches*. I've had enough of men and their inches." I turn back to the tank. "But I could use a friend."

"You need a man who knows how to give it to you slow and easy-like." The husk in his voice tells me he's serious. It's not a line to get in my pants.

I slant an eye toward him. "I had one of those. He did. Often. The problem is, I fell for more than his inches. But that's all he was willing to offer."

"He's an idiot."

"No arguments there." I swivel and motion forward. "What else you got for me?"

Tucking my hand in the crook of his arm, he leads me down a row of smaller tanks full of brightly colored frogs. "We can feed the manta rays."

My smile nearly breaks my face. "We're gonna get along fine, Darkboy." He's a kindred spirit, comfortable dwelling in the darkness, but not afraid of the light. Plus, he brought me to an aquarium. I mean, that's the bomb. My father, Austin, Gabriel never did anything like this. It seems simple, small, but it's exactly what I needed to avoid the light all around me when all I feel is dark. This place is a reminder—the world is bigger than me and my troubles—and amazing, if only you open your eyes to see. Even in the darkness there is beauty.

I throw back the rest of my whiskey and revel in the burn.

"You're up." Jonah passes over the cue.

We're playing Jess and Walker, who suck at pool. I don't know why they insist on teaming up. They might learn a thing or two or have a shot at winning if they'd pick other partners.

"Cap and Frankie coming back tomorrow?" Sloan tosses out right as I take my shot.

I give it a little too much power, causing me to miss. Jess and Walker woot, patting Sloan on the back with a, "Thanks, man."

Sloan shrugs. "Sorry, Gabriel."

"Coach says they're coming back with a new kid who's got a thing for our girl," Patrick offers up like his comment isn't a punch to my gut.

"Whose girl?" I growl, burning them all with my fiery gaze.

"You sure she's still yours?" Walker dares, obviously not caring if I knock his teeth out.

"I'm sure." No, she hasn't returned a single one of my calls. But Cap assures me she's fine, and this new kid and her are only friends. He taunted me with it at first, but decided for my training's sake it was best to level with me. My Angel put him firmly in the friend zone where all these dumb motherfuckers belong.

I pass off the cue to Jonah and tap my glass to Jake, the bartender, letting him know I need a refill. As I wait at the bar, glancing over my shoulder at the game, a familiar form shimmies up to my side. Blonde Tits.

"Long time no see, Gabriel." She looks around like she's looking for something, or someone. "Where's your girl?"

"Home." I don't even give her the pleasure of my attention. My stone-cold stare is straight ahead.

"Really." She walks her fingers up my bicep. "I coulda sworn I heard Walker say she's out of town. Something about checking out new meat."

I nod my thanks to Jake with a generous tip when he fills my glass three-fingers full.

"You know, it's awful understanding of you—" Blonde Tits continues talking like I give a fuck what she thinks.

I check my phone and lay it on the bar as I take a drink and check out the status of our pool game.

"—I mean, who knows what goes on out there on the road. For all you know, she's in a meat sandwich with these new guys as we speak."

"What the fuck did you say?" I pin her with daggers for eyes.

She pushes into my side, her hand moving up my chest. "I could keep you company while she's gone. No one has to know." She turns an imaginary key like she's locking her lips. I wish she had a real key.

Stepping out of her grasp, I grab my drink. "Not interested." I can't believe I took this chick home a few months ago thinking *she* could knock Frankie from my thoughts.

What the fuck was I thinking?

CHAPTER 22

CAP, ROWDY, AND I WRAPPED UP OUR LAST DAY of our scouting trip. We've picked up two more fighters with the potential for a few others who felt they needed more time to think about it. What's there to think about? Nobody takes better care of their fighters than Cap. But they don't know that. Word of mouth is good, but fighters also don't like to give up a good thing. If new blood is coming in, the older guys feel like maybe that means they're out, so established fighters are more tight-lipped to be sure their good thing remains *their* good thing.

The ones who fit end up finding us one way or another. It's a karma kind of thing. You get what you give, and Cap gives good karma.

I may have celebrated a little too much at dinner. The guys egged me on. I rarely drink. They don't know that, and I didn't want to seem like a goody two shoes. It's hard enough living in the testosterone-laden world of MMA. I don't need to remind them I'm a woman by not drinking... But also, I wanted to cut loose for a change. At least a little.

So, yeah, I'm a little drunk. My room is too quiet and way too empty. And I'm homesick. Which can't be true because I don't even have a home. I'm officially homeless. All my worldly belongings are stuffed in trash bags, sitting in my office at Black Ops.

How did my life come to this? My professional life is on track, but somewhere along the way my personal life jumped the rails. It's not even a runaway train. My life is a derailed train car, missing wheels, listing to one side, spray-painted with graffiti, the door broken off its hinges, scraping the ground. Yep, I'm a broken down railway car.

I flop back on my bed, my phone tight in my hand, resting on my chest. I want to hear his voice. I've deleted every voicemail he left. I didn't listen to a single one. Now I wish I had. I'd at least know what he's thinking. He hasn't called me today. I'm not even worth him chasing me for three days. He gave up after two. Hell, he didn't even fight for me when I was in the same house. I packed and left his home without a peep from him.

Out of sight. Out of mind.

Sitting up, I click on his name before I can chicken out. It's late. He should be home. He's a stickler when he's in training.

Ring. Ring. Ring. Ring. Ring. Click. Voicemail.

I hang up, tossing my phone on the bed.

Maybe he's in the bathroom. Maybe he's already asleep.

He'll see I called in the morning.

Maybe he'll call back.

Or maybe he won't.

Shit.

I pace my room. I shouldn't have called.

I should have left a voicemail.

And say what?

I miss you?

Hey, I'm homeless. How are you?

Are you still an asshole? No?

Do you think you could love me?

Fuck. I'm pathetic.

I jump when my phone chimes with a text.

Slowly, I reach for it. The text notification appears, but not the actual message. I click the notification and my phone unlocks with face recognition. I'm surprised it recognized me, because at the moment, I feel nothing like myself. It's not smart enough to know I'm completely devastated on the inside.

One word appears on the screen.

Gabriel: *Busy*

WTF? Three dots bounce on the screen. I wait, trying not to read too much into his *busy* response. He's typing something else, so that has to be good. Right?

The dots disappear a millisecond before a picture pings on the screen.

It takes me a second to register what I'm seeing. It's a woman with blonde hair. Her face is distorted, and she's—"Oh my God!" I scream and drop the phone.

He didn't.

He couldn't.

I look at the screen, my phone lying face-up on the floor.

He did.

"Asshole!"

I pick up the phone, turn off the screen, and set it on the nightstand instead of hurling it across the room.

On the edge of the bed, I scrunch up my eyes, trying to unsee some blonde woman giving Gabriel a blow job.

A. Blow. Job.

I'm a fucking idiot.

I wasn't there. He found someone else's holes to fill. Of course he did. Why would I expect less? Austin had no trouble cheating on me. Apparently, neither goes Gabriel. Though in all fairness, I did move out and not return his phone calls.

But he didn't have to send me a fucking picture!

"I'm not going back to Sunnyville." I grab my duffle bag. I can't see him right now. I don't know when I'll ever be able to see him again without seeing that woman's face. But I know I can't take a chance of seeing him or her tomorrow.

I don't even bother folding. I toss everything in the bag: clothes, toiletries, shoes, iPad, laptop, cables. I'm packed in two minutes flat. It's a record. Yay, me.

I throw my purse in the bag, zip it up, and sling it over my shoulder. One last glance around the room confirms I've got my train wreck of a life packed.

I pull out my phone and call him. I want to hear what a douche he is from his lying, cheating lips.

"Hello?" a saccharine sweet voice answers.

I check the screen to be sure I called him. I did. "Who is this?"

"Amber. Who's this?"

"Frankie." I bite my lip, trying to keep calm and steel my emotions from ripping her a new asshole.

"Oh, Frankie. We were just talking about you."

"We?"

"Well, Gabriel, of course. You did call his phone, didn't you? Who else would I be referring to?"

God knows. I hoped I'd called someone else, even though the screen confirms I didn't.

"Can I speak to him?" Do I still want to?

"Oh, honey. I'm sorry, but he stepped into the shower. In fact—" Rustling noises have me pulling the phone back until she speaks again. "He's expecting me to join him."

Of course he is. Gabriel loves shower sex.

"I'll tell him you called."

"You do that." I hang up, stick my phone in my pocket, and walk out of my room.

There are no tears as I make my way to my next stop. I'm too angry to cry.

It only takes one knock and a few seconds before a smiling Rowdy greets me. His eyes fall to my bag before his smile falters.

"What's wrong?"

"I'm heading to Vegas. Wanna come?" I probably should go alone, but I don't want to be alone. Plus, Austin is there, and, well, it would be nice to have someone big and strong by my side to be sure he doesn't try something again. Though, I'm pretty sure he's moved on. But yeah... Rowdy... Vegas... Me. It's the closest to a game plan I have for such short notice of my life continuing to spiral out of control as it circles the drain.

He studies my face, looks me up and down. Then smiles. "Sounds like fun."

I sigh in relief at his willingness to jump onboard my sinking ship without even asking any questions or wondering if I even have any life preservers. I don't. Obviously.

Ushering me inside, he takes my bag. "Give me a minute, and I'll be packed."

I sit in the desk chair and watch as he does nearly the same thing I did. Throwing everything he has in his suitcase. Though, he does have a little more than me. He was planning on moving to Sunnyville from here. He packed up his car a few days ago and has been following Cap and me as we make our rounds. He was planning on driving with us back home tomorrow, along with the other guys.

He stops packing and focuses on me. "What about Cap? Won't he be mad I'm not going with him in the morning?"

"I'll handle it."

As if my word is gold, he smiles, nods, and finishes collecting his things.

On the way out, we stop by Cap's. Once I'm standing in front of his door, I call him instead of knocking.

"Frankie? Everything okay?" He doesn't sound like he was asleep.

"No. Can you open your door?"

"What?" The turn of the deadbolt clicks, and a startled Cap

blinks at me. "What's going on, Frankie?" He scowls at Rowdy over my shoulder.

I disconnect the call with him and pull up the lovely picture Gabriel sent me. "I'm not going home."

"Why? Where you going?" He looks at Rowdy again. "Why's he packed?"

"I'm going to Vegas. Rowdy is coming with me." I hold up my phone so he can see it. "Gabriel texted me this. I can't go back there. Not yet, anyway."

Cap grabs my phone; his fingers whiten from the force of his grip. "Motherfucker."

"Yep."

Cap sighs and pulls me into a hug. "He's an idiot." I nod my agreement, not trusting my voice. "You take care of her, you hear me?" he says over my head.

"Yes, sir. I plan to," Rowdy answers from behind.

"Good." Cap pats my back. "Do what you need to do. But don't let Gabriel keep you away from your family. You hear me?"

"Hear you," is all I can manage.

"I'll send him back to Vegas. He'll go. He won't have a choice if he wants to keep his fight," Cap insists. He kisses my head and pulls back, holding my hand. "You deserved better than those idiots have given you."

Maybe, but maybe not.

People treat you the way you let them.

It's time I stop letting people treat me like shit.

Like I don't matter.

Like I'm nothing.

CHAPTER 23

I ARRIVE AT BLACK OPS EARLIER THAN NORMAL. Cap got back late last night according to Jonah, but I haven't heard from Frankie. She's not answering her phone. I'm worried. I don't know where she is. Where she's staying.

I need to be sure she's safe.

I need to get her home.

I need to show her what I have to offer is enough. I can make her happy. I'm sure of it. I just need to convince her.

Making it as far as the training room, I stop when a red-faced Cap heads my way. Except he's not stopping. He's out for blood. Mine, apparently. "Whoa—"

Smack!

He tags me right on the chin. I step back, shaking my head as dots dance in my vision. "Fuck, Cap. What was that for?" I get my bearings.

Jonah is in front of Cap, holding him back. Walker is running in from the locker room after Jonah called for reinforcements.

"You son of a bitch!" Cap ducks and throws an unsuspecting Jonah over his hip.

Stunned by an impressive move from the old man, I put my hands up. "Cap, what the fuc—"

Smack! His fist connects with my right eye.

"Fuck!"

"Cap, come on." Both Jonah and Walker drag Cap backwards. "Calm down. Tell us what's going on."

He points an angry finger in my direction. "I told you if you hurt my girl, I'd end you."

True. He did. But I promised him I only had good intentions. "It was a misunderstanding. I need to see her, make her understand—"

"A misunderstanding?" The old man pushes both Jonah and Walker off like they're nothing.

Jesus Christ, he's pissed. I hold up my hands. "I'm not fighting you, old man. But lay another hand on me, and I will knock you the fuck out."

He closes in, nose to nose. His angry breath washes over me like fiery steam from a dragon's exhale. "Tell me, Gabriel. What was the misunderstanding? You letting Amber suck your cock? Or you sending Frankie a *picture* of Amber sucking your cock?"

"The fuck?" Jonah's good nature goes out the window. I have about two seconds before he's on me too.

Walker doesn't look too far behind.

"Stop!" I urge the three of them but address Cap. "I don't know what you're talking about. I never sent Frankie any such picture." I run my fingers through my hair, ignoring my pulse pounding in my face where Cap's blows landed.

They're still looking like they want to murder me, so I continue, "Clarification. There is no picture of Amber sucking my cock." I look between the three of them. "Who the fuck is Amber?"

Jonah smiles like I'm an idiot.

Walker crosses his arms over his chest. "She's the ring-chaser who hit on you last night."

"Tits?"

"*Tits?* That's what you call her?" Jonah is shocked, like it's not the first thing he noticed about her.

"Sometimes *Blonde Tits*, but yeah, that's what I call her." I turn to Cap. "Whatever the fuck her name is. She may have sucked my cock in the past. *Before. Frankie.* But there is no picture of her doing it. And even if there was, I sure as shit didn't send it to Frankie. So, explain. In detail. Now."

Cap sinks down to the nearest bench. "I don't know any more details. Frankie showed up at my door the night before last, upset. Said she wasn't coming home. She couldn't. Then held up a picture of Amber sucking your dick. Said you texted it to her."

This is a shit show. I can't imagine how fucked up my Angel is over this. I'd murder someone if she sent me a similar type picture. "You saw my face?"

He scowls. "No."

"Then how the fuck do you know it was my dick?" Damn, he hit me twice and didn't even see my face in the picture.

"Well, hell." Cap scrubs his face. "I took her word for it." He points at me. "It came *from* you."

Jonah clears his throat, garnering our attention. "Didn't you lose your phone two nights ago?"

"Yeah."

Walker chuckles. "One guess who has it."

"Fuck me. Tits stole it from Davenport's." Has to be her. It's the last place I remember seeing it.

"You're telling me you didn't send Frankie a blow job pic?" Cap asks.

"Yeah, Cap. That's what I'm saying. Not only didn't I send it, I didn't even have my phone at the time. And Tits...err Amber hasn't been anywhere near my cock in months. Not since the night Austin went crazy on Frankie." I cringe at the thought, remembering Austin calling me, spurring on my fantasies of Frankie being mine. And then Grant's call about my Angel being in the hospital. "And for the record, I'd never cheat on Frankie. *Never.*"

"Christ, I'm sorry, Gabriel," Cap offers.

I shrug. "It's done." I look around as if my girl is hiding out. "Where is she? I need to talk to her."

"She's not here."

"Where the fuck is she?"

"She's in Las Vegas."

I pop up. "You let her go to Vegas alone?" I pace to the wall and back. "Upset and alone." I point to his sternum. "Austin is there. If he harms one hair on her head, I will end you, old man. Hear that!"

I make it as far as the door before Cap and the guys catch up with me. "She's not alone."

Turning, I wait for Cap to continue.

"Rowdy is with her."

"The kid?"

"He's the same age as Frankie. He's big. He'll keep her safe."

"While trying to get in her pants?" I scoff. "I doubt he's got any blood flow to his brain, his dick is so hard for her."

"It's not like that. They're friends," he tries to reassure me.

"*She* said they're friends. Did *he* say it too?"

He pales.

"I didn't think so." I flip them off as I head out the door.

Guess I'm heading to sin city.

"What are we doing, Frankie?" Rowdy shields his eyes from the sun as his head rolls toward me from his adjacent lounger. "Don't get me wrong. I'm enjoying the sun and the view." His gaze follows a scantily clad chick as she saunters past us in a swimsuit that could only be described as dental floss with triangular scraps covering her nipples and coochie. "I'm trying to figure out where your head is. What's your plan?"

I close my eyes and tip my chin toward the sun. "My plan is to eat, drink, relax, and forget about Gabriel." I haven't thought much past that.

Turns out Darkboy is rich. He comes from Texas Oil and has money up the wazoo. That's how I've found myself staying at this swanky place and currently soaking up the sun at the pool outside our private cabana. Yeah, I knew Rowdy was a keeper—and I don't mean for his money. He's kind and generous, yes, but he's also thoughtful and deep in a way I can relate to. He's quickly becoming my new bestie.

What is it with me and men? I've only ever dated Austin, except for my short stint with Gabriel, which I'm pretty sure wasn't called dating. It more resembled a territorial fuck buddy who stole my heart but had no clue what to do with it, nor had any desire to find out.

Besides those two and Emmy, I've only ever had guys as friends. And I don't mean friends with benefits. I mean the truly would-do-any-thing-for-you kind of friends. Maybe even more brothers than friends. They don't necessarily treat me like one of the guys, but I'm definitely not in the girl-you-date bucket either. Granted I've been with Austin from the age of fourteen, and given that I'm twenty-three now, it's not like I was fair game for dating.

Still, I don't have many female friends. Emmy has kinda adopted me, and her friends and sisters-in-law have welcomed me into their group. But if it wasn't for moving to Sunnyville, I'd still be strictly Y chromosome-abundant in my life.

Perhaps it's my chosen line of work. Actually, I'm sure it's that. Yet a nagging part of me is screaming daddy issues. You know, looking for approval from the men in my life since I never got any from my sperm donor of a father.

"You're way too deep in thought over there to be doing any relax-ing. Your foot is either tapping out Morse Code, or you're working the Fibonacci Sequence in your head. Either way, we should go do some-thing. An idle mind is a dangerous mind." Rowdy sits up, slinging his legs over the side, facing me.

I immediately still my foot. I can't disagree with the idle mind remark. My thoughts have turned wayward and entirely too cavernous for poolside enjoyment. "What did you have in mind?"

His face lights up like he's been waiting for me to ask that very question. "I wouldn't mind checking out that rollercoaster. You know, the one at the top of that casino."

My stomach tumbles at the idea. I clutch my midsection and take a long drink of bottled water. "I don't think so."

I need to cut back on the booze, like altogether. Me and alcohol don't seem to be destined for friendship. It seems to only want to fuck me over too. Who knew Gabriel and alcohol where in cahoots?

Standing, I stretch and ignore Rowdy checking me out. We're friends. That's all we'll ever be despite his appreciation of my body, his golden tongue, and his charming wit. I don't know if I need another guy friend, but I definitely don't need any more MMA fighters for boyfriends or even fuck buddies. I've had my fill. Been there done that. Got the t-shirt and the smashed heart to prove it.

"How about a little blackjack, an overinflated buffet, and then maybe I watch *you* ride the make-you-puke-it-all-up rollercoaster you're dying to try?" I don't mind watching, but I'm all out of participation chits at the moment.

Maybe forever.

Life on the sidelines doesn't seem so bad at the moment. I could use less drama in my life. Except the buffet. I'm all in. This girl's gotta eat. You know, feed a broken heart, starve a cold… Or something like that.

His dimpled grin stirs the darkness out of his pale blue eyes. "I'm all yours, darlin."

Damn, it's too bad he doesn't do it for me. Or maybe I'm too far up misery creek to know if he does or not.

Life with Rowdy seems like it might be fun. Maybe not completely drama-free, but he sure as fuck wouldn't break my heart. But he'd also never make the universe move with a simple touch or a heated gaze. Life with Rowdy would be safe. He'd never send me a picture with his cock in another woman's mouth.

And if he did, maybe I wouldn't care.

Loyal. Brave. True. The words of Gabriel's tattoo come to mind.

Fuck *loyalty.* I'm done. It's about me now.

Me.

I'll be *brave* for me.

I'll be *true* to me.

He can go screw himself and that blonde ring-chaser he rode in on.

I'm D-O-N-E. Done.

CHAPTER 24

ROWDY'S CHIPPERNESS IS HARD TO IGNORE. It's kinda contagious. He's like a dog with a new chew toy. I can nearly see his tail wagging. I open the door to the Black Ops MMA Gym, Vegas edition, and pounding rock music and the smell of sweat assault my senses. Darkboy is all smiles.

"If you like this, you're gonna love the gym in Sunnyville. Be happy Cap is sending you there instead of leaving you here." The door closes behind us. I take a moment for my eyes to adjust to fluorescent lights compared to the blaring Las Vegas day outside. "Don't get me wrong—" I direct him past the empty reception desk and swipe my card to enter the private training space for the fighters. "This place is great, but once I saw what Cap had in store in Sunnyville, this place seems old school now."

Rowdy's gaze ping-pongs around the room, landing on a few hulking guys working it out on the mats. "It's incredible. Way better than Guy's gym, or where I started back home, in Beaumont, Texas."

I'm glad he's happy with what he sees. It only gets better once we get to Sunnyville. Though, admittedly, I'm not ready to go back—he needs to go. I can't keep him here as a crutch. I need to stand on my own two feet. It's been a nice escape, but I have to figure out what I'm doing and *where* I'm doing it.

I introduce him to a few guys and step back as he gets lost in MMA talk.

"Frankie?"

No. I spin around coming face to face with Austin and sway on my feet.

"Whoa." He catches my elbow. "You okay?"

It takes a millisecond after the dizziness disappears for my anger to rise. I've been with Austin for so long, I forgot for a split second I'm pissed at him. That the last time I saw him he nearly choked me out and accused me of some nasty things. That the time before was even worse. I knock his hands free. "Don't touch me."

He puts his hands up. "I know. I had no intention of touching you. Honest. But you looked like you were about to pass out for a second."

"I'm fine." I glance past him into the eyes of Rowdy, who's scowling and moving toward us. "I'm fine," I repeat when he stops in front of me, angling his body between me and Austin.

"You sure?" Rowdy studies my face. "You look like you might faint."

"I turned too quickly." I've been drinking more than I ever have before. I have to stop. It obviously doesn't agree with me, and the stress of everything going on with Gabriel isn't helping. I motion to Austin. "Rowdy, this is Austin."

Rowdy's brows shoot up as if to ask, *The Austin?*

I give a quick nod. "Austin, this is Rowdy. He's one of Cap's new fighters."

Reluctantly, they shake hands with short grunts of acknowledgment, as if they'd rather whip their dicks out and mark their territory. *Fucking alpha males.*

Austin is the first to break the stare-off. "Uh, Frankie, do you think we could talk?" He glances at Rowdy before returning his gaze to me. "In private?"

"Not happening." Darkboy steps in front of me, his arms crossed, blocking me each time I try to step around him.

The surprise on Austin's face is priceless.

Cap must have filled Rowdy in on my history with Austin as I shared minuscule details beyond my Gabriel troubles. I'd hoped to ease Rowdy into my shit show of a life, rather than bash him over the head with the details of my pathetic existence.

"Who the fuck are you to tell me I can't talk to her?" Austin, obviously overcoming his stupor, gives Rowdy a shove to dislodge him as the barrier between us.

"I'm the motherf—"

"Stop!" I quickly step between them when Rowdy comes back ready for a fight.

Rowdy's stormy eyes lock on me. "Don't do that." He pulls me away. "Don't ever step in front of me, Frankie." His voice is a pained whisper, his hands fisted at his sides. "I can't see straight when I'm angry." He runs his hands through his hair, making the waves of shoulder-length locks bounce back into place. "I don't ever want to hurt you."

I grip his arm, tilting my head to catch his eyes he has trained over my shoulder. "Okay." So, this is his dark streak I've been sensing but haven't seen. "Understood."

He nods. "Never hurt you." His eyes are full of more apology than necessary.

"I never thought you would, Darkboy."

He smirks, letting out a punch of air. "You tagged me in the first few minutes of meeting me, calling me *Darkboy*. How is that?"

Maybe my gauge on trusting people isn't broken after all. It had been blinkered by love, but knowing it's still there and working bumps up my confidence. I shrug. "I'm just that good."

He smiles on a nod, but frowns when he motions behind me. "You're gonna talk to him, aren't you?"

Glancing over my shoulder, I spot Austin holding up the far wall, waiting. "I think I need to. There are things to be said." Peace to be made. Hatchets to be buried. Adulting shit.

"I'm not comfortable leaving you alone with him. Cap would have my head if something happened to you."

If he's worried about Cap, he should meet Gabriel.

Damn, I forgot. My stomach sours, and my heart flutters. I forgot Gabriel doesn't give a shit about me either. My mind is mush. The force of that reality makes me want to get in my car and drive, never looking back.

But before I can move forward, I have to put Austin behind me. Then, someday, I can do the same with Gabriel.

The idea of saying goodbye to him saddens me more than saying goodbye to Austin. Maybe because Austin and I have been saying our goodbye slowly over the last year, emotional distance wedging us apart with each disappointment, each lie, each heartbreak. His latest attacks were simply nails in the coffin of our relationship.

Whereas Gabriel and I barely started before we ended. But the impact is profound, cavernous, and aches in a way Austin's betrayal never did.

Well, fuck. I guess I should get one bad decision over with and behind me.

After arriving last night, I couldn't track my Angel down. She was nowhere to be found in any of our normal haunts. She's not answering her phone. The asswipe she's with hasn't answered any of my calls or texts either.

The guys at the gym said they hadn't seen her but promised to give me a call if they did. They didn't have any idea about Frankie and me being together. They knew she and Austin had broken up and the cliff-notes version of his meltdown, but if they know the whole story, it's not from me or any of the guys in Sunnyville. We're a tightknit family, and the guys left here in Vegas haven't earned their place. Doesn't mean they're not great guys. It just means they're not family. And the shit Frankie has been through is family business.

I hate that family knows about my business. About my fuckup. But I'm here to make it right, make her understand I didn't cheat on her. I never would.

The idea of her even believing I would not only cheat on her but be callous enough to text her proof in the form of a blowjob pic eats at my insides. She went through hell with Austin, and here I am putting her through even more cheating humiliations—true or not—she believes it to be. And it kills me.

Truth be told, I fucked up before she even left by not making my intentions clear, by not telling her she means more to me than sex. Except, I'm still not clear on where I see our future. I just know I want her in it.

Leaving my sister's apartment, I give the new guy a call, hoping this time he'll pick up.

It rings twice, and my heart jumps when he answers, "You're a determined fuck."

"You have no idea. Where is she?" I should probably go easy on the guy, after all I'm looking for his help, but damn if his attitude isn't rubbing me the wrong way.

"Trying to forget you."

Fucker. "She can't. She never will." I won't let her.

"Yeah? Well, she's talking to her ex as we speak. You're already a distant memory." His words hit me right in the heart and send my pulse racing.

"She's with Austin?" I pull over. My hands shake with rage. "You fucking let her meet up with the man who hurt her in more ways than you'll ever know?"

"Like your blowjob pic didn't send her running to another state. I don't even know you, but I know you're an idiot for letting her go. How could you cheat on her?" He lets out a heavy sigh. "*He's* an idiot too. What's with all the guys in her life?"

This is going downhill fast. "Listen, Rowdy—"

"Cameron."

"What?"

"My friends call me Rowdy. You can call me Cameron or Mr. Jenkins."

The fuck? This kid has balls, I'll give him that. "Okay, Cameron." No way in hell I'm calling him mister anything, except Mr. Pain-in-my-ass. "She can't be alone with Austin. This isn't just an asshole ex. Austin *hurt* her. You have to protect her. Promise you'll get to her."

The line is silent for a moment. "I tried to stop her. She's a stubborn one."

"That she is."

"She said she needed to do this…" I can nearly hear him pacing, torn between giving her what she wants and what she needs. "His tail-feathers ruffled a little when he met me, but he quickly backed down. He looked like a beatdown dog with his head hung low and his tail between his legs more than anything else."

"Where are you?"

Silence.

"Listen. You don't know me. I get that. I know I fucked up. But I need to see Frankie. I need to talk to her, make things right, but I also need to know she's safe. Please. Tell me where you are."

"We're at Cap's gym."

CHAPTER 25

I HEAR AUSTIN'S WORDS. I SEE HIS MOUTH moving, but what I hear can't be right. Pregnant? Some chick he was screwing around with while we were still together is having his baby. *She's* having his baby.

His. Baby.

Not. Me.

Her.

And he's happy.

Fuck. Me.

I sit on Cap's couch in his office he uses when he's here, my hands locked between my knees, trying to still their trembling. But it's of no use, just as the tears streaming down my cheeks don't listen when I tell them not to fall.

It's only been a few months, and he looks happier than he has in years. He's thinner, not bulked up by the steroids he'd been using since his car accident. He's clean. No drugs. No alcohol. No women. Except the one he impregnated when he was with me.

He put his dick in her vagina and got her pregnant. He wouldn't even do that with me. But he could with her.

God, I'm an idiot.

I hate that I'm shocked and jealous. He hurt me so badly, treated me like shit—like yesterday's trash—and yet he's the one walking off into the sunset with a happy ending and the family I always wanted.

"I love her." He twists the knife a little deeper.

All I can do is nod like a damn bobblehead and try to stop my chin from trembling.

He loves her.

He doesn't love me.

He hasn't for a while now.

He's getting married.

He's gonna be a father.

And he's happy.

Fuck my derailed life. She took it.

No. He jumped the fucking tracks and gave my life to her.

I don't want that life with him anymore, but why the hell does he get to be happy when he hurt me so badly?

What the fuck kind of karmic bullshit is this?

"I'm sorry, Frankie. I never meant to hurt you."

I scoff, a laugh nearly bubbling free. *He can't be serious!* "Did you really *try* not to hurt me? Do you really, actually give a fuck how much you did?" I'm proud of the bite in my tone. I feel like such a putz for believing a word he fed me. The dreams he promised. The hope he grew and then so easily trampled on.

His head drops. "I was out of my head. It was the steroids."

Bullshit. "You cheated *before* the accident. *Before* the steroids. By your own admission." Lies. They come to him so easily. "So we're clear. These tears aren't for you." I swipe angrily at my wet cheeks. "They're for the man I loved. The promises broken. The dreams that will never come true. The babies *we'll* never have!" I stand to leave. "These tears don't be-long to you."

My vision spins as a wave of dizziness hits me. I grip the door han-dle to steady myself.

"Frankie, please."

Please? "What do you want from me?"

He comes closer. "Forgiveness… Understanding… Why can't you be happy for me?"

"Happy for you?" I balk with disgust. "You cheated on me for years. You lied to me over and over again. You were emotionally abusive. You assaulted me, not once but twice. You have yet to apologize for any of it. The fact you could do what you did to me and actually expect me to be happy for you now…"

I open the door to step out but pause, meeting his eyes. "You haven't asked for forgiveness. Telling me your sins isn't the same as being remorseful. I'm not a priest. I'm the woman who was foolish enough to waste the last nine years of my life on you. I gave you all of my firsts." My admission brings a new wave of tears. "Such a waste," I whisper as I slip out the door, hurrying down the hall to the stairs as the world spins around me.

At the top step, he grips my arm. "I'm sorry, Frankie." His teary eyes hold mine, and for a second, I see the boy I fell in love with. "Please forgive me."

He's unbelievable. He may mean it, but the fact he only apologized *after* I said he hadn't diminishes its impact—its believability. "Maybe someday I can forgive you, Austin. Maybe even be happy for you. But that day is not today."

I pull away, and he releases me as I hear the gruff voice I haven't heard in nearly a week. "Angel."

My heart jumps as if it heard its other half, as if the owner of that voice didn't shatter what was left of its already broken pieces.

I whip around, moving away from Austin, the motion doing nothing to help my unsteadiness. Coming about, I find Gabriel standing at the bottom of the stairs. His frown morphs into concern as he takes in my face, my distress evident even from a distance.

He steps forward.

I take a step down, only in my frazzled state, I misjudge the lip of the step and stumble.

I reach for the railing, but miss.

Oh, God.

Panic races through my body as I try to right myself. It's a lost cause.

The cry I hear can't be Gabriel or Austin's. It's too high and way too panicked to be either of theirs.

It's mine.

The minute I realize what's happening—what's unavoidable, as my vision distorts and my angle is hideously wrong for descending stairs in an upright position—I roll to my side, balling up as best I can and prepare for impact, praying hitting my side will do less damage than tumbling headfirst.

When the impact comes, it's delayed as the world stills and the seconds stretch into minutes, but the delay does nothing to diminish the pain as I smack my ribs and head on the first step and the feeling of being skewered through my skull rips through me. With each hit, roll, bounce, the pain is excruciating. I give up my attempt to roll down the stairs in lieu of grabbing for anything to slow my descent.

It's on the fourth or fifth roll I lose the battle—or maybe I win—with another strike to my head all goes dark, and I cease feeling anything at all.

I'm going to kill that son of a bitch is the first thought that crosses my mind when I see—even from my side view—the tears streaming down my Angel's face and the sight of Austin's hand on her arm as she jerks away.

I barely catch the end of their conversation, but it's evident something is very wrong. She looks unsteady on her feet. My gut clenches, and I move with purpose to get to her before she can get to me.

But I'm not fast enough. Her wayward first step is catastrophic.

The fear on her face and the terror in her scream has me bolting up the steps in horror as I watch her fall in slow motion. Her attempt to minimize it by rolling into a ball is admirable, but there is no way she's getting out of this unharmed. I can see it happening, and I'm helpless to stop it. Once again, I'm not here in time to save my Angel.

I've heard the soundtrack of war. I know what grown men screaming in pain sound like. I know the sight and sound of flesh being ripped from bones. The cries and pleading of the enemy to have mercy on their souls.

But I will never get the sound of her body hitting the first step out of my head, or the sight of her bouncing to only hit again and again before I reach her.

When I finally do, I catch her head before it slams to the hard surface, but the impact of our meeting is not gentle. If it wasn't for Austin coming from above, and Cameron hot on my heels, our collision—all 240 pounds of me slamming into her—could have caused her more damage than the fucking stairs. Somehow, in perfect timing they slowed our joining and each cushion a part of her body before it lands again and brace me to stop my forward momentum.

We still on the steps, frozen, afraid to move, our breathing the only sounds I hear besides the rush of blood in my ears as I look down at a lifeless angel.

"Frankie?" Breathlessly, I shout her name. When not much comes out, I take a deep breath and try again, "Frankie?"

Getting no response, I check for a pulse, careful to move her neck as little as possible.

"Is she breathing?" Cameron asks as Austin cries, "God, don't let her die."

"She's got a pulse." I keep my fingers steady, judging the strength of her heartbeat. "It's strong." Her chest moves with each breath. "She's breathing."

I tell Cameron and Austin not to move, and bark orders to anyone listening to call 9-1-1, and get the backboard and medical kit from her office. I've never been so happy I'm a medic in all my life. The training, the hard work, the pain, the tragedies I've seen and experienced have led me to this place of holding her life in my hands.

Once on the backboard, straps in place, we move her to the lobby where I assess the damage while waiting for the ambulance to arrive. She's bleeding from a cut above her left ear. I place a cotton bandage against it and put Cameron to work holding it in place with slight pressure. Her lip is busted. Her nose is bleeding. Her eyes are swelling shut, but I'm able to confirm her pupils are reactive. The blood coming from her ears is concerning. I have no doubt she has a concussion, but a brain bleed will have to be assessed at the hospital.

"How is she?" Austin asks every few minutes.

Letting one of the other guys deal with his panicked state, I tune him out as I continue my exam. I go through a mental checklist as I feel across her collarbones, shoulders and arms. "Nothing broken."

I lift up her shirt and ignore Cameron's gasp at the sight of the contusion on her left side. "Probably broken ribs." I note her right side seems to have taken less of a beating.

I move lower, palpating her abdomen, feeling her hips and down both legs to her feet. I glance at Cameron, his concern evident, but he's keeping his shit together, which I appreciate. "I think it's only her ribs and her head, but we won't know for sure until imaging is performed."

Sirens approach as I check her blood pressure again. It's a little low, but steady. "She's doing good. My girl's a fighter."

"Where did you learn to do all of this?" Cameron asks, adding more gauze to her head wound.

"I was a medic in the army."

"He was Special Forces—a Green Beret," Warren, the gym manager adds with pride.

Cameron's eyes go wide. "Wow."

"*Former* Green Berets," I stress.

"Still. That's impressive." Cameron scans Frankie's face. "She's lucky you were here."

145

"I'm not sure." I sit back and hold her hand. The emotions I'm trained to hold back seep through my restraint, knowing the EMTs are close and my time to be the first responder is nearly up. I run a hand over my face. "Maybe she wouldn't have fallen if I hadn't called her name."

CHAPTER 26

REGRET AND SORROW ARE MY DAILY COMPANIONS for two days now. My Angel hasn't woken up. She's banged up pretty bad, bruising all over her body. Her left side and head took the brunt of the damage. A few broken ribs, a concussion, and a face that looks like she lost a prize fight. But her scans came back clean, no internal bleeding, no brain bleeds, no brain swelling. She's breathing on her own. IV meds to manage the pain and keep her hydrated. Yet, she still sleeps.

Rowdy hasn't left her side, or mine for that matter. Yeah, I progressed from Cameron to Rowdy. He deemed me worthy. I guess it's a good sign. If my Angel would just wake up, I'd have a chance of convincing her I'm worthy of her.

Though, I'm not. I knew it the first day I met her, and I reinforced it every day since, with maybe a blip or two where I really thought we had a chance. But the longer she stays unconscious, the harder I pray and the less I believe I deserve even a moment of her precious time.

I'm no good for her. I've proven that over and over again. Her latest tumble, the most obvious proof. The pain I've caused her, indirectly or not, is hard to come back from. Hard to see past. Hard to forgive. Hard to forget.

For the past five years, I went out of my way to avoid her. When I couldn't, I went out of my way to make her feel like she meant nothing to me. In truth, she meant the world. Every day she seeped in further.

I couldn't fight her out of me.

I couldn't fuck her out of me.

I couldn't knock her loose.

She's here to stay.

Even if I end up calloused and alone, she'll still be with me.

Even if she ends up with a guy like Rowdy, she'll still be mine.

My Angel. My own personal hell.

"Hey."

I scrub my face and blink up into the eyes of a concerned Cap. "You need to rest. Shower. Eat."

"I'm good." I'm not leaving her side.

"It wasn't a suggestion."

I chuckle my dissent. "I'm not up for taking orders, Cap."

He grips my shoulder, bending down so we're eye to eye. "I know you're worried. But running yourself into the ground is not going to help her when she wakes up. She needs you strong and not smelling like a ripe locker room." He straightens up. "Now, get your ass out of the chair before I have you removed."

"Fine." I stand, pocketing my phone. "I'll shower and eat, but I'm not sleeping anywhere but at her side."

I find Rowdy in the waiting room. His feet are propped up, head back, eyes staring at nothing. I nudge his shoulder. "Come on."

He jumps to attention. "Where?"

"Food. Shower."

"Nah, I'm good."

Nodding my understanding, I note his tired eyes and disheveled state. Maybe we both could use a little sleep, too. "I don't want to leave either. But she'll need us when she wakes up. She needs us strong and healthy." I pull him toward the exit. "Which requires we sacrifice being by her side for a few hours."

He follows, his reluctance equaling mine. Neither of us want to leave, afraid of what will happen if we do.

"She'll be fine," he offers.

"Yep."

"I believe that." I'm not sure who he's trying to convince. Me or him.

"Me too."

"You don't seem like you believe it."

"My Angel's strong. She'll bounce back. She always does."

"Then, what's wrong?"

I unlock the car, motioning him to get in. Once we're on the road to their hotel—the suite he's kept even though he hasn't stepped foot in the door since the accident—I offer up my truth. "She's better off without me."

"I thought the same... At first." He slants his eyes my way. "But now I've witnessed how much you care for her... I believe I was wrong."

I have no response. I don't know if you can love someone enough to make what is inherently bad *good enough* for someone who is inherently good. I think it's a leap too far to traverse. I may be named after Gabriel the avenging angel, but I am no saint. My mortal form is deficient. I was made for one thing and one thing only. To fight. It's what I know. It's what courses through my veins. It's what keeps my tin can in my chest silent.

I know how to survive.

I know how to fight.

I know how to fuck.

I don't know how to love an angel.

Rowdy and I step into Frankie's room and pause at the sight of Austin crying at her bedside. He nearly looks like the guy I was best friends with for five years...nearly. The version before me, though, he's caused my Angel a lot of pain. Pain he could have avoided if he had the balls to leave her *before* he started cheating. Before he decided he no longer saw forever in her eyes.

"What are you doing?" I give him a wide berth, moving to the other side of her bed, unsure if I'll listen to what he has to say or kill him straight out.

He sniffs and rubs the disgrace from his face. I've got nothing against a man crying. I've felt like it a few times in my life, and if you pressed me, I'd admit I shed more than a few tears the first night I sat by her side watching her sleep and praying for God's mercy. Not for me. For her.

"I had to see her." His red-rimmed eyes stare at me like I have the answers he seeks.

Sorry, man. I can't give you absolution.

"I don't think she'd want you here. Especially while she's defenseless." Rowdy stands at the end of the bed, arms crossed. His stance is wide, looking like he'd rather piss on Austin than share the same air.

I can relate. And I like Rowdy all the more for it.

"Who the fuck are you to tell me that? You've known her for, like, two seconds." Austin stands. His balls make an appearance. It's good to know he hasn't turned into a complete pansy-ass.

Rowdy raises a brow, his mouth tight as his gaze slides to me and back to Austin. "I know the two of you have caused her more pain than she deserves."

I'm not pissed or taken aback by his words. He's not saying anything I haven't already said to myself.

Rowdy points at me but speaks to Austin. "But he wasn't the one making her cry two days ago. He didn't have her running down the hall in near hysterics." He leans over the bed getting closer to Austin, rage rippling off him like steam. "And he sure as fuck didn't cheat on her for years, making her feel like she didn't deserve better than a piece of shit like you."

In seconds Austin is in Rowdy's face, going toe to toe. Their nostrils are flared, hands fisted at their sides.

"Enough." I pull them apart, one hand braced against Rowdy's chest as I push Austin in the other direction. "I understand you want to be here. You want to know how she is. But you gave up that right the minute you left her bleeding and unconscious months ago. You fucked up, brother. But it started years ago. You've moved on. You've made your choice." I back him to the door. "Man the fuck up, and let her go so she can move on."

"I need to know she's okay." His anger is gone. He knows he fucked up in ways they may never come back from.

"She will be. But she doesn't need the reminder of your failed relationship by waking up to your face. Don't make her suffer to make yourself feel better. Cap will let you know when she wakes up. Then she can decide for herself if she wants to see you."

In the hall he turns, his hand over his mouth as his eyes fill with tears. "She was my everything for so long." He fights to keep his emotions in check. "I can't imagine a future without her in it—in some way." The crack in his voice, I feel deep in my bones.

His words ring too true for me. "You crushed her dreams, Austin, in a really shitty way. You have to give her time to discover new ones. If it includes you or not—it's up to her. Not you. You made your choice. Now you need to let her make hers."

He moves down the hall like a man who left more behind than he bargained for. Like the best of his life is behind him—lying in a hospital bed—better than anything that could possibly lie ahead.

I know as soon as my Angel wakes up, the man I see walking down the hall could be me. I just might be mirroring his steps, his regrets, his fear that there will never be anything better than Frankie in his life.

The only difference? I know for a fact, there is nothing better than Frankie.

I walk into her room and nearly crumple at the sight of my Angel's eyes open and her sights on me.

"Angel."

"Gabriel."

CHAPTER 27

THE SIGHT OF GABRIEL AT THE DOOR OF MY hospital room brings me back to the last time he stepped into my ER room after Austin dislocated my shoulder. It's not the pain I remember, it's the look on Gabriel's face, the desolation, the compassion, the air of protectiveness that washes over me. He's devastatingly handsome in a way that makes my heart ache and brings tears to my eyes. I've missed his face.

"Angel."

"Gabriel." Anguish tugs at my resolve while Austin's words float to the surface, bringing me back to the moment I stepped away from him and toward Gabriel, only to tumble down the stairs injuriously.

Before my sob breaks free, Gabriel is at my side. "I'm so sorry," he whispers, tenderly clasping my face between his hands, wiping at my tears. "I tried, but I couldn't get to you fast enough." His lips are feather soft as he kisses my forehead, cheeks, chin, and finally my mouth. "I'm so fucking sorry, Angel."

"Not your fault," I rasp around the tightness in my throat as I fight for control.

"It's my fault you were there in the first place." He squeezes his eyes closed as if he can eliminate whatever thoughts are pressing to be heard—to be seen.

His thumb tenderly swipes back and forth over my cheek. "I didn't cheat on you. I swear. That chick stole my phone from Davenport's. I wasn't with her."

"She said you were in the shower, and she was going to join you." I hate the quiver in my voice, the hurt, coming back in full force. "You broke my heart."

"I didn't." He shakes his head. "I wasn't with her. I didn't cheat on you. She stole my phone. The picture she sent you, the text, wasn't me. There's no picture of her sucking my cock." He flinches like the words leaving his mouth hurt nearly as much as the image did me. Shaking his head, he adds, "I didn't know she talked to you too." His head falls to my neck. "Jesus, what you must have been thinking... Feeling. I'm so sorry, Frankie."

"Why would she go to all that trouble?"

He meets my eyes. "She hit on me that night, tried to talk me into going home with her. I told her I wasn't interested and walked away. I didn't realize I'd left my phone sitting on the bar until hours later. By then it was too late. She'd already taken it and hatched her scheme to get back at me."

"The guy in the picture wasn't you? You weren't with her?"

"Not me, but—" He bows his head, hiding his eyes. "I was with her the night things went down with Austin. The night at the bar when I was such an ass to you. I took her home. But there are no pictures, and I haven't seen her since." His eyes rise to mine. "I'm not a cheater. I only want you. There's no one else but you, Angel. For the past five years, you're all I see. I haven't been a saint, but I'm not a fucking cheater. Once you were mine, that was it. No one else but you."

He didn't cheat. I nod, too many emotions running rampant to respond.

Tenderly wrapping me in his arms, he buries his head in my neck. "Please forgive me."

"You didn't cheat, so there's nothing to forgive," I mumble into crook of his shoulder, trying to wrap my mind around the turn of events. *I was upset for nothing?*

"Yes, there is. You wouldn't be in this hospital bed if I didn't send you running to Vegas." His mouth finds mine for a short but tender kiss. "I'm guilty as hell in so many other ways I've hurt you. Forgive me, Angel."

A new stream of tears starts to fall. "I forgive you, Gabriel."

"Thank you," he kisses across my lips. "Thank you." His reverence is overwhelmingly welcomed. His hold on me tightens.

I suppress a groan as my body protests. Being in his arms again is worth the pain.

"I'm sorry to interrupt."

Gabriel pulls back enough to see the nurse at the end of my bed.

"Hi," she says to me. "I'm Dawn. Your nurse."

"Hi, Dawn. I'm Frankie."

She smiles. "It's good to see you awake. I need to check your vitals, and Dr. Ryals will be here in a moment to talk to you." Her eyes dart to Gabriel. "Privately."

Reluctantly, Gabriel releases me, standing to his full height, and grips my hand with a squeeze. "I'll be outside."

Once again, I'm shocked into silence. I see his mouth moving. I hear his words, but it can't be true.

"Could you repeat that?"

Dr. Ryals takes the seat closest to my bed and kindly takes my hand. "I can tell this is a shock." He places his other hand on top and pats. "You're pregnant, Frankie. About six weeks as best we can tell without knowing when your last period was."

"I can't be." I'm not even sure I said it loud enough for him to hear.

"You are, quite assuredly." He glances at the door and then back to me. "I assume the big guy outside with the permanent scowl is the father."

Shit. Gabriel.

I nod. Panic rising. He doesn't want kids. He doesn't want to marry—have a family. He's happy with status quo. A fuck buddy.

Dr. Ryals hands me a tissue. "Don't cry. It'll be okay. Give yourself time for the news to settle. You don't have to tell him now if you're not ready. Your care is strictly confidential. No one besides the hospital staff have to know. Beyond that, it's your discretion."

My head bobs, bobblehead mode in full effect. I can't tell him now. I need time to process. To figure out what he really wants, what he's willing to give. If I tell him I'm pregnant, and he wants to get back together, I'll always doubt his feelings for me. Plus, I'd never trap him into a relationship. I just… Need a minute to process…

"Have you been having any symptoms? Nausea, light-headedness, fatigue, smells or food turning you off?"

"I've thrown up and been dizzy." *Oh God, I drank!* "Um, I've had some alcohol. I don't drink often, but it's been a stressful week. Could I have harmed the baby?"

"You don't usually drink?"

"No, but this past week I probably drank three days, maybe. I thought throwing up and being dizzy was because my body wasn't used to it."

His smile is genuine. "More than likely it was the pregnancy and not the drinking. I'm sure the baby is fine. But"—he arches a brow—"no more alcohol. Okay?"

"Of course."

"The baby looks good, by the way. You're in great shape. You'll bounce back quickly. Be patient with the ribs. They'll take the longest to heal." He goes on to tell me he'll start me on a prenatal vitamin, and I'll need to see an obstetrician as soon as I get home.

Home? And where is that, exactly?

I pace the hall. Cap and Rowdy keep eyeing me like I'm a ticking time-bomb. I feel like I am. I know she's fine in there with the doctor. I just need to see her to confirm for myself. I only had a few minutes with her after she woke up. I'm guessing Rowdy alerted the nurse to her wakened status. It's good they came to check on her, but I would have liked a few more minutes with her, comforting her, feeling her forgiveness wash over me like a blessing.

I may not be guilty of cheating, but I'm guilty of so much when it comes to my Angel. Things I may never be able to come back from.

My father was a piece of shit, and what I gathered from Austin over the years, hers wasn't much better. I can still hear my old man's voice in my head telling me what a loser I was, and I'd never amount to a sack of shit—the world would be better off without me. If it wasn't for my mom and sister, I might have believed that last part, but I know for a fact their lives are better because of me.

I put food on the table. Not him.

I kept the roof over our heads. Not him.

I made sure they were safe. Not him.

The only thing he did was beat me and my mom and look at my sister in a way a father never should. By the time I was fifteen, I was bigger and meaner than him. I'd been fighting for years on the streets, making enough money to get by. I was the underdog, the surprise they never saw coming. A no-good kid with a bum for a dad.

But I showed them each and every time. I showed them all.

I kicked his ass out and never looked back.

It if wasn't for special dispensation to get me in the army at seventeen, who knows where I'd be now. Probably still fighting on the streets, except not for Cap, but for some greedy mob boss who would take most of my earnings and shoot me like a lame horse the second I showed any signs of weakness or injury.

The army saved my life, gave me a livelihood to fall back on—a marketable skill that didn't include fighting or killing people. Cap gave me a chance at a real career as a fighter, not a street fighter, but a legitimate MMA fighter with real skills and discipline.

It was tough going. I had more bad habits than good ones. More anger than skill. More emotional baggage than a bus could carry, but he and coach were patient. They saw something in me. Something I couldn't see. They were my honing rod, removing the rough edges and sharpening me to knife-edge precision.

They made me the fighter I am today and gave me a family where I belong. Where I'm only told I'm an asshole when I act like one—which is often. The beatings only happen in the ring. The smack talk, all good-natured. I'm admired and looked up to instead of spit on and told I'm a waste of breath.

Cap gave me purpose.

Frankie gave me life.

What do I have to offer her that could possibly compare to what she's already given me?

The door to her room opens and out steps the doctor, his eyes landing on me instantly, something unwritten on his face. "Gabriel, is it?" He offers his hand.

I shake it. "Yes, sir. Gabriel Stone."

His eyes widen in recognition as he continues to shake my hand. "The fighter?"

"Yes, sir."

"Well, it's nice to meet you. My sons and I watch you fight at every opportunity. I hear you have a big matching coming up soon."

"Yeah, in about eight weeks." I don't even let myself go to the place where I know I've blown off training for the last four days for my girl.

"We look forward to it." He nearly blushes when he realizes he hasn't let go of my hand. Releasing me, he motions to the door. "She'd like to see you."

CHAPTER 28

R EELING FROM THE NEWS, I TRY TO BLINK AWAY my tears and focus through my foggy brain that has me only wanting to close my eyes and go back to sleep. Though, I doubt it would be a peaceful rest with this weight on my chest.

He doesn't want children.

Dread beats down any hope I had before the nurse interrupted us earlier. I'd forgotten why I'd moved out in the first place. Why I'd spent the night at the gym instead of meeting Cap the morning of our trip.

When I woke up, I was so overcome with joy at the sight of Gabriel, I'd forgotten myself. But reality is a bitch. She doesn't like to be ignored. She wants her due, which apparently is my relationship with Gabriel, as messy as it is.

Gabriel "No Mercy" Stone held me until my broken pieces healed. He protected me. Worshipped my body. Made me feel like a goddess.

He didn't want my heart. I gave it to him anyway.

He made no promises. No declarations of love or a future.

He gave me his body, then gave me a baby.

But he still won't give me his heart.

Once, only being with someone I loved was enough. Now, I know I deserve more. I deserve someone willing to be as all in as I am. I deserve to be loved and cherished openly and honestly—outside the bedroom as well.

Gabriel's heart isn't open to me, or, if it is, he's keeping it captive. I know he cares, but it's not enough if he can't give me his all.

I have to set him free.

I'll put myself out there one last time before I walk away from the man I just might love forever.

No Mercy for me.

"Hey." His deep voice draws my attention as he nears my bed.

I want to sit up, but the ache in my side tells me it would be a mistake. Three broken ribs. Maybe their pain will override the agony of breaking my own heart.

We'll see.

"Hey." A weak start to a devastating conversation I'd rather avoid.

He studies me from head to toe and back. "Everything okay?"

"Yes. No. I mean…"

He sits on the edge of the bed, barely enough room for my hulking Big Man. "Take a breath. Tell me what's got you all teary-eyed and nervous."

I take as deep a breath as my ribs will allow and let it fly. "I'd forgotten. Seeing you made me so happy, I'd forgotten—"

"What'd you forget?"

"—we were broken up."

He scowls. "We didn't break up."

"Maybe *broken up* is too formal since we really weren't anything more than… lovers."

"What the fuck, Frankie? We had a fight. That's all."

I shake my head. "No. It was more. I'd moved out. We were done. Even if you had been with that woman, it really wouldn't have been cheating because I left you days before."

"We weren't fucking done." Steam nearly rises from his ears. "We'll never be done."

"But we are. Don't you see? It's inevitable. Why string it out, make it more painful than it has to be?"

"Why are you doing this?" He looks around the room, motions to my body. "Why now, when you need me? You're still in the fucking hospital. On painkillers. You shouldn't be making rash decisions."

"No. It's not rash. I'd already made the decision the night before my trip." I grip his hand. "Gabriel, my fall doesn't wipe away what happened before I left. I'm a little freaked out from the accident and maybe you are too, but nothing has changed."

"It has."

"Really? What am I to you? What do you want from me?"

"I want you to come home. Let me take care of you."

"But why?"

"What do you mean *why?*" He stands and paces before the end of the bed, tugging at his hair. "Because I want to!"

"I want to get married and have babies. Can you say the same?"

"Don't do this, Angel." Agitation flickers all around him like flames.

An image of Gabriel flashes before my eyes, not the one before me now but the one on his back tattoo. The avenging angel, wings spread, sword and shield at the ready as flames lick at his feet. Agony contorting his face as the angry flames grow higher, consuming him slowly, painfully.

I flinch from the sight of it, sorrow taking my breath, tears taking my sight.

He's at my side before I can catch my breath. "Are you in pain? Here—" He pushes the button to release more pain meds. "We shouldn't be doing this now. You just woke up after being unconscious for two days."

"Are you going to want children next week? Next month? Next year?"

"Don't." He draws back like I landed a fatal blow. I suppose I have.

"*Loyal. Brave. True.*" I finger his tattoo under the sleeve of his t-shirt. "You are all those things, Gabriel. Except when it comes to your heart, you keep it closed off, sheltered, unavailable." I swipe my tears away. "I wasted nine years of my life on Austin, believing we had a future, a shared future *he* wanted as well. I can't do that again. I *won't* do that again."

"Please." Gabriel's pleading eyes watering nearly do me in. I've never seen Gabriel cry. Such a strong beast of a man brought to his knees by his inability to love me.

"I know you're capable of love. I've seen the love you have for your mom and sister. It's inside you. I know you care about me. I feel it. You're too afraid to let it out. Tell me there's a chance, and I'll wait. I'll try."

He shakes his head and stands, turning away from me, tucking his emotions back in place behind his armored heart and hard façade. "I can't give you what I don't have." The coolness in his tone matches that of his heart.

"*Truth,*" I quote his tattoo under my breath. "Then this is goodbye."

Brave is what I am as I watch him walk out the door without so much as looking back.

There's no need to look when there's no one there you care about.

Then this is goodbye. Her voice haunts me as anger has me shaking with the need to smash something—hit someone. Hard.

Walking out her door was the hardest thing I've ever done. What could I say? I wouldn't lie to her. She deserves better than that. She asked for truth. I gave her my truth, and she didn't want it.

No, she wanted more.

Fuck!

I can't do more. I don't know how to do more. I'm pretty fucking sure there is *no more* in me to give.

Kids?

Fuck.

No, I don't want 'em. But they sure as shit don't want me either. I'd be a shit-tastic father and probably an even worse husband.

I'm a fighter. It's what I do. It's what I'm good at. It's what I know.

Then fight for her.

Shut the fuck up. My inner voice needs to get a life and leave me alone.

The door bangs against the wall when I slam through the waiting room door. Cap jumps to his feet and stalks to me. "What's wrong?"

I shake my head and press my lips together, blowing steam out my nose as I fight for control. "She broke up with me."

"She… Wow." He's as shocked as I am.

"I'm moving back to Vegas." I spot Rowdy coming in from outside. "You and he will have to look out for her. Promise me she'll be safe."

Cap clutches my arm, shaking off Rowdy, silently telling him to stay back. "Always. She was mine before she was yours."

"No, Cap." My throat tightens, and my chest seizes. "She's always been mine. Always will be."

The shake of his head and his deep sigh reflects his disappointment. "I still have hope for you two."

"Don't. I can't give her what she needs." Or what she wants.

"And what's that?"

"A heart." Love. Children. Marriage.

I leave him with his promise to get her home safely—to my house. I have no plans on selling it or living in it again without her. She made those walls a home and my bed a haven. Besides, I'm packing up and moving back to Vegas. I won't be there.

I'll be here, in sin city.

Where the rich get richer. The poor get poorer.

And the broken find sanctuary in the lecherous darkness where my Angel can never dwell.

I've always known she was meant for heaven, and I was destined for hell. I just didn't realize I'd have to walk through fire with every step I take away from her. The heat—melting my flesh, thick air—taking my breath, cloudy vision—bringing tears to my eyes, and the pain of that broken organ in my chest as it stills—only ever beating for her.

I saw a glimpse of forever in the eyes of my Angel.

I felt the darkness lift.

My own personal hell turned heavenly when she was in my arms.

But today, the gates of hell opened up to welcome me back.

There's no room for a devil in her dreams of a family.

No compromise.

No living in the now.

No living with what I have to offer.

She's got no mercy for a broken asshole like me.

CHAPTER 29

ELL DWELLS BETWEEN THE WALLS OF Gabriel's home. Yet I can't bear the idea of leaving. I love his house. I loved it more with him here. I ache when I walk through his bedroom to use his bathroom so I don't have to share the guest bath with Rowdy. I'm staying in my old room, Rowdy, in the room across the hall. I can't bring myself to sleep in Gabriel's room—his bed—without him. Maybe a part of me hopes he'll come to his senses and fight for us. Fight for me.

No one's ever done that. Not my father. Not Austin. And now, not even Gabriel. It seems I'm not worth fighting for.

Except I am.

I am fighting for me. I'm fighting my every instinct to run to wherever Gabriel is and make him see he is capable of loving me. If he'd only give us a chance, stop believing the negative crap in his head. I know he had a tough childhood. His dad was an ass, and though Gabriel may have learned how to be an ass from his father, he's not him. Gabriel would never beat me or his children. He's afraid. My Big Man with the strength to pin a heavyweight fighter to the mat time and time again, who's undefeated, is afraid he's not strong enough to overcome his past.

I fear it too—for myself. I know nothing of being a mother, but it looks like I'm going to be one nonetheless. Not necessarily sooner than I thought, but definitely not the way I pictured it. I never thought I'd be a single mom. I envisioned having children with Austin, loads of them.

I wasn't with Gabriel long enough to dare dream of having his children. I shied away from such thoughts, knowing how he felt about kids. He doesn't hate them. He's great with Gwen, Emmy and Grant's daughter. He lights up when she smooshes his face between her hands and plants a big kiss on his lips. He's like putty in her hands. A big tub of goo, there to do her bidding. And he loves every second of it.

But having his own children is a different story. I understand. I don't blame him. I don't hate him. I'm not even mad at him. I'm just sad. Sad that a future with me isn't worth fighting for—whatever that looks like.

I need a man who'll put me first, ahead of his insecurities. His fears. A man who will fight for *me*. Gabriel may be letting me live in his home. But it's not enough. I know I can't stay here forever, but for the immediate future, I'll take advantage of his generosity. I'll relish every moment and remember a time when he was here with me—sharing his space but not his heart.

I eye the containers of frozen food. Pulling out a casserole dish big enough to feed an army with the word 'lasagna' written across the tinfoil, with reheating instructions, I stick it in the oven.

He can cook. I'll miss that too.

I peel a banana to take with my prenatal vitamin and set the timer. It'll be a while before the lasagna's ready. Refilling my water, I pop the pill, barely getting it down before Rowdy appears in the doorway.

"What's that?" He eyes the prescription bottle on the counter.

I take another drink of water and answer around a bite of banana, "Nothing."

He picks up the bottle, reading the label. "It appears you need to take *nothing* once a day." He pins me with his eyes. "It's a ninety-day supply with four refills. That's a lot of *nothing*."

"It's a multivitamin." Finishing off the banana, I throw the peel in the trash and stick my head in the pantry. I need something else to tide me over.

"Hungry?"

"Yeah." Starving, actually. We've been home for two days, and when my appetite finally came back, it came back full force, like, I-need-to-eat-every-few-hours full force. I give up on the pantry and start pulling stuff out of the fridge.

I'm about three slices of ham wrapped around cheese in when I note Darkboy leaning against the counter, arms folded, eyeing me.

"Is there something you need to tell me?" His brow quirks in interest.

"What?" I mumble around the excessive amount of food in my mouth. I'm hungry and eating for two here. Clearly.

"Didn't you just have a bowl of cereal?"

I nod.

"Two pieces of toast?"

I shrug.

He glances to the left. "Put food in the oven?"

"It's frozen. It'll take a few hours," I clarify.

He nods on a smile. "A banana, and enough meat and cheese for more than a few sandwiches?"

"Your point?" I finish off another ham-cheese wrap and my glass of water.

He grabs my cup and refills it while munching on a slice of cheese. He places my water on the counter next to me. "I just find it curious."

"I'm healing. I'm hungry."

"Obviously." He stalks closer, nabs a slice of ham and cheese, rolls it up and hands it to me. "You've either got the metabolism of an elite athlete, a tapeworm, you're eating your feelings, or..."

God, don't say it.

"Pregnant."

He said it. A wash of dizziness has the room spinning and my ears ringing.

"Whoa." Rowdy grips my hips. "Breathe, Frankie." He places me in a kitchen chair, gently forcing my head down. "Just breathe."

I breathe in through my nose, out my mouth until I feel better. By the time I sit up, my ribs protesting each and every movement, he has my glass of water in my face, and he's sitting in a chair in front of me, knee to knee. "So, pregnant, huh?"

His face distorts as my eyes well with tears, and my trembling chin is a sure sign I'm about to lose it.

"Ah, hell. Don't cry, darlin.'"

I find myself on the couch, at his side, my face buried in his chest as he holds me. "It'll be okay, Frankie," he assures me more than once, and each time I cry a little harder.

A knock at the door has him cussing as he extricates himself from me and the couch. "Don't move." He reaches to the end table and hands me a box of tissues before heading to the door.

"Where is she?" Emmy's voice reaches me seconds before she stomps to a stop at the edge of the living room. "Oh, God." Her face crumples as she takes me in. She hasn't seen me since my fall. I'm still pretty beat up, but my eyes are barely swollen—well, except for the crying—and the bruising has lightened considerably. But from her perspective, I didn't have black eyes the last time she saw me. My busted lip has healed, and the staples in my scalp are hidden beneath my hair, and the rest of my body—healing ribs and contusions—are hidden from sight as well.

"I'm okay," I assure her, holding up my hand when she charges, getting ready to hug me.

"She's got broken ribs." Rowdy grips her arm to slow her forward motion.

"Oh." She stops, then sits ever so slowly next to me. Her worried eyes spot my tears. "You're upset."

"Was," I sniff.

"Can I give you a little hug if I'm really careful and don't squeeze?"

"Yeah," I exhale on a new wave of tears. I've missed her. I've forgotten what it's like to be so seen by Emmy.

"I've missed seeing your face," she whispers into my cheek. Her hug is gentle like she promised.

"Me too." I glance at Rowdy once she releases me. "Emerson, this is Cameron Jenkins. He's one of Cap's new fighters."

She stands to shake his hand. "It's nice to meet you, Cameron. You can call me Emmy."

"Likewise, ma'am. You can call me Rowdy."

Smiling, she reclaims her seat next to me. Rowdy sits on the adjacent couch. "Welcome to Sunnyville, Rowdy. Where are you staying?"

"Thank you, I'm happy to be here." His eyes stay locked on her. "I'm staying here."

Her eyebrows shoot up. "Here?" She looks between us. "As in, here with Frankie?"

"Yes." Rowdy replies as I say, "No."

"Yes, I'm living here with Frankie in Gabriel's home," he reiterates.

Protective alpha males, what am I to do with them?

"You know Gabriel?" Emmy asks, still eyeing the two of us.

"I met him at Cap's Vegas gym but got to know him while Frankie was in the hospital."

"And?" Emmy prompts.

"I think he's an idiot for letting Frankie go."

"Agreed." She smiles, satisfied with his answer.

"He didn't let me go. I told him to leave."

She pats my knee. "Semantics. He could have fought for you."

Yep, he could have, but he didn't. I battle another wave of tears. I'm going to blame it on the pregnancy and not my weak backbone when it comes to all things Gabriel.

"Stay for lunch? Lasagna's in the oven."

She smiles at the two of us. "Love to."

CHAPTER 30

I T'S BEEN FIVE DAYS SINCE I WALKED AWAY FROM my Angel. They say it'll get better with time. I don't believe it. My dark thoughts and the hole in my chest only grow each day I can't get a glimpse of her. When I was deployed, there were hours, days she didn't come to mind. It was a peaceful reprieve, my thoughts occupied with staying alive or saving the lives of others. There was nothing peaceful about that time except the breaks I got from wanting her.

The idea of finding peace again is nearly enough to make me reenlist. But that's stupid talk. Running away from her and into the peril of deployment would be a suicide mission. I am many things, but suicidal is not one of them.

Besides, I'm a different man now. She changed me. I doubt any emergency could pull her fully from my mind, my gut, or my cock that only wants her. She's ruined me, and I'm pissed as hell about it. Which isn't really a bad thing if you're a fighter. I've been training hard, harder than ever. Cap sent Jonah to Vegas with me. Coach stayed back to continue training the other guys in Sunnyville, where my other half works and lives—in my house.

Even though I offered, I resent her for living there, in my space, the space I shared with her. The space where I brought her to heal when Austin hurt her in ways I never would. Though, in the end, I hurt her in my own unique way. If she's feeling the pain of our separation half as much as I am, I don't envy those around her. My Angel lashes out when she's hurting. The idea of me being the cause is a difficult burden to carry. But carry it I do, as my penance. Though the idea of her taking out her frustrations on those assholes who get to see her every day nearly brings a smile to my stone-cold face. Nearly.

"Gabriel, get a move on," Jonah's voice echoes through the locker room.

"Coming."

I step into the training room to a scowling Jonah and a nervous newbie—not new to the sport, but new to me—by the name of... *Fuck, I forgot his name.* Doesn't matter, I'll knock him on his ass like I did to the guys who came before him. He won't come back—at least not to spar with me.

Jonah halts my progress with a firm hand on my chest. "Listen." He pushes, garnering my dead stare. "He's a sparring partner. The point is for you to use him to test yourself, to work your skills, to get you ready for your match."

"Yeah," I grunt.

"So, knocking him out in the first few minutes defeats our goal and scares everyone from wanting to get in the ring with you." He pushes hard enough for me to take a step back. "Got me?"

I slap his hand off. "Maybe you need to find tougher guys."

"Maybe you need to lighten the fuck up and stop taking your breakup with Frankie out on them."

"Cap taught me to use my anger."

"Yeah, in the octagon, not to kill sparring partners."

Melodramatic much? Whatever. "Are we doing this?" I could just as easily beat the shit out of the bag than deal with these pansy-asses. I miss Walker and Sloan. They could take whatever I unleashed. They never won, but they sure as fuck didn't whine about it and not come back the next day.

170

Obviously exasperated, he steps aside, letting me pass. "Don't kill 'em."

"No promises."

I've got the kid in a chokehold he should've escaped in seconds—I'm barely trying here, it's like I'm *his* sparring partner to help *him* get ready for a big fight instead of the other way around—when I see a familiar face enter the gym. I release the kid and roll away, jumping to my feet, and watch Austin cross the training room floor like he doesn't have a care in the world. Like he hasn't left the best part of him behind.

I guess I was wrong. He never saw Frankie for the gem she is. Maybe he knew her too long. Maybe growing up with her made her seem like a given, like he had a right to take all he wanted before discarding her when someone new and exciting came along. From what I've gathered, there were quite a few *new and exciting things* who caught his eye over the years. *Piece of shit* is all I can think as he disappears inside the locker room.

"You're done," I throw over my shoulder to the kid as I leap the ropes, landing easily on the other side, stalking to where Jonah glares at me. "You need to find me some real heavyweight competition. No more of these kids. If you have to, tell Cap to send me one of the new guys he brought to Sunnyville."

I step past him and pause. "Not Rowdy. He stays there." I pin him over my shoulder. "I need a challenge, Jonah. I've got seven weeks, and at this rate I'm better off conditioning and taking on a boxing bag than these dipshits."

I leave him to stew as he grumbles some response I can't make out. I'm so over it, I can't even be bothered to find out.

Asshole in full force. *Check.*

Pushing through the door, I find Austin shooting the shit with some of the other small-time fighters on Cap's roster—where Austin is going to stay if he doesn't get his head on straight. He has such potential and had come a long way in the last two years. Except now, I don't trust if what I saw was him or the steroids. He never got caught. He never failed a test before a fight. So, career wise, he's in good standing. But reputation wise, he's got a way to go.

Leaning against the wall, I stare them down, waiting until one of them notices and shuts the fuck up about the skank-talk coming out of their filthy mouths. One's bragging about how hard he gave it to some ring-chaser last night, how she was gagging for it, how dirty she let him get. Another how he got head in the laundromat from a stranger under a table while his woman was across the room folding laundry. Assholes. All of them.

When my wilting patience doesn't pay off, I clear my throat. Arms crossed and death glare in full force, they nearly cower out the door, tripping over their own feet—all except Austin.

"Hey," he greets with a chin nod, not a bit affected.

"They shouldn't talk like that about women. About anybody." The disgust is apparent in my voice, and in case he missed it, I'm pretty damn sure it's all over my face.

"They're messing around. It's harmless." He straddles the nearest bench and eyes me up and down.

"Yeah? You think it's harmless if they were talking about your mother or sister in such a way? Or what about Frankie or whoever you left her for? You okay with them talking about her pussy like that?"

He cringes, eyes lower, not so cocky now. "I get your point."

"Good. Next time, tell them to shut the fuck up. Set the example. Be better. *Expect* better."

"I said I heard you. Get off your high horse." He shoves his phone and bag in his locker. "What are you doing here, Stone? I thought you were living the dream in Sunnyville with my girl."

The fuck? I'm on him before he fully turns around. My forearm restricts his airway. My body plasters him to the nearest wall. "You want to rethink those words, Tamer?" Rage is asking for blood. Reason has me slowing my roll, understanding he's trying to find his footing in this new reality where Frankie is no longer his but mine. He doesn't know I'm fighting my own new reality where she isn't mine either, not in any tangible sense.

"Fuck," he grates, short of breath.

I ease up before letting him go and stepping back.

He slides to the floor, getting a few good breaths. "You're right. Sorry."

I sit on the bench closest to him, admitting, "I've been an ass to everyone. I get it."

"You? Shocker." He smiles, meaning no offense, and I don't take any.

"She dumped me." I lean forward, arms resting on my knees, my head buried in my hands. "I couldn't give her what she wanted, and she wasn't settling for less." I let out a punch of air and meet his eyes. "You taught her that lesson."

"I guess I did." He nods, remorse contorting his features as he looks past me. "I never meant to hurt her." He sniffs, turning away. "It kills me knowing I did." He swipes at his eyes. "I'm such an ass."

"You learned from the best."

"Nah, you didn't make me an asshole. I did that all on my own."

We're silent, lost in our own thoughts as seconds tick by before he speaks again.

"I upset her the night she fell down the stairs. I'm the reason she was so distraught and probably why she fell." A sad smile crosses his lips. "My girl's pregnant. I'm gonna be a dad."

For a split second I think he's talking about Frankie. "The girl you cheated with?"

"Yeah, Natalie. She's about five months now."

"Fuck, man. When you screw up, you go all in."

"Don't I know it." His head falls back, hitting the wall. "What the fuck do I know about being a dad?"

"You'll figure it out." Hopefully he's a better dad than he was a boyfriend.

His gaze meets mine. "What about you? You could do it too, you know? You could be what Frankie needs." He picks at the square carpet tile. "Maybe it was always you."

"Fuck." I run my fingers through my hair.

Maybe it was always you. His words pack a punch, stealing my breath, and have thoughts racing that are better left alone.

You could be what Frankie needs.

The vision of Frankie's abdomen swollen with my baby has my feet moving before my brain commands it.

Fuck. Fuck. Fuck.

CHAPTER 31

CAP SAID I HAD TO WAIT TWO WEEKS BEFORE
returning to Black Ops Gym. It's been three. I've always loved
coming to the gym, working with the fighters, and Cap. But
a part of my joy is missing now, taken by Austin and Gabriel, the two
faces I looked forward to seeing most throughout my day. That was my
reality for nearly nine years with Austin, and if I'm being honest, nearly
five years with Gabriel too. I've always felt the pull of Gabriel even
when I was madly in love with Austin. Or maybe I wasn't as in love as I
thought. For as much of an asshole as Gabriel was to me, he still turned
my head, had my heart racing, and my girly parts lusting.

In hindsight, I hadn't been as repulsed by Gabriel as I pretended to
be. In fact, I wasn't repulsed at all. I was hurt by his disregard and confused by my body's reaction to someone who treated me so poorly. And
no matter how he treated me, I still wanted his approval. I never would
have cheated on Austin, but I still wanted to be seen by Gabriel.

Daddy issues, clearly.

Gabriel's absence and the failure of our relationship feels like it
will be more daunting the moment I step foot in the gym. His absence
from one of his favorite places is more proof I'm not worth fighting

for. He moved to another state to avoid me, for God's sake. I know. I said I was worth the fight. I'm still working on believing it myself. My doubting inner voice is hard to silence. Plus, the pregnancy is taking its toll, sapping my energy, and I just may puke more food in a day than I actually consume. I'm not sure. Could be a draw.

As I stand in the parking lot outside the gym, I'm reminded of the last time I returned to work after Austin dislocated my shoulder. Only that time, I had Gabriel by my side, holding my hand and promising to fuck me on the training room floor so everyone knew I was his.

Crap, no more tears! These stupid pregnancy hormones have me crying at nothing. And don't get me started on my heightened sex drive. I want sex all the time and no prospects in sight. Though I don't want somebody new. I want somebody old, and grumpy, who shows me no mercy when it comes to loving my body. It was only my heart he didn't want. My body? He couldn't get enough of.

"You comin' in, darlin'?"

I dry my tears with my sleeves, thankful I don't wear makeup most days, and nod at Rowdy as he nears.

He smiles softly as he takes in my undone state. "You don't have to do this today. Cap won't mind giving you more time, I'm sure."

"Tomorrow, next week, next month—it's all the same. Nothing will be different. The man I love is no longer in there, no longer in my life. He doesn't want me for the long haul. And I'm in a long-haul kind of situation." I hold my stomach, wondering if Gabriel gave me a girl or a boy. Either way, I hope he or she has his blue eyes. I'll love this baby with all the love its father didn't want from me. I have a new reality, and stepping through those doors cements its last pillar into place. Single momdom, here I come.

Rowdy pulls me in for a hug, careful of my healing ribs. "It'll be okay, Frankie. I know it."

I nod into his chest, my tears getting his t-shirt all wet. "I'm sorry I'm crying again." He's comforted me so many times over these past weeks. He has to be sick of it by now. I know I am. I've never cried so much in my entire life as I have since Gabriel broke my heart and left me a gift to remember him by.

"No apologizing." He reaches in the back pocket of his jeans and pulls out a travel pack of tissues. "Now, blow your nose, put on your big girl panties, and let's go inside."

I pull a tissue from the pack. "Since when do you carry Kleenex around?" His thoughtfulness nearly has me crying again.

"Since my roommate started crying pools of tears on a daily basis."

"I'm pitiful." I blow my nose and wipe my tears.

When I'm ready, he grabs my bag, rests his hand on my lower back and urges me forward. "Not pitiful. Just pregnant with a broken heart."

"You're gonna make me cry." My voice cracks as my chin wobbles, and I blink rapidly trying to stop the waterworks.

"It's okay, Frankie. You cry all you need to. I've got broad shoulders to comfort you and enough Kleenex to dry up those tears." He kisses my head. "And extra t-shirts to catch the rest."

I lean my head into the crook of his shoulder. "God, Darkboy, what would I do without you?"

He wraps his arm around me, his hand on my waist. "Lucky for both of us, we don't have to find out." He stops before the door, his head bent so I can see his full face. "It's not a one-way street, Frankie. You give as good as you get." He sighs into my hair and kisses my forehead. "Now, let's go face that demon you've built up in your head."

"How you doing, Frankie?" Cap enters my office as one of the new guys exits after I treated his pulled muscle.

"I'm good." I wash my hands and dry them off, my back to him. I need to tell him my situation, but I haven't cried a tear since I walked in with Rowdy this morning. I'd rather keep it that way. I turn and cross my arms, leaning against the counter. "I was afraid to come back," my admission comes easier than I thought it would.

He shuts the door and moves farther inside. "I thought maybe that was the case when you didn't come back after two weeks. I thought for sure you'd show up after week one." He laughs and steps close enough to rub my arm. "I'm really sorry how things turned out. I never thought Austin was good enough for you, but I had high hopes for Gabriel. I still do."

"He doesn't—"

"He does," Cap interrupts. "He just needs time to get out of his own way. Give him till after his fight to get his head clear."

I shake my head in disbelief.

He continues, "He loves you, Frankie. I think he always has. Five years is a long time to want someone."

"No—"

"Yes." He draws me closer, holding my hand. "Listen to me. I'm not the only one who noticed the way he looked at you, the way he protected you. You have no idea the fear he put in every man who crossed your path. You got respect, not only because you deserve it, but because he demanded it. He wouldn't let anyone look at you wrong much less say anything derogatory toward you. He loves you, Frankie. I think he has all this time. He just doesn't know it. But he's showing you by giving you his home and keeping an eye on you even from Vegas. He wouldn't let me send Rowdy to spar with him. He insisted Rowdy stay here to keep you safe."

"Gabriel asked Rowdy to stay with me?" He's only my friend out of obligation to Gabriel?

"No. He didn't have to. Rowdy is protective over you too. Gabriel sees that, and as much as it hurts him to send you into the arms of another man, he'd rather you be with Rowdy than be alone."

"But I'm not *with* Rowdy." I pull away and move toward the window. "You know that, right? I don't have any intention of getting involved with anyone else for a long time." Even if I was interested.

"Okay." His tone is hesitant.

Scowling, I turn and face him. "You think I'm sleeping with Rowdy? It's only been like a minute since Gabriel,"—my arms motion wildly—"and then the hospital. I... I can't—"

"Hey." Cap softly grips my shoulders. "Okay, I got it. You're just friends. Which is good, because I still see you with Gabriel. He's the horse I'm betting on."

A humorless chuckle exits my mouth by its own volition. "Money's too precious to waste. You should only bet on sure things."

His grin is too big for such a stone-hard face that rarely smiles, much less grins. "My point exactly." He tweaks my nose before departing with these closing words, "Trust me. He'll be back." He catches me over his shoulder before he's out the door. "He's a stubborn ass, but he's no idiot. He'll figure it out, and when he does, you better be ready."

Leaving me stunned, I stare after him. *What the hell just happened?*

CHAPTER 32

THE NEW GUY CAP SENT CAN AT LEAST TAKE A punch and challenge my takedowns. I haven't knocked him out yet. Though, he's earned my respect enough to actually spar with him instead of trying to kill him like the last handful of idiots Jonah put in the ring with me. Landry "Cowboy" Pierce is gonna be a title contender someday.

But not today. I've got him on the ground in a Kimura hold, his arm locked behind his head in position to break or dislocate if he doesn't submit. "Come on, Cowboy. You know you're done for." A slight tug has him groaning in pain. "Give me what I want, then we can both take a shower and get those drinks Jonah has been holding over our heads."

"Fuck. You suck," he growls with his face smashed to the mat.

"Don't break his arm, Gabriel. Cap will be pissed," Jonah calls from outside the ring.

I'm not going to break his arm or dislocate it, but the boy needs to learn to submit so he can come back to fight another day.

Another tiny tug has his eyes watering. "Give me what I want," I seethe in his ear.

"Landry, for God's sake, tap out. He's got you. You know it. He knows it." Jonah motions to the room. "The whole damn place knows it. Tap the fuck out. Now!"

Tense seconds pass in strained silence until Cowboy's other hand taps my leg. He doesn't say it. He doesn't have to verbalize his submission—his tap is concession enough. I release him slowly, helping his arm back into a normal position, and stand up, offering my hand. When he takes it, I pull him to his feet and pat his shoulder. "You did good."

I swing out of the ring and take the water Jonah offers, catching the look of defeat on Landry's face. "Hey." I wait until his eyes meet mine. "Submission doesn't mean you're no good. It means you live to fight another day. *Always* choose submission over injury. A bruised ego heals faster than a broken arm."

He nods, hardly convinced.

"We'll work on techniques to get out of the Kimura hold next time."

He lights up. "Yeah?"

"Yeah. Don't beat yourself up. I'm a tough motherfucker. You put up a good fight. I outmaneuvered you. Maybe next time you'll outmaneuver me."

That grants me a full smile. "Thanks, Gabriel."

I don't miss Jonah's approving grin.

"Don't mention it." I swipe the sweat off my face with a towel and crush the bottle of water after downing it.

"Those drinks?" Jonah prompts as we head to the locker room.

"Food first." I pat my stomach. "I could eat an entire cow."

Cowboy groans. "A steak sounds amazing."

"Shower. I'll meet y'all out front." Jonah leaves us to talk to Warren, Cap's Vegas manager.

A hand on Landry's shoulder stops his progress. "Think about what I said. Keep things in perspective. You've got talent. You could go far, but don't let your ego think you deserve more than your skills are capable of. Submission might mean defeat today, but it also means you get a chance to win tomorrow. Injury means your chance at winning is further down the road." I release him and strip on my way to the shower. "It doesn't mean you don't fight like hell. It means when you get stuck, you need to be man enough to realize it. You feel me?"

"Yeah, I feel ya. Thanks for the advice. I really appreciate it." He steps in the shower stall down from me.

"We all start somewhere. The key is to listen and learn." I was him once. Thought I was tougher than every other fighter out there, and most times, I was. It took some hard knocks and guys better than me, willing to show me the ropes, to knock me down a peg or two. Submission is a hard lesson to learn for guys like us who believe we're better than that. Learning to pick your battles is key to a successful career. Maybe even in life.

As I soap up, my mind wanders to Frankie. Did I give up too easily, or did I only submit to come back and fight another day?

"Have you heard from her?" Jonah leans in, his voice quiet so his question is only for my ears.

I shake my head and take a drink of the only beer I'm allowed to have tonight. When I'm in training, which is all the damn time, I don't drink often, but this close to my match—three weeks away—I limit it to one beer a week and usually on Fridays, and never, never the hard stuff. I savor the cool ale as it slides down my throat like it's my hand sliding down my Angel's body to her sweet spot. My heaven on Earth.

"Have you reached out to *her*?"

His question receives the same negative reply. *Nope.* His disbelief is apparent. What he doesn't get—what none of them get—is I'm an all-in or all-out kinda guy. Frankie told me I don't know how to live in the gray spaces, and she's right. I'm a black or white kind of guy. Gray is for pansies who don't have the balls to stand up for what they want.

But after five weeks without my Frankie Angel, I can see the appeal gray holds. It allows for compromise. It allows you to keep what you cherish while giving up something that holds less meaning. The thing is, she deserves my all—my black or white—not my gray that can't commit to the future she desires. She deserves a man who's all in.

After what Austin said weeks ago, *maybe it was always you*, I keep seeing Frankie by my side, our children at our feet laughing and playing as I hold my Angel, my hand resting on her extended abdomen, full of another baby I put there. My vision of her and me together for the long run, all in, husband and wife—with children—doesn't send me running like it did when Austin planted that seed. It warms my gut, makes my chest ache in the place only she has ever occupied, and stings my eyes like I might actually fucking cry.

Damn, I need to get drunk.

I break my rule. Finishing off my beer, I order another. "I'll be back," I tell the guys, stepping outside and punching a contact on my phone.

"Hey, asshole." Rowdy can never just say *hi*. It might piss me off if it wasn't so like me.

"How is she?" I pace the parking lot, keeping my eye out for anyone who might be listening, but the only people out here are arriving, leaving, or getting it on in the back of their cars. They couldn't care less about a schmuck like me. I lean against the far brick wall, welcoming the cold stone against my back, reminding me to keep my emotions in check. I'm only calling to ensure she's okay, she's safe.

"She's fine." I hear noises in the background and then silence, assuming he stepped away from the crowd he was with. A long pause and a deep exhale have him admitting, "Still crying over you."

Shit. Not the news I want to hear. "Still? Can't you distract her? Make her forget?" I thought she'd have given up on me by now. She's the one who pushed me away. Made me put up or shut up. We could've still been together if she hadn't been so hardheaded about committing to a future I didn't know if I could handle.

"Sounds like you're either asking me to keep her in a state of inebriation or fuck her until she can't remember *her* name, much less *yours*." I don't miss the edge in his voice. It only serves to piss me off nearly as much as his words.

"You better not lay a hand on her, or so help me God—"

"What are you gonna do, Gabriel? Fight for her?" He chuckles. "That's rich coming from you. All she wants is for you to fight for her. Show her she's…" He stops.

"What? Show her… What?" I need him to finish his thought. I need every morsel he can give me about my Angel.

"Show her she's worth it. Prove you're capable of doing something her own father wouldn't do, and what Austin couldn't do."

"She's worth everything." Even breaking myself to stay away from her.

"Really? You've got a weird way of showing it."

"I can't—"

"Listen, Gabriel, I'm done playing your informant. You want to know how she's doing, you need to call her. Or better yet, don't, and let her move on." He hangs up before I can get my brain around what he said.

Stuck in my head, I reenter the bar, grab my beer off the table and finish it off in one long pull.

Soft hands run up my sides to my pecs and still as hard tits press into me. "Buy me one of those, handsome?"

I eye the raven-haired beauty looking up at me. For a split second all I see is Frankie before I blink the vision away and stare into the green eyes of a dark-haired stranger. "Not interested." I step out of her grasp and up to the bar. "Another beer."

I down it in one gulp. "Another."

"Whoa. Cancel that." Jonah steps into my side. "Time to go, brother."

"I want another beer," I protest, trying to get the bartender's attention.

Jonah pulls my arm down. "You know as well as I do what you want isn't going to be found in the bottom of a beer or the pussy of some ring-chaser. What you want and need is back in Sunnyville, and as soon as you pull your head out of your ass, I'm sure she'll be happy to see you."

"What's with everyone telling me what I need? Of course she's what I need, but it's not enough. *I'm* not what *she* needs." I let him guide me out of the bar and to his truck.

"Then *be* what she needs."

"What if I can't?"

"Then let her the fuck go."

CHAPTER 33

THE LAST THREE WEEKS I'VE BEEN BACK TO work have gone relatively smoothly. Gabriel has been gone for six weeks, and I'm now twelve weeks pregnant. The end of the first trimester. My doctor swears I should stop puking any day now as the placenta starts to produce the hormones the baby needs instead of relying on my body for them—which means the nausea should dissipate.

Please, God, let it stop.

I'd like to say it's getting easier to live without Gabriel in my life, but it would be a lie. I'm convinced the hole in my heart will never mend. I'll need a transplant or the will to ignore the pain with each beat it takes without him by my side. I'm not sure I'd know how to even breathe without the tightness in my chest and the ache in my soul.

One step at a time, one moment, one breath, one day, one broken dream at a time my day passes into weeks, bringing us to two weeks from his big fight.

I know I have to tell him he's going to be a father, even if he wants nothing to do with our baby. He deserves to know. This is too big of a decision for me to make for him. The burden too large. The stakes too high. The potential heartbreak for him, for me, for our child is immeasurable. I can't take this decision out of his hands. I know that, and yet I can't even think how to tell him. A letter? A text? A phone call?

What is the appropriate medium to give him news he'd never hoped to hear?

A future he never intended to have?

A legacy that could break the mold of his past or shatter his future entirely?

Yeah, I don't know either.

So, I wait.

I'll defer the decision until after his fight. I can't be the reason he doesn't step into the octagon focused and ready to win. My future may have jumped the track, but I won't purposely impact the course of his. He has tunnel vision when it comes to training for a title match. He's destined to win, hands down. He'll be the heavyweight champ. I'd bet my life on it.

On one of my many trips to the restroom, I stop by the private training room to say *hi* to the guys. I arrived earlier than they did and none of them needed me today, so I focused on catching up on paper-work with the intent of making my presence known at some point. I just finished lunch and figure it's a good place to check in before starting something new.

I step inside and still when the smell of sweat and dirty socks inundates my nostrils. My stomach flips. I clasp my hand over my mouth when saliva starts to pool.

I cannot get sick, I chant as I scan the room looking for a safe haven from the noxious smell, or maybe backing out of the room before anyone notices I'm here is a better solution.

"Frankie!" Jess calls from the far end of the room with a smile and a wave.

Great, so much for a clean escape. I wave with my free hand, the other one still covering my mouth.

"What's got you too busy to hang with us today?" Sloan drops his weights and moves closer. "You haven't worked out with us in ages."

I shrug and point to my ribs, not trusting my mouth to do anything but puke.

He scowls, eyeing my hand over my mouth. "I thought you were given the okay to start light workouts like the treadmill or light weights."

Panic rises when I notice all of them have stopped what they're doing and have moved toward me, nearly in slow motion, their faces full of concern and confusion.

"What's wrong, Frankie?" Patrick touches my arm. "Why the hand over your mouth?"

"Not feeling well," I manage around my hand, but regret it when another wave of nausea hits with the stench of their close proximity.

The aroma of sweaty men never bothered me before. I usually find it rather calming as it means I'm in the presence of athletes in peak condition, pursuing their dreams and overcoming challenges. It can be exhilarating on the skin of a guy I'm attracted to, an aphrodisiac even, like it's proof of his masculinity.

But today, it's like skunk spray. My eyes water, and I spin away from them, running for the trashcan I spot in the corner. My stomach lurches, sending my lunch the wrong direction. Kneeling, I barely make it before it all comes out in hideous retching, leaving me gagging and gasping for air.

"Fuck." Rowdy's voice comes from behind seconds before hands grip my hair, holding it out of the way. "Get a wet towel and some water," he barks in true Gabriel-like alpha fashion. "Breathe, Frankie." He pats my back lightly as he soothes with calming words my stomach refuses to hear.

Embarrassed, with the contents of my stomach expelled into the trash can, I sit back on my heels, my eyes still closed as I catch my breath.

"Here." Rowdy hands me a wet towel.

The cool towel feels amazing on my face. I exhale a few more times before I wipe my face and dare to open my eyes. The trash can has been removed and replaced by a clean one. I glance around and watch Cap tie the used trash bag closed before placing it inside a larger container.

"Are you done?" Rowdy's concerned face comes into view at my side. He knows by experience my trip to worship the porcelain god can involve multiple waves of upchucks.

"I think so." I take the water someone else offers and avoid all eyes except Rowdy's. "I'm so embarrassed. But the smell..."

He chuckles. "You guys hear that? Your stench made her sick."

The number of grumbles and remarks from behind me tell me I didn't escape an audience, and my embarrassment is not yet over.

"Mint?" I ask Rowdy, but a hand from my other side has me looking into the face of a scowling Cap as he hands me a peppermint, already unwrapped. He keeps a stash in his pocket at all times. I should have remembered. "Thanks." I slip it in my mouth, sucking and moving it around, the smell and taste a sweet relief.

I reach for Rowdy. "Help me up?"

"You sure?"

A nod from me has two sets of hands, Rowdy and Cap's, helping me up, not letting go until I'm steady on my feet. Reluctantly, I turn, facing my audience of concerned fighters. "Show's over." I fake a smile and hope they let it go.

A mix of scowls and frowns mars their faces as all eyes land on me, then slowly move down my body to still on my middle section. I quickly remove my hand. I hadn't noticed it was cradling my abdomen. *Shit.*

"Fuck."

"Oh my God."

"Oh, fuck."

"No way."

Their reactions hit me all at once. I don't know who said what, but it's clear they have no doubt I'm with child.

"Frankie?" Caps voice pulls my eyes to his. The concern and hurt there has my vision blurring and my hand reaching for Rowdy's in support.

He clasps my hand and leans down. "Maybe we should take this to a more private location."

I shake my head. This needs to be addressed now. I can't have any of them running to tell Gabriel. I focus on Cap. "I'm sorry. I should have told you." My eyes scan the guys: Sloan, Patrick, Walker, Jess. "I didn't want to have to ask you to lie for me." I wobble on my feet, and before I know it, I'm swept up in Cap's arms and set down on the nearest bench.

"He has a right to know," Cap whispers for only my ears before he pulls away. "It's Gabriel's, right?"

Nodding, I catch each of their gazes as they near. Cap and Rowdy sit on either side of me, holding my hands.

Sloan pops open a lemonade Gatorade and hands it to me. "How far along are you?"

I take a drink and close my eyes while I wait for it to settle. When it does, I open my eyes to them kneeling and sitting in front of me, having moved in closer for a family powwow. "Twelve weeks," I admit.

Walker eyes Rowdy's hand on my knee. "Gabriel doesn't know?"

"No. And you can't tell him," I implore each of them, stopping on Cap. "He only has a few weeks before his fight. I'll tell him afterwards. Telling him now would just be cruel." I look back to each of them. "Promise me you won't tell him. This is my secret to tell. Not yours."

They nod, but it's not enough. I take each of them by the hand and make them promise on my unborn baby they won't tell Gabriel, or anyone else. They all promise and seem more concerned about me than keeping this secret from Gabriel. I let out a relieved breath until I realize Cap hasn't said a word or made me any such promise.

Stepping to him, he pats my shoulder. "I promise." Then he walks away, his disappointment trailing behind him.

We leave the guys in the gym, fumbling to clear their heads so they can get back to training. Inside my office, before I sit, I grab my spare toothbrush and toothpaste and brush my teeth, rinsing more times than needed.

When I finish, I plop down on the couch in my office with Rowdy pacing in front of me. "Considering all things, I think that went pretty well." I leave out my concern for Cap. I know I hurt his feelings. I should have told him. I was afraid of disappointing him. As it turns out, I did it anyway.

"Mm-hmm." Rowdy's hands are in his hair, messing up his man bun. Laidback Rowdy is usually the calm one unless he's seeing red, ready to fight.

"What's wrong?"

He stops, his eyes locking with mine, sad and full of something I can't put my finger on. "I like you."

My brows shoot up. "I like you too."

He nods. "I think if we decided to, we could even love each other."

"I already love you, Darkboy. You get me in ways no one else does."

His megawatt dimpled smile loosens the knot in my gut. "Ditto." He takes a seat next to me, gripping my hands in his. "But that's not the kind of love I'm talking about." He worries his lip while his thumbs run back and forth over the back of my hands. "Marry me, Frankie." He drops to his knees on the floor before me.

"What—"

"Marry me. I'll love your baby like it's my own. We could be good together." He sweeps his hand across my cheek. His eyes fill with a heat I've only seen a few times from him. "Real good, darlin.'"

What he says is probably true. We could make it work, and it might be good. We get along. We click, understanding each other in a deeper way than most. The idea of loving him or being loved by him doesn't turn me off. Though I've put him clearly in the friend zone, I'm not oblivious or unaffected by his charms. I am attracted to him. But could I do that to him? Could I do this to Gabriel without even giving him a chance?

I stand and step around him. "I... I appreciate—"

"Don't say *no.*" He stands, stalking me to the wall. His hand rests above my head as he leans in. "Think about it." His other hand squeezes my waist, and my breath catches. His eyes land on my parted lips. He's gone alpha on me, and my ignored libido takes notice, sending alerting shivers down my spine. His eyes slide to my thrumming pulse-point on my neck before he whispers across my skin in the same place, "I could love you so good, Frankie. Make you come in ways you've never dreamt of."

Oh, shit. My pregnancy hormones have my body screaming, *yes, please,* as my heart cries, wanting to know why it's not Gabriel here saying these things to me.

Rowdy presses his mouth to my throbbing pulse, licking and sucking gently. I brace my palms against the wall, refusing to give in, refusing to pull him toward me. But when he kisses a trail up my neck to my ear and across my jaw, pausing momentarily to catch my eyes before his mouth covers mine, I lose my battle and sink my fingers into his hair, moaning my approval and begging for more with the press of my body to his.

He's not the man I love, but the man I love chose not to fight for us.

Delving in deeper, Rowdy's tongue caresses mine, his arms ensconcing me in his embrace as his hands knead and urge me closer. His moans mix with mine. Urgent and needy hands roam until he slows with tender, light kisses and gentle caresses at my sides. "Yeah, so fucking good, darlin.'"

He pulls back, hands on my hips to keep me on my feet. "Think about it." He kisses my cheek and leaves me breathing heavily, clutching my belly like I can protect my baby from my confused, racing thoughts of Rowdy's promises of family amongst Gabriel's echoed promises of nothing more than sex and shelter.

A love that rocks the universe but has no future?

Or a love that rocks my baby as a surrogate father and could probably make me happy?

Yeah, I'm screwed and confused as hell.

CHAPTER 34

MY EMERGENCY CALL TO EMERSON HAS HER dropping off Gwen with Grant's mom and rushing to meet me. Her guys keep Wings Out running without her having to be there full-time since Gwen was born. Luckily, I caught her on a day off, but not too early to mess up her mommy-daughter time.

Like a chicken shit, I'm avoiding Cap and Rowdy, leaving early with the excuse my pregnancy grants me. Of course, I don't actually tell them in person. No, that would make me less of a chicken. I sneak out the back and walk around the building to my car, pull out of the parking lot in blazing glory. *Yeah, that won't get anybody's attention!* Then stop at the corner market to blast a text to each of them with my excuse—the same excuse—knowing Darkboy will probably head home to check on me only to not find me there. I can't very well tell him I'm not feeling well and leaving work to then meet Emmy for an early dinner and girl time.

I hate lying. I make a habit of not doing it. I've been lied to enough to last me a lifetime and then some. I'll make it up to them. I don't know how... Yet.

As expected, I beat Emmy to the new wine bistro. Though I can't drink, I can appreciate the ambiance. But mostly, I appreciate the secluded rooms they have in the back, sequestered by partitioned walls and sliding doors, reminding me a little of a Japanese Minka-style home, though the walls are not thin like those in a traditional Japanese home. The rooms aren't overly large, at least not the ones I've seen, but big enough for a rounded booth and a sitting area for lounging in privacy.

Leaving Emmy's name up front, I slip into the designated room with a request not to be bothered until she arrives. I sit in the booth, drumming my fingers on the mahogany-topped table, fidgeting with nervous energy. My stomach rumbles, amazingly bold enough to ask for food after its mass exodus only a few hours ago. *The nerve!*

Giving up on the booth, I try for the couch, then the chair. Determining sitting may not be the best state to force myself into, I opt for pacing from one end of the sectioned-off room to the other. I shake my hands and blow out puffs of air, trying to calm my heart and racing thoughts.

Rowdy proposed to me!

He kissed me!

Holy moly, what a kiss.

"Stop." I cover my eyes. *What a freakin' mess!*

"It's not good if you've taken to pacing and talking to yourself." Emmy's compassionate smile greets me as I take in her t-shirt and cut-off jean shorts, looking more like a hot teenager than a momma.

My lip trembles with relief at the sight of her. "No, not good at all."

Hugs and a few tears later, we're sitting on the couch facing each other. She has a glass of red, and I have an iced tea with extra lemon and no artificial sweetener.

"First things first." She eyes my glass. "Why am I the only one drinking? I thought this was an emergency calling for commiserating over libations."

"It does. Only..."

Her gaze flits to my growling stomach and back to me. "Only?"

I set my tea on the coffee table and scoot to the edge of the cushion, ready for a quick departure if her reaction to keeping this secret from her turns bad. Which I fear is the only way it can go. "Let me preface this by saying I wanted to tell you, but I couldn't. I didn't want to put you or Grant in a tough spot by keeping a secret from Gabriel."

Her brow puckers, and she takes a drink of her wine. Setting it aside, she mimics my position on the couch. "Noted. There's nothing you could tell me that would make me have to take sides between you two. Except maybe—"

"I'm pregnant."

"—that! Oh…" She stands and walks away and then back to me. She takes a deep breath, visibly shaken by my news. "To be clear: you're pregnant with *Gabriel's* baby?"

"Yes! Who else's would it be?"

"Rowdy's?"

"No! We aren't… We haven't… It's not like that," I settle on, finally finding the thought I need to convey.

"And it's not Austin's?"

I rear back. "God, no. But he did knock up the woman he cheated with."

"What?"

"Yeah, he told me the day I fell down the stairs. It might be why I fell down the stairs. I was pretty messed up. Not because I wanted him back, but because he was living our future with someone else. It's a hard blow to take." I sit back. "Turns out I was pregnant too. I just didn't know it."

Contemplative, she sits next to me, leaning back. "Wow. Give me a sec. It's a shocker." She takes a large gulp of her wine. "You sure you don't want a sip?"

I drank too much when I was first pregnant, not knowing I was. I have no intention of having another drink while this precious one is still inside me. "I'm sure. But I could eat." I rub my stomach as it rumbles in response.

She smiles. "Obviously."

We order food as she processes my news. Once the waitress leaves,

I turn to Emmy. "I feel I should get all the news out, give you a chance to digest it all at once instead of hitting you over the head again and again."

"Whoa, that bad, huh?"

"Maybe not bad, but shocking."

She sits up, bracing herself. "Go for it."

"Well, first Cap and the guys found out today. Not by choice, I kinda got sick in front of all of them, and, well, they figured it out. They promised not to tell Gabriel. Cap too, but he's upset with me for keeping it from him. Understandably."

"Cap will forgive you. He needs time to process." She pats my leg. "Do you *plan* on telling Gabriel?"

"Of course, but not until after his fight. He's made it clear he doesn't want kids. I wouldn't feel right keeping it from him, but there's no reason to sidetrack his focus when he's so close to his goal."

"Yeah." She sighs. "I can see why you wanted to keep this to yourself." She grips my hand, leaning into me, shoulder to shoulder. "I hate that you've been going through this on your own."

"Not entirely on my own," I admit.

"Oh?"

Please don't be hurt. "Rowdy figured it out pretty quickly. When he asked, I couldn't lie to him. He's been my rock."

Her eyes lower, and she bites her lower lip. "I'm glad." She sounds anything but happy about it.

"I'm sorry. I really did want to tell you."

She nods, repeatedly. She's got my bobblehead impression down. "I know." She swipes at the corner of her eyes. "I get it." She locks eyes with me. "I really do. I'm just sad I couldn't be there for you. Not hurt you didn't tell me."

Thank God!

"So, the shocker…"

"Besides being preggo?" She eyes me expectantly.

"Yeah, besides that." I grip her hand, linking our fingers. "Rowdy asked me to marry him."

"What?!" She squeezes my hand so hard I struggle to get free.

"I know, right? Totally out of left field." Her silence has me turning to face her. "Right?"

"Not really. It's obvious you're good friends. He cares for you." She shrugs. "It's not a big leap to see you guys going from friendship to… More."

"But we aren't *more*."

"But you could be."

I blow out a punch of air, my lips vibrating in the process, as I sink down on the couch. "He kissed me." He did more than kiss me. He turned me on.

"And?"

"It was hot." *Really hot.*

"But?"

"But he's not Gabriel. He'll never be Gabriel. And I'm not ready to give up on the idea of there being an us. At least not until he closes the door permanently, after I tell him about the baby."

"In the meantime?"

"In the meantime, I tell Darkboy *no*. I can't ask him to give up his future for me and my baby. Even if Gabriel wants nothing to do with us. I have to believe there's someone out there who wants me for me and not out of obligation or sacrifice." I lay my head in Emmy's lap, and she strokes my hair. "Besides, Rowdy deserves a girl who fell in love with him from the get-go. Not someone who has to *learn* to love him. He might turn me on, but at this point—" I rub my belly, "—this little one is making my hormones so crazy, I think a stiff breeze could get me off."

"God, I remember those days." She wags her brows. "Some of the best times too. Grant can't wait to knock me up again just for the hot pregnancy sex."

"Please." I brush her off. "You guys do it like rabbits as it is."

"Yeah, but a pregnancy orgasm—or should I say *orgasms*—is not to be missed." She sighs at the thought. Her hand rests on my baby bump that's becoming more prominent every day. "You need to get yourself a toy, or hit Rowdy up for some pregnancy sex. You may not want to marry him, but you two could enjoy the rest of your pregnancy like nobody's business."

"I think sex would take our friendship way past the friendship zone. A kiss we can come back from, but fucking like monkeys, probably not."

"I see your point."

A knock at the sliding door brings me to a sitting position as our food is placed on the table.

"If we can't get you laid, we can at least feed you and satiate one need."

"I'm all for food right now." I might become as big as a house, eating my hormones into silence. Is that even possible?

Maybe a toy is needed after all…

CHAPTER 35

MY TRAINING FOR THE PAST FOUR MONTHS culminates in tomorrow night's fight. For the past week, besides training, I've done nothing but promotional crap. Cap arrived in Vegas a few days ago. He's been acting off—more of an asshole than normal—especially to me. He's still upset about me and Frankie not working out. I get it. I want to tell him to chill, that I've been having second thoughts, but honestly, I'm not sure.

Yes, I still want her.

Yes, I want to see her every fucking day.

And yes, the idea of committing to a future with her isn't as scary as it was a couple months ago when I walked away, unable to tell her I wanted more than sex.

Even then I wanted more. I just couldn't promise it. I couldn't commit to it. My fears of being a fuck-up for a husband and father are real. But despite my past, after the fight, I'm heading back to Sunnyville to win her back.

Living without her is worse than the uncertainty of what our shared future could hold.

I don't know what I'll say. What I'll promise. I'll get on my knees and beg if need be.

Life has been hell without her, and I need my Angel to bring me back to heaven.

I had my weigh-in early this morning for a fight that doesn't feel nearly as important as it did months ago. To continue my promotional hell, I'm currently at a breakfast held by WickedTuff, the promoter for tomorrow's fight. I've done the rounds, shook the hand of the current heavyweight champion, Killer González, for the required photo op. I even let him think he had me with his tough-as-nails act and stone-crushing grip. I smiled, nodded and told him, "Enjoy your last night as champ. Tomorrow, your title is mine."

"You son of a—" He didn't care much for my conversational skills.

He actually tried to lure me into fighting him right here. I simply smiled, patted his arm as his guys held him back, and told him, "Save your energy for the octagon. You're gonna need it."

He left shortly after. I guess his team couldn't calm him down enough to make staying worthwhile.

Biding my time till I can leave, I grab a handful of grapes off the buffet and scan the room for a friendly face who doesn't want to fight me, sign me, or fuck me. Near the entrance I spot a frowning Cap and two unexpected faces: Grant and Emerson.

Shoving the last of the grapes in my mouth, I make a beeline for them. "Hey, I wasn't expecting to see you two until tomorrow."

Grant shakes my hand with a half hug. "I decided to surprise Emmy with a few extra nights in Vegas."

"Nice." I hug Emerson. "It's great to see some friendly faces amongst these sharks."

"Hey." Cap takes offense, giving me the evil eye.

I chuckle. "Cap, you barely tolerate me, much less feign friendliness."

"Not true. I like you just fine. Might even like you as a son if you'd pull your head out of your ass."

Whoa. Surprised by his admission—not the *ass* part but the *son* part—I actually stagger back a step, my hand rubbing the familiar ache in my chest. He had to go and remind me of *her*. My Angel. "I'm working on it."

His brows meet in the middle, eyeing me skeptically. "Really? Leaving her high and dry for two months isn't what I'd call *working on it*."

"She said we were done. *She* dumped *me*," I remind him.

He scoffs and snags a mimosa off a passing tray. "You'd better hurry the fuck up before you're too late."

Glowering, I notice the silent conversation shared between the three of them. "What's going on?"

Emerson shakes her head, studying her feet intently.

Cap shakes his head, lips tightly closed.

Grant clears his throat, glances between Cap and Emerson before focusing on me. "Don't wait too long."

My skin prickles as alarm bells go off. "What the fuck does that mean?" I look between them. "Somebody better tell me what's going on before I start ripping this place to shreds."

Emerson stares daggers at Grant. "Don't," she whispers through clenched teeth.

Sighing, Grant squeezes her hand. "He has a right to know."

"Oh, fuck, not good," Cap murmurs to my right.

I'm done with this cat and mouse game. "Know what?" I step into Grant, apparently the weak link, or maybe just a better friend to me. "Grant."

"Fuck." He runs his palm down his face, lingering on his chin, his eyes pleading with Emerson, not wanting to betray her by revealing whatever secret they're keeping. "He's going to find out."

"*After* the fight," she says, not even moving her lips. Apparently, lockjaw is a real thing.

What she said and not how she said it hits me. "Wait. You're not telling me something because of my fight?"

Emerson meets my eyes for the first time since this whole debacle started. "We love you, Gabriel. She lo—" Her hand smacks over her mouth, halting her words. Her eyes go round like saucers.

My anger fizzles, but my worry doesn't. I touch her arm. "Please, tell me."

Emerson looks at Cap and back to me. "She made us promise. She wanted to wait until after your fight to tell—"

"Tell me what?" I interrupt. Is something wrong with my Angel?

Her eyes water, and now I'm starting to really freak out.

"You can't lose this fight because of her. She'll hate me." A tear slips down Emerson's cheek.

Christ.

Grant pulls her into his arms, kissing her head. "Shh, no more." His eyes lock with mine.

"My fight is not worth whatever secret you're keeping for Frankie," I implore him. "Please, tell me. Is she okay?"

He nods. "She's fine. Or she will be. It's just… Fuck—" He sighs like the weight of the world resides on his shoulders. "I hate to tell you this, man."

I can tell by their reactions I'm going to hate *hearing* it.

"Rowdy—"

"Rowdy?" What the fuck does he have to do with anything? Then it dawns on me he's the only one who didn't come from Sunnyville with the rest of my Black Ops fight team. He and Frankie are the only ones.

A solemn mask transforms Grant's face. "He asked her to marry him."

"Marry him?" I grip my hair while my world crumbles around me. "I thought they were only friends." My words are more an expression of disbelief than a query to them.

Grant just shrugs. He has no more words for me. What is there possibly left to say?

My Angel has moved on.

Found a man who could promise her forever.

Give her her happily ever after.

Fuck me.

I stumble out of the hotel ballroom, ignoring their calls, and punch the down arrow for the elevator. It dings, the doors opening nearly instantaneously as if it was waiting to whisk me away on an express ride to hell.

Maybe it is, but not before I make a crucial stop.

CHAPTER 36

WHEN I TOLD ROWDY I COULDN'T—wouldn't—marry him, he took it like a man.

He didn't cry, like I did.

He didn't puke right afterwards, like I did.

And he sure as shit didn't remain celibate, like I am.

It seems all the men in my life find it easy to move on. All except Cap.

He's still pouting. It's been two weeks since he found out I'm pregnant. He checks on me every day, offering me food, water, protein drinks, my own pack of peppermints. Yet he's holding his forgiveness hostage. No matter how much I apologize, it doesn't seem to be enough. I don't have the right words, the acceptable amount of remorse, or the promises to warrant his mercy.

The sad part is, I love that he's so upset. At least he cares enough to stick around and be mad with me. He still cares for me. It's obvious by his daily check-ins. He's just not ready to forgive me. And that's okay. All I can do is ask for forgiveness. I can't force it or expect to receive it. Some pains take time to heal. I know that all too well.

So, life goes on. Cap is mad. Rowdy is distant. And the guys at the gym treat me like a princess who can't lift a finger without their help. That part I secretly love, though I'd never admit it to them.

Tomorrow is Gabriel's big fight against Killer González in Las Vegas. He's a big guy, originally from Brazil but trains in Florida. He's evenly matched in weight and height, but the weight doesn't sit the same on him as it does Gabriel—who's all muscle. Killer looks more like he's seventy-five percent fighter and twenty-five percent Pillsbury Doughboy. He didn't always look like that. I think this past year as the reigning champ has gone to his waist. Except in the interview I saw earlier this week, he still thinks he's hot shit and that taking down Gabriel will be a breeze.

He's delusional. Gabriel will grind him up and eat him for a late-night snack. The guys will all be there to cheer him on too, even Cap. They've all gone to Vegas. I didn't even go into work today. There's no point. No one was even there except Rowdy, and he's avoiding me. So, like I said—there's no point.

Pounding on the front door has me setting down the knife I'm using to spread mayo on two slices of bread. The beginnings of a sandwich. It's just after noon, and I'm starving. I check the living room to see where Rowdy disappeared to. He breezed in and out of the kitchen, looking for food a few minutes ago. I thought he might stick around to eat with me. Guess not.

The banging on the door begins again, and then the doorbell rings.

"Jeez, I'm comin'. Hold your horses."

Rowdy appears at the top of the stairs, frowning at the door like that alone will make it stop.

More banging.

I reach for the deadbolt to unlock it.

"Check the peephole first," Darkboy hisses from his roost.

When I see the meaty frame on the other side of the door, I nearly faint as my heart starts pounding like it's responding directly to his banging on the door—like it's a secret code only they know. My breath hitches when he lifts his oversized hand and bangs again, jolting me back a step. He doesn't even look around. It's like he *knows* we're home.

Backing away slowly, I glance around, trying to figure out my escape route. I can't bring myself to open the door. I haven't seen or heard from him in two months—since I told him goodbye at the hospital. The day I found out I was pregnant. The day my life changed forever, heading down on a road he wasn't willing to go, its destination nowhere on his life plan.

I yelp when Rowdy touches my arm. I didn't even notice or hear him come down the stairs. "What's wrong?"

Shaking my head, I back up to the wall. "I can't." I feel like I've finally started to get my feet under me in the last few days. Like I can live without him.

I don't want to, but I *can*.

Him being here will only undermine any progress I've made. I know I said I was going to tell him about the baby after his fight, but I'd decided the best thing for me is to write him a letter—not tell him in person. Seeing him again, being rejected all over again, would be too painful, set me back too far. I have to be strong for our baby. I'm determined to set an example for our child, be good, be strong, be present. The cycle of shitty parenting stops here. The next generation will know they are loved, cherished, and most of all—wanted.

"Tell him I'm not here. Tell him I died." I run for the living room. When I hear the click of the lock, I realize the living room is not a great hiding place. I should have gone for my room or—the garage!

I dart toward the kitchen, planning to grab my keys and make a dash for it when I hear Gabriel's familiar voice.

"Where is she?" He's not happy, but God, that voice. It calls to me like a homing beacon.

"She's not here." Rowdy sounds like he's up for the confrontation I'm avoiding.

"No? Well, I'll wait." I hear movement, but I can't tell where he's heading, the living room or the kitchen.

I'm stuck in the doorway between the two. Nowhere to go without being seen.

"That's not a good idea." Rowdy's voice meets my ears about the time I catch sight of Gabriel at the entryway across the room from me, on the threshold of stepping into the living room.

My heart soars, and my stomach plummets. I'd nearly forgotten how handsome he is, especially in all-alpha mode.

Gabriel turns, missing me in the process. "You forget who owns this house and lets you stay here rent-free."

"I actually pay rent to Frankie. I don't know what agreement you have with her. So, if it's all the same, you should leave."

My gasp at Rowdy's boldfaced lie draws their eyes to me. *Oh, shit.*

Gabriel pins me with his laser focus and heated stare. "Not here, huh?"

Rowdy shakes his head and shrugs, letting me know I'm an idiot for giving myself away. Leaning against the doorframe, he crosses his arms and legs, getting ready for a show.

Gabriel moves into the room. I do the same but stay behind the couch, hoping to hide my growing middle section from his keen eye. At nearly four months, I'm not big by any means. But I have a definite baby bump, and my waist is thicker—not to mention my thighs and ass. What the couch won't hide are my enlarged boobs. Yeah, I'm totally screwed.

"Angel." His pet name for me has my knees about to buckle and a sob ready to take flight.

I swallow through the lump in my throat to ask the obvious, "Shouldn't you be in Vegas?"

"No." There's no hesitation in his weighted response. "I'm right where I need to be."

No? "What about your fight?" I grip the couch to not only keep me on my feet but to stop myself from crossing my arms over my chest as he studies my face before lowering his gaze to my breasts with a puzzled brow raise. Maybe he'll think I got a boob job.

His confusion aside, he locks onto my face again. "I don't give a fuck about the fight."

What? I couldn't have heard him correctly.

His eyes narrow, and he tilts his head one way and then the other before stepping closer.

Shit, he's gonna figure it out before I know why he's here.

"I needed to see you," he offers before I can ask.

"Why?"

"You can't marry Rowdy."

I jerk back, not believing my ears. These past five minutes are confusing the hell out of me. I never in a million years expected to see Gabriel the day before his fight. Even to stop a marriage that is never going to happen.

Crossing my arms over my chest, I scowl right back at him and catch a glimpse of a smiling Rowdy over his shoulder. "And why not?" I can't help myself. Gabriel has hurt me too deeply for me to let him off the hook that easily.

"Because I love you."

"What—" My tough exterior crumbles as I collapse to my knees.

I barely make it to the floor before Gabriel is gripping my shoulders. "Are you okay?"

Shaking my head to clear the fogginess, I need to be sure he said what I think he said. "Say it again." I don't even recognize the sound of my voice as mine.

He tips my trembling chin till his turbulent blue eyes lock on my stormy grays. "I love you, Angel." He captures my cheek with his palm. "I think I always have."

"What took you so long?" My voice wobbles to match my chin as I try to hold it together.

"I didn't think I could be what you needed," he admits.

I knew that. "And now?" I'm cautious. I can't let hope spring free when I don't know what he's offering. For all I know he's only here because he's jealous.

He holds my hands, his thumbs rubbing across the tops. "I know I'm not good enough for you. But I want to spend the rest of my life trying to make you happy—giving you want you want—what you need. I damn well know no one will try harder than me to make you happy."

Hope blossoms like a flower breaching a crack in the sidewalk. Leery, I ask, "What are you offering?"

He brings our joined hands to his mouth with a kiss. "Everything, Angel. Marriage. Kids. Whatever you want, it's yours." He pulls me closer, leaning in, forehead to forehead. "Only, don't send me away again. It nearly killed me the last time. I won't survive another minute without you."

"So, you're not here because Rowdy proposed?"

He glances at the entrance where Rowdy stood only a few minutes ago. He's gone. "Oh, I'm here because of that. I've got tons of questions, but they'll have to wait. Right now, I need to hear what you're thinking."

"I'm afraid you're only here because you're jealous."

He's shaking his head before I even finish. "I was coming to you as soon as I won my fight, but when I heard about the proposal... Nothing was more important than getting to you to show you I'm all in. Please, Angel. Say you love me too. Say you don't love him. Tell me you're still mine."

"I'm not marrying Rowdy. I do love him. He's been by my side since you left. I can't ever repay his kindness or express how much his friend-ship means to me. But I'm not *in* love with him." I catch his eyes. "You understand the difference?"

"I do, and I'm relieved as hell to hear it."

"Good. But now I need you to tell me what you want. You said all the things you'd do for me. I can't ask you to sacrifice your happiness, your dreams, for mine."

"The hell you can't." His scowl creases his forehead, and I press my thumb to calm its edges. When he sees I'm still waiting for an answer, he concedes. "As you know, I never saw marriage and kids in my future."

Yep, painfully aware.

"But you've always made me feel things I've never felt before. The world comes alive when you're near, and it dies when you're away. I don't want to live in the land of the dead. I want to step into the light and live with you. Forever. I want to marry you so every motherfucker knows you're mine. I want to put so many babies in you, you'll be begging me to stop. I want it all a million times over, and then a million times more. But only with you, Angel. Only you. It's always, ever, only been you."

I don't know how I've managed to keep my tears at bay, but I can hardly hold them back on my next words. "I need to tell you something."

CHAPTER 37

MY HEART DROPS AT THE SIGHT OF HER unfettered tears and the fear in her eyes. "Can we get off the floor?"

That gets me a sniffled chuckle. "Not until I tell you what I need to."

God, she's scaring the hell out of me. "Tell me. Rip off the band-aid."

She worries her bottom lip, and I can't help but dislodge it with my thumb.

Leaning in, I whisper across her freed lip, "It's okay, Angel. You can tell me anything."

She keeps shaking her head, and when a sob escapes, my fear shoots sky-high.

Is she sick? *Fuck. What will I do without her?* "Please, baby, spit it out. What are you so afraid of?"

Her face morphs into an ugly cry, only my Angel doesn't look ugly at all. Her gaze meets mine, and my gut clenches, waiting for her to say what she's so afraid to. "That you'll leave me again," she finally confesses.

Fuck. Relief floods me. "I'm not going anywhere. There's nothing you can tell me that will make me walk away. Nothing. Ever." I kiss her forehead and breathe in her familiar vanilla scent. It's intoxicating and smells like home. "You hear me?"

She nods.

"Tell me," I encourage with a squeeze of her hands.

Her mouth opens, then closes. She takes a big, cleansing breath and shakes her shoulders and head, releasing the tension. "Gabriel."

"Yeah, Angel?" I can't stop my smile at hearing my name on her lips. It's been too long.

"When you left, you didn't leave me completely. You left something behind."

What? "No riddles. Not now. Plain. Short sentences only."

She takes my hand and places it on her stomach. As the words, "I'm pregnant," pass her lips, I feel the swell of her abdomen, and the same thought leaves my mouth and whispers across her admission, "You're pregnant."

"Yes," she answers what I already knew.

My eyes take her in with a different sight. Open and aware, I now see her face is a little rounder. Her eyes, tired. Her breasts, fuller. I scan lower and see hips widening to accommodate my child growing within, and under my hand, I feel her belly's tautness as it expands.

"Holy fuck." I sweep her into my arms and set her on the edge of the couch, urging her back so her head rests against the cushions. I push her t-shirt up and her yoga pants down so I can get a good look at what our love has done to my Angel.

"Gabriel?" She's hesitant and afraid.

"Shh." I kiss her lips. "Give me a minute."

When I can't see enough, I hoist her into my arms and bound up the stairs to my bedroom. I don't know where Rowdy is, but I'll be damned if I'll let him see her in the state of undress I'm aiming for.

Locking the door behind me and flipping on the light, I set my precious cargo in the middle of the bed. She eyes me cautiously, still trying to figure out my frame of mind.

When I'm done, she'll have no doubts about me or our future.

Stripping her till she's in only her bra and panties, I take in the sight of her. "You're so fucking beautiful, Angel."

She blushes and sucks in a breath when I kiss up her leg while crawling up her body till I'm hovered over her baby belly that's more noticeable now that she's flat on her back. It's not much, but it's definitely not the way she looked when I left her two months ago. I did this to her. Our love did this.

I settle between her thighs and press my mouth to the swell above the top of her panties. I'm so close to heaven, but all I can see is my baby. *Our* baby. I close my eyes. My hands cradle our baby and place tender kisses from side to side. I say a silent prayer for the health of our child and my woman, *let nothing I do cause my Angel another moment of pain.*

With moisture clouding my vision, I look up to find her watching me in awe, her tears running free. "I'm devastated in the most profound way that we've been granted this gift—*you've* given me this gift. I've hurt you so deeply over the years, and I'm so fucking sorry, Frankie." I move up her body to settle at her side, wrapping her in my arms. "I'm all in, Angel. I'm all yours if you'll have me."

Have him? Does he not know me? He offered himself up on a platter, granting me every wish I ever had for myself, except it's a hundred times better because it's with him. My bobblehead in full motion, my lips pressed together to sequester a sob, all I can do is give him my eyes and hope he can see the truth.

His smile is warm and indulgent as he presses closer, nuzzling into my neck. "I've missed you, Angel." His hand skims my waist and up to my breast, squeezing ever so lightly.

My head swims with the idea of having him inside me again, and my hormones have me pressing into him, racing for the finish line before we've even begun. With a hand on his arm, I pull him closer till he's nearly lying on top of me. "I haven't—" I shake my head in embarrassment—"since you've been gone."

His heated gaze searches for my meaning. "You haven't had sex?"

I shake my head. "No, but that's not what I meant."

He scans my body pressed into him, his thumb running across my sensitive, beaded nipple through my bra. "Haven't come?" His gruff tone is making me wet.

"Uh-uh, but God, I want to." *Need to.*

His tender reverence as he takes me in and absorbs the idea of me abstaining in his absence brings a tender smile to his lips. "Fuck," he whispers against my lips, a soft press before he pulls back. "Let's remedy your ache."

"Yes," I mumble into his mouth as his lips return to mine.

It's a slow kiss, with an undercurrent of unrequited desire that's been building for months. As I'm about to break free of the riptide, he breaks our kiss instead. "I haven't been with anyone either, Frankie. I couldn't—didn't want anyone but you. Only ever you."

His confession has a moan escaping as I sink my fingers into his hair. Our lips meet in desperation, a clash of forces coming together—like the universe becoming one again. With a little prodding from me, his caress roams lower, my hips guiding him as I tremble with need.

His tongue breaches my lips as his hand deftly slips below my panties. He groans when he finds my want more than apparent by the moisture coating my needful place. His string of curse words and dirty promises has me begging for mercy by the time he slips his fingers inside me, pulverizing any ideas I had about surviving without this man in my life, by my side, over me, inside me.

"Unhook your bra. I need my mouth on your tits," he hurriedly commands, not releasing my mouth or slowing the thrusting of his fingers when I arch up to reach the clasp at my back. Once freed, his heated gaze blazes a trail over my breasts. "Fuck, Angel." He locks on me. "I don't know how knocking you up made your tits any more glorious, but fuck if they aren't."

I don't get a chance to respond before his mouth is on them, kissing, licking, sucking. "Oh, God." I nearly come when he pulls my nipple in deep and teases it with his teeth.

"Not God, Angel. Remember?"

How could I forget? "Gabriel."

"That's right. Only me. Ever. Only. Me."

This man and his words, his touch, his passion. I think I've died and gone to heaven.

"Not yet, Angel, but I'm working on it," he answers what I didn't mean to voice.

His mouth teases my breasts as his fingers bring me closer and closer to the edge, but when he whispers against my mouth, "I need to be inside you," I come so hard I swear moisture pours out of me, and my cries deafen my hearing, leaving me shaking and crying with relief in the arms of the man I love.

I love him.

I haven't told him. Somewhere deep inside, I fear this is all a dream, and he'll come to his senses and remember he doesn't want a happily ever after with me. The high from the blessedly overwhelming orgasm he just gave me fades with my reality check.

When a man shows he has no mercy, you should believe him.

CHAPTER 38

STANDING TO GET NAKED, I WATCH MY ANGEL go from pure bliss to saddened certainty of whatever her inner voice is telling her. Barefoot, shirtless and my jeans undone, I lean over her, hands planted on either side of her head. "Don't listen to your doubts, Angel." Her shocked expression has me grinning. "I know you. I know the men in your life always let you down in a big way." I sit on the edge of the bed, running a hand down her body to rest on our baby. "I know I've fallen in that piece-of-shit category, but not anymore." Our eyes meet when I look up from where my hand rests. "I love you, Frankie. I always have. I pushed you away with my asshole ways to save you from my broken ass." I shake my head, knowing I need to lay it all out there. "But I also kept myself from you out of fear. You represent all the things I was afraid to want. Like yours, my father was a…" I don't really want to get into his sins. "I don't know anything about being a father or a husband, but I'm willing to give it my all with you. Not only because *you* want it, but because *I* want it too."

"What if you change your mind?"

"Not happening. You know once I commit, I don't give up."

"Black or white."

I press my smile to her unconvinced lips. "I'm looking forward to exploring the gray with you." Nose to nose, our eyes lock, and the love I have for her soothes that ache in my chest I always felt when she was around. "I came back for you, Angel. I didn't know about the baby, but now that I do, I'm still here for you. The baby is a bonus, not the prize. *You* are my prize, my grand championship title win, my now, my tomorrow, my forever after."

Her worried eyes glisten with new hope, and a smile spreads across her lips, lighting her up. "I love you, Gabriel."

Jesus, fuck. I gasp and squeeze my eyes shut, never expecting those words to carry such a punch.

I'm tense and shaking, reeling from the words I never thought I'd hear when a soft hand caresses my cheek and warm lips press to mine. "I love you." Kiss. "I love you." Kiss with a slide of her tongue teasing my lips. My tension fades and my cock returns to life. "I love you."

Her hands grip my shoulder, demanding I reduce the space between us, so I do. Her mouth is back on mine, coaxing mine open, where she breathes into me, "I love you, Gabriel Stone. You may have shown me no mercy all those years you were trying to keep me away. But now that I have you, I'm going to love you with no mercy." She kisses me hard and deep, forcing her words down my throat, and I groan, gripping her tight and kissing her just as intensely.

Though I'm panting and ready to fuck her into tomorrow, she pulls back. "You hear me?"

Her stealing my line makes me chuckle. "Yeah, Angel, I hear ya."

Finally naked, I carefully situate myself between her legs, my weight braced on my forearms bracketing her shoulders, her head captured in my hands. I kiss her slow and easy, taking my time. I wanted to fuck her. Now, I want to make love to her with the soundtrack of her confession of love echoing in my head.

When she's squirming, begging me with her body and plaintive cries, I enter her gradually, inch by inch.

"More, Gabriel," she pleads.

"I want to love you, Angel." I kiss along her jaw, flexing my hips, casually going deeper each time.

She grips my ass and tightens her legs around my hips. "Love me next time. Fuck me *now*."

We lock eyes. "You sure?"

"Yes, I've missed you. I need you to show me you missed me too."

Her words hit me hard. She needs my passion, my pain, my longing for her, my wanting to love her so hard she can't walk for a week. "But the baby?"

"Survived a fall down the stairs. He's good."

"He?"

She shrugs. "Or she."

She? A girl? The weight of being a father to a girl seems so much heavier than a boy. I know boys. Girls? They hold the mysteries of the world. What would I teach a girl? *To stay the fuck away from boys.*

"Gabriel?"

"Yeah, Angel."

"Fucking, remember?"

"Yeah, baby, I remember." I put my thoughts of fatherhood aside and take the time to appreciate how my Angel's body has changed.

Sitting up, I pull her legs over my thighs, raising her ass off the bed, giving me a perfect view of her fuller tits as they bounce and the shape of her hips as they accommodate the life hiding within. I thrust harder, the idea of getting her pregnant again driving me deeper each time.

I grip her tits and squeeze her nipples, teasing and twisting. She nearly bows off the bed with a, "Yes!"

I swear I've never been this hard or this turned on. The idea of being inside her fueled every jerk-off session for the past five years—including the last two months, but the reality of feeling her wet, tight heat around me again has me ready to explode. I pound in deep with a swivel, making her mewl my name.

She braces her hands against the headboard, giving her leverage to push back with every thrust. She fights to keep her eyes open and locked on me. Her mouth, open with streams of sighs and moans, feeds my hunger. With one hand playing her tits like a master craftsman, I slide the other one down, dipping it low to wet my thumb with her juices. The feel of her excitement makes my spine tingle with the need to come.

Fuck, not yet.

Rubbing my moistened thumb over her clit has a stream of cuss words flying out of my girl's mouth. I'd smile if it wasn't so fucking hot hearing my Angel be so dirty.

"You gonna come for me?"

"Mm-hmm."

I sacrifice the feel of her tits to brace myself as I lean forward, my thumb still rubbing her into a frenzy. I need her mouth when she comes. But first I need her eyes and ears on me. "I'm gonna love you like this every day of my life, Angel. Deep and hard, or slow and easy. You're gonna know you're my one and only. Ever only you. Every. Fucking. Day."

"Gabriel!" Her face contorts, letting out a scream as she squeezes me and comes, her entire body racked with convulsions.

She doesn't let up. I start moving again, chasing my own release but rubbing her clit to keep her gripping me like she never wants to let me go.

Never let me go, Frankie Angel.

A few more strokes and I burrow in deep, barking out my own release to the heavens as she comes again, crying and clenching me so fucking tight.

"Love you so fucking much," I whisper in her ear as I catch my breath, resting my head on her shoulder, careful not to put my weight on her or the baby.

"Forever." Her whispered reply has my eyes glistening and my cock twitching.

"Forever fucking after."

CHAPTER 39

I'D LIKE TO TELL YOU I WON MY FIGHT, BUT THE truth is, I have no intention of leaving this bed to actually make my fight. Killer González will win by default. And I'm perfectly fine with that. I have my Angel back, and no championship title could ever come close to beating that. I may hang up my gloves forever. The fire to fight has been diminished by the love of my girl.

Who would have ever thought a devilish beast like me could be tamed by an angel?

As if on cue, sleeping beauty stretches next to me, her tits slipping into view as the covers lower. My cock hardens, remembering the feel of her wrapped tightly around me. Blinking awake from a cat nap, she smiles when she notices me watching her—lusting after her. "What time does your plane leave?"

"There's no plane." A steam train couldn't drag me away from my Angel.

Her eyes narrow as she tries to find meaning behind my words. "You're planning on driving? It's too far. You'll be exhausted by the time we get there and in no condition to fight."

We? Love that so much. I prop up on my elbow and kiss a nipple that's begging for attention.

"Hey." She plants a palm on my shoulder and pushes me away, frowning and pulling the sheets up to her neck. "Talk, Big Man."

Big Man. Her love name for me she barely got to use before we broke up makes me smile and my healing heart leap. "I'm not leaving you. I don't give a shit about winning the title when I just got you back."

"Who says you have to leave me? I'm going with you."

"No, you're not. You're staying right here—in bed, with me—where I can love you, feed you, and watch our baby grow inside you."

"The things you say..." Her eyes water.

"Hey... Hey." I pull her close. I can't tell her not to cry, I know her hormones are running rampant. And hell, if I haven't given her enough mean words to last her a lifetime, getting used to me being kind is gonna take a while, I suppose. "Besides, you're in no shape to travel by plane or otherwise."

She rears back, looking at me like I'm crazy. "Says who?"

"Really? My pregnant woman who was puking up her guts a few hours ago says."

"Pfft." She dismisses my concerns with a wave of her hand. "I hadn't eaten."

I study her, not following the correlation.

She pats my chest and sits up against the headboard, tucking the covers below her arms. *Darn it.* "I guess you've never been around pregnant women, huh?"

"And you have?" I laugh, joining her, side by side.

"Point taken. But as a pregnant woman, let me tell you a few things." She starts counting on her fingers. "One: pregnant women throw up. Usually when they've waited too long to eat, or a smell turns our stomachs, or..."—she shrugs—"Honestly, sometimes I turn my head too quick, and it makes me nauseated. Two: I'm hungry all the time. Three: My nipples are sensitive as fuck, which leads me to four: I'm horny." She touches my leg, squeezing hard. "Like, all the damn time."

"The last three sound amazing." I'm sure I have a stupid smile on my face.

"Yeah, well, it also comes with the need to pee more than I drink, heartburn strong enough to burn down a city, and mood swings that have me crying or laughing so hard I pee my pants—so there's a lot of fluid either way."

God, I know she's not meaning to be funny, but she's cracking me up. I try to stifle my laugh behind my fist, but her last remark has me losing it. "It sounds like quite a ride." I sober as it dawns on me. "I'm sorry I've missed it all."

"It's okay. You didn't know."

Somberly, I pull her on my lap. "That's no excuse. I should have never left. But I'm here now, and I'm not leaving your side." I kiss her forehead, coaxing her to lay her head on my chest so I can hug her close. "God, I don't even know how far along you are."

"Fourteen weeks. I'm in my second trimester."

"I missed the first one." Nothing she says will reduce the guilt of knowing I left her alone and pregnant.

"Be glad you did. It was lots of puking and crying."

"And Rowdy helped you through it?" I already know the answer. He told me himself she cried a lot. But he left out the news of her being pregnant—with my baby.

She nuzzles into my neck. "I'm sorry it wasn't you too, Gabriel. But I'm glad he was here. I'm not sure I would be this sane if he hadn't been there. Heartbreak and pregnancy were a full bag to carry."

Jesus, fuck. I guess she's not trying to reduce my guilt, after all. Nor should she. I've been a dumbass.

I squeeze her tighter. "I'll make it up to you. Every fucking day of our lives. I promise."

She sits back, a hand flat on my chest, her eyes clear of remorse. "We needed that time. I needed time to find my way and realize if I had to, I could live without you." Her voice cracks, and a tear slides down her cheek. She quickly wipes it way before I can, but not before my heart that's been thumping away since I laid eyes on her skips and falters, breaking a little more for the pain I've caused her.

She pats my chest until she's able to continue, "You… You needed the time to realize you couldn't live without me. Your fear of having a future with me wasn't bigger than your fear of no future at all."

No lie. "Damn, my Angel is smart." Forehead to forehead, I give it up. "I promise you, here and now, I'm a better man for knowing you. I'm a better man for leaving you. And I sure as hell am a better man for coming back, begging you to love me and forgive me for all the shit I've put you through."

She presses her lips to mine. "Never forgotten. Always forgiven."

I kiss her back, but before I can get my tongue inside her delectable mouth, she bounces from the bed. "Now that we've got that settled." She picks up her phone and dials, putting it on speaker and tossing it on the bed as she starts to collect her toiletries from my bathroom. Her clothes aren't in here. She admitted earlier that while using my bathroom was practical, she couldn't sleep in here without me. It made my absence more painful, a fact I'm distracted from dwelling on due to her current state of nakedness. Not a bit of shame in her as I watch my baby mama move about the room.

When a familiar voice answers, I sit forward, glance at the clock and wonder what my Angel is up to.

"Cap?" She pauses her packing and sits next to me, her phone now on my lap.

"Hey, honey. How you feeling?" His love for her is apparent by the warmth in his voice. I guess he's not pissed at her.

And I just figured out he knew she was pregnant too. *Who else knows?* The thought is dismissed by the sound of my name.

"Gabriel has some crazy idea he's throwing his fight. I need help getting him back to Vegas. Can you help?"

"That depends." Cap's cool tone comes through loud and clear. He has a demand. I'm not sure I want to hear it.

She frowns. "Depends on what?"

"Gabriel?" He must have figured I was close by.

Here comes the demand. "Yeah, Cap."

"Did you get that thing we discussed dislodged yet?"

I chuckle and pull my girl close. "Yes, sir. My head is fully out of my ass, and I'm staring at my future as we speak."

"I'm glad to hear it, son." His voice has turned husky.

I can only imagine he's feeling the same emotions I am. Elated I've worked it out with my Angel and thankful I'm back in his good graces.

"Then, Frankie, you need to get yourself packed. Gabriel, Rowdy is downstairs waiting on you two to catch the next flight out." He surprises both of us with a game plan already in place. Typical Cap move.

"What if I hadn't called you?" Frankie asks.

"I gave him strict orders to give you lovebirds till 9 p.m. before banging on your door."

Her eyes meet mine, and a devious smile takes over her face. "So, we have a little more than an hour before we need to leave?"

Cap clears his throat. "I suppose so. Give or take."

Oh, I'm gonna give and take, alright. "See you soon, Cap." I disconnect the phone and text Rowdy to make some sandwiches for the ride to the airport.

My girl's gonna be hungry after I make her come a time or two.

CHAPTER 40

WAKING UP IN VEGAS THIS TIME ISN'T tarnished by the sadness I felt the last time I was here, or honestly, the last year here with Austin. I want to bound out of bed, but I've learned to take it slow in the morning, easing onto my side and getting the feel of the land—the state of my stomach—before making any rash movements.

A kiss on my shoulder has my heart jumping and my pulse thrumming, remembering who I'm here with, and why I'm no longer sad. "Morning, Angel."

"Morning, Big Man." I squirm into him, feeling his hardness pressed against my backside.

He smacks said rear. "Don't tease what you can't have." He kisses up my neck. "At least not until after the fight."

Some fighters abstain from sex before a major fight. Last night after we got to his hotel suite, Gabriel shared the news he usually stops a week before, but since he hadn't had sex since we broke up, he wasn't missing out on loving me. Until this morning. He draws the line on fight day, says he wants to use the desire he has for me to fuel his win and then claim me as his reward.

Naked, his impressively hard dick bobbing against his abs, he saunters to the bathroom. He smirks at me over his shoulder when he catches me watching. "Hungry?"

"Famished."

He chuckles and shakes his head, pausing at the door. "Check out the room service menu. I'll order when I come out."

I stretch over his side of the bed to get the menu.

"And, Angel?"

"Yeah?" I catch him checking out my ass as I look over my shoulder this time.

His heated gaze has my pussy clenching with want. "I promise fight days are the only day I'll deny you sex. All other days of the year, your wish is my command."

Sitting up, I wrap my arms around my bent knees, resting my chin on my arms. "I've gone without sex so much over the last few years, one day, now and again, isn't going to kill me." My revelation is honest, but maybe not what he needs to hear today.

He glowers and comes back, sitting on the edge of the bed, his arm wrapping around me. "You and Austin—"

"Rarely," I interrupt before he can say the words I'd rather not hear from his lips. "And at the end, even less so." Shame pinkens my cheeks, and I turn toward the window, unable to hold his gaze.

"Frankie?" He pulls me into his chest, allowing me to hide there. "What are you not saying?"

A sob I tried like hell to hold in has me shuddering in his arms as it escapes. "I'm sorry." I can't imagine what he's feeling, comforting me from the pain caused by another man.

"Hey." He captures my chin, urging my eyes to his. "You never have to apologize, be ashamed, or hide your hurt from your time with Austin." He wipes at my tears. "You were together since you were fourteen. You became who you are with him. I don't begrudge you that or expect you to act like being *with him* or *without him* doesn't have a lasting impact on you."

"Who are you?" I'm in awe of him. I knew Gabriel had more beneath his asshole exterior, but I had no clue he was capable of being so attuned to my needs, or so deep and profound in the way he supports me.

He chuckles with a tender smile and gently cups my cheek. "I'm the man who fell for you even when you were his. Who dreamt about you more than I had a right to. Who will always protect your heart even when it's been broken by another."

God blessed me with this man.

"Now tell me."

I nod, keeping his gaze this time. "I don't remember when it started—or really when it stopped. I imagine it was when he started seeing his current girlfriend."

His eyes narrow as he considers my words. "What stopped?"

"Vaginal intercourse." My chin wobbles, and I start to look away.

But he captures my face, holding me in place. "Meaning...?"

"Meaning..." *I can't.* I bury my face in my hands. I can't say the words and witness what might flicker across his eyes before he locks it away. I couldn't stand to see him think less of me.

"Angel." His hand caresses over my head and down my back. "I need you to look at me. I know it's hard. But I need you to know I'm here. I'm all in, and nothing you say will change that. But you need to look at me to know for yourself."

Lifting my head, I'm greeted with an encouraging smile. How can a man this big and beastly be so incomprehensibly gentle? My hand is on his cheek before I realize I've even moved. I brush his lips with my thumb. "I love you, Gabriel 'No Mercy' Stone." My tears flow and cloud my vision, but I don't stop. "Don't you dare think for a minute what you give me is not enough. I've never—and I mean *never*—felt as loved and cherished as I have in the last twenty-four hours since you came back into my life." I pull him closer, lightly touching his mouth with mine. "No one has ever made me feel so loved, not even Austin in our best of times. You remember that when you think you have nothing I need."

I grip his face in both hands, squeezing not too tenderly. "I need you. Only *you*. Exactly as you are."

His mouth crashes over mine, not a bit tender, either. His moan fuels mine as he lays us down, him on top. His weight is comforting and just enough to remind me of his power, his strength, but not enough to squish our baby. Palpable need rolls off us in waves. The smell of desire washes over me, and I wrap around him—all arms and legs—urging him to give us what we both need.

With a single thrust, he enters me. I arch into him in shock and elation at the feeling of being full of him again as he stills, fully seated. He grinds his hips before barely pulling out, and entering me again—over and over—again.

Desperation has me clinging to him, pulling him tighter. Our kiss never breaks. His tongue slowly loves mine into a rhythm that matches our hips and consumes our cries for more and answering moans. I shake with need and fear my heart will burst from the fierceness of each beat.

When the tingle starts at the back of my legs, I whimper and gasp for air. He groans in protest and chases my mouth, unwilling or unable to make love without every part of us being connected. The intensity of his need, uninhibited vocalizations, and the power of his thrusts send me to the heavens like a shooting star. Blindly, I come, my cries of pleasure like stardust trailing behind the eruption of my release.

My Big Man follows, comets bursting free when I feel the pleasure of his release deep inside, the throbbing stutter of his cock with each surge of cum. Every inch of my man is big and powerful, and the strength behind his ejaculation is no less so.

His breathing is heavy in my ear, his lips pressed to my neck. I hold and caress him until our breathing evens out and life comes back to his limbs. Slowly, he peels himself off me, sliding to rest at my side. His hand lingers on our baby's hiding place.

"Did I hurt you?"

A smile breaks free. "God, no." He did anything but hurt me. "Unless you call coming so hard you lose sight hurting."

His smile matches mine. "That good, huh?"

"Better."

His nods as his smile fades, his hand coming to cup my cheek. "He'd only come in the rear entry." He refers to Austin's preferred way of having sex with me at the end.

He gets a chin nod as my brow creases and my face breaks into an ugly cry. "He rarely touched me near the end, but if he did, it was only from behind and, like you said, rear-entry style. He avoided my vagina like I had the plague. It never dawned on me why. I thought there was something wrong with me."

"Angel," his voice cracks, and I clear my eyes in time to see a tear slide down his cheek."

"I don't know why he stayed. It's obvious now, he wanted to leave a long time ago. I guess he was hoping I'd break up with him."

"But you did. I remember he came running after you."

"He did. Making more promises he would never keep. They were all lies. I don't even know how far back they go. Two years for sure." I swipe at his damp cheek, meeting his gaze. "I have two things to say, and then we need to stop this sad-fest. Okay?"

"Yep."

"One. I'm not really crying over him. I'm embarrassed to tell you these things that are so private, really only the two people inside a re-lationship should know. Yet it really isn't even that. It's the shame of it. Feeling so unwanted. Putting up with it for too long. The humiliation runs deep."

"I can see that." He grips my chin tightly. "But hear me when I say I see the strength in you for trying for so long, for taking so little and giving so much. I don't see shame or embarrassment. He humiliated *himself* by cheating, by his lies. Not you." He presses a kiss to my swollen lips. "I'll never cheat on you. I'll never use your body for anything but worship. And I promise to never lie to you." He moves his head from side to side. "Well, unless it's for a good reason, like to hide a surprise." He holds up his hand like he's taking an oath. "But other than that, it's all truth between us."

"I think I can live with that." I grab his hand and hold it over my heart. "Two: I feel so bad we broke your fight day rule."

He rolls to his back and lets loose a belly laugh. "God, Angel, I'm not." He links our fingers, still holding his hand to my chest. "Sex with you is spectacular. Always has been. Always will be. The testosterone rush will keep me going all day until we can do it again tonight."

"You sure?"

"Positive." He kisses my cheek and rolls out of the bed. "Now, I've got to piss and get some food in you before you feel the need to worship at the altar of the porcelain god."

"Yes, please feed me. Besides, there's only one deity in this room I'd kneel before."

He stops in his tracks. "You mean me, right?"

I giggle. *Lord, since when do I giggle?* "Yeah, Big Man. I mean you."

His toothy grin has me laughing again as he slips into the bathroom.

It's a heady feeling to be in his presence, to feel his appreciative gaze, his words claiming me with every syllable.

It's an amazing thing to be loved by Gabriel, my avenging angel. He deems himself the devil, but I see the purity of his soul, the integrity of his beliefs, and the strength it takes to come from nothing, expect nothing, yet offer up everything you have.

Yeah, I'm a lucky girl to feel the pull of his heart tied to mine.

CHAPTER 41

S ITTING ON THE COUCH IN OUR SUITE, MY KNEE
bobs with nerves as I wait for Grant and Emmy. The fight is hours
away, but Gabriel is getting ready to meet up with Cap, Coach
Long, and Jonah, leaving me in the capable hands of Rowdy, who arrived
a few minutes ago.

Gabriel's mom and sister are meeting us at the stadium. Our seats
are on the same row, but all of the guys are here too. So, I don't know if
I'll end up next to his family or in the middle of mine. It's Gabriel's biggest fight to date, and definitely the largest fight venue I've ever attended.

I'm nervous as hell. He's calm as a cucumber but still buzzing with
excitement, revved up, ready to fight.

He pulls me aside, sequestering me in our room. "You okay?" His
brow pinches together as he stills my hands.

"Yeah. Just nervous."

A quick kiss and a squeeze of my hands is all it takes to ease my
nerves. "I got this, Angel. Don't worry." He hugs me close, his nose buried in my hair. "You'll come see me once you arrive at the stadium, right?
I want to see you before I go out. Don't forget." His adamancy makes me
second-guess my opinion of him not being nervous.

There's no place I'd rather be, but—"I'll be there as long as you don't think I'll distract you."

He gives me a lingering kiss, his mouth confirming his words. He wants me there. "I've waited a long time to have you in my corner on fight day. I want to see you before the fight. I want to know you're sitting in my seats, reserved for my team, my family." His hand covers my baby bump. "You're my family now, Angel. You and our little one. I can't lose with you on my side."

I rest my head against his chest, saying a silent prayer for his safety. "Don't get hurt."

"I won't be the one hurting." He rubs my back, his mouth pressing to my temple.

Meeting his eyes, I grip the lapel of his suit jacket. "You show him *no mercy*. You hear me? Only I get your mercy. Not him."

He chuckles his response. "I hear you, Angel. No mercy. I got it."

I had my weigh-in for the fans hours ago after leaving Frankie in our suite in the capable hands of Rowdy. I left shortly after Grant and Emerson arrived, and I gave them grief for keeping the pregnancy secret from me. I understand where my Angel was coming from—she didn't want to sidetrack me from my goal of winning this fight. What she fails to understand is, fighting is no longer the most important thing in my life. She is. *They* are.

I can see how it might be hard for her to understand, since neither her father nor Austin managed to put her needs first. Rowdy, who'd only known her a few months, did what they couldn't. He put her needs and those of my baby above his own when he asked her to marry him. I'm sure he didn't see it as a great sacrifice. He's attracted to her, after all, but I don't believe he's *in love* with her. He loves her, and as Frankie pointed out, there's a marked difference. That difference is the only reason I haven't put my fist through his face.

If I had known she was pregnant, Frankie would have doubted my love for her over my obligation to our baby. A fact I'm quite sure Grant considered as well, and why he only spilled the beans about Rowdy's proposal and not the fact my girl was growing a bean of her own in her womb.

Changed and warmed up, Jonah rubs my muscles, keeping me loose as Coach wraps my hands. Jess, Sloan, Walker, Patrick, and Landry linger around the door keeping watch for my Angel and Rowdy. They'll take their seats when she does. I've tasked them with looking out for her, but I trust Rowdy to protect her as if she were his own, as he has been the last few months. I owe him a lot. More than I can ever repay.

When the guys start glancing my way and back down the hall, my heart rate picks up. I know my Angel has arrived. I can feel her in my bones. I always have. Always will.

"You gotta calm down, darlin." Rowdy pulls me into his side, facing away from the hallway where the fighters reside. "You go in there crying and shaking, you're gonna mess up his mojo. He's a tough motherfucker, but he was ready to throw this fight for you. You give him one reason to doubt your desire to be here, and he'll forfeit in a heartbeat."

"I know." I shake my hands, roll my shoulders, loosen my neck. I gotta get ahold of myself.

I've been to hundreds of fights. I've seen how Gabriel rules the octagon. He doesn't mess around unless he's feeling really cantankerous, then he'll play with his prey for a while before taking them down. He's undefeated. A fact I need to remember.

Tonight feels different, though. Immensely important.

"If you freak out, blame it on the baby. Don't say you don't feel well, as that will get him out of here even faster. But you know, hormonal and all. Emotional. Delusional. Crazy."

I whack his arm. "I'm not crazy and delusional."

He rolls his eyes. "I've doubted your sanity a few times over the past few months. It's a valid excuse."

He's ridiculous. "Whatever. Ready?"

He grants me a dimpled smile. "Always."

His hand firmly placed on the middle of my back, he guides me forward. Our backstage passes get the onceover before we're let in. The halls are cluttered with all kinds of people. My eyes wander to the ring-chasers, easy to spot by the lack of clothing, the abundance of cleavage, and usually hanging on or flirting with some fighter, no matter how big or small. They all start somewhere, but the bigger cards get more ring-chasers. I better not find any near Gabriel.

Rowdy walks right on by like he doesn't even see them. Impressive. I wonder if it's an act for me, or if he really doesn't roll that way.

"Not my style." He reads my mind.

"Glad to hear it."

As we pass a few doors with predatory assholes lingering outside, Rowdy pulls me closer.

When a guy looking like his ego is larger than his stature can support steps toward us, Rowdy puts up a hand with a one-word warning. "Don't."

Ego Dude stops in his tracks, glaring but not saying a word. Rowdy gives a good I-could-kill-you-and-not-break-a-sweat glare. It's an art form. He's perfected it.

Tension radiates off him, daring anyone else to make a move. No one does, but I feel a little dirty for all their eye-probing.

"Don't let 'em get to you, darlin'. Their bark is worse than their bite." He looks down at me with a wink. "They couldn't handle a firecracker like you."

I let loose a laugh, having no doubt he could. He proposed, after all.

My gaze falls to the other side of the hall, and I spot familiar faces coming our way. Sloan and Walker fall into step, escorting us the rest of the way. My guess is they spotted potential trouble and came to offer reinforcement. No doubt at Gabriel's urging.

Outside the door with Gabriel's name on it, the rest of the guys filter out, waving me through. No time wasted on greetings. Also, on Gabriel's orders, I'm sure. I step inside as Cap, Coach, and Jonah step out with mere nods of *hello*.

My eyes lock on Gabriel bouncing on the balls of his feet, dodging and swinging at nothing but the competitor in his mind's eye.

When he spots me, his movements slow as he rakes me from head to toe. I wore a dress, maybe a little too formal for a fight, but it felt like I should dress up for him. Make him proud to have me on his arm. Though, in reality, no one is going to see us together. It's not like I'm escorting him down the aisle to the octagon.

"Angel." His hands squeeze my waist, and his mouth crushes mine before I can respond. Diving in deep, he pulls me tight, pivoting so I'm hidden from view by the bulk of his body.

"Gabriel," I gasp against his lips.

"Fuck. You look incredible. I can't wait to get inside you."

A full body shudder in response has him pulling me closer, his hand gripping my ass.

"You saw me at the hotel," I remind him.

"Yeah, but against this backdrop, full of testosterone, your sexiness is amplified." He kisses my neck and whispers in my ear, "It's like you're full HD color in a black and white world."

My hands rest on his hard pecs, bulging by his state of readiness. I squeeze in admiration. He squeezes my ass in response, tweaking my chin to get my attention. "You want me, Angel?"

My breath catches. The sight of him all alpha, predatory, and ready to hunt is such a turn on. "Yes. Can I have you?"

He chuckles and nips at my ear. "You wet for me?"

I squeak my response, which only makes him chuckle more.

"I'm inconveniently hard for you, Frankie. I can't wait to get you back to our room.

"Me too." I squeeze my thighs together.

He notices, mistaking the movement for something else. "Use my bathroom. I don't want you going to the public restrooms if you can help it." He motions to the door behind me.

Being pregnant and having to go to the bathroom every hour or so, it's not a bad idea to take the opportunity to use what is surely a cleaner facility. I slip inside. Murmurs come from the other side of the door. I do my business and wash my hands, noting as I glance in the mirror, I look like a woman who's been thoroughly kissed and turned on by her sexy-as-hell baby daddy. The thought makes me smile.

I open the door to a hovering, hulk of man, looming in the doorway like he could barely stand to have it closed between us. "Everything alright, Angel?"

I press a kiss over his heart and finger his tattoos on each bicep, breathing them across his skin, wishing them to life. "*Loyal. Brave. True.*" I lay a kiss on the word *brave*. *Be brave, my Big Man.* I secretly pray.

"*Mercy is granted not earned.*" Another kiss on *mercy*. *May you have mercy for me but none in the octagon.*

He cups my cheek, his breath quickened by my touch, my reverence. "I love you." His kiss is soft and tender, reflecting his words.

"I love you, Big Man." I pat his side, laying one more kiss for luck in the center of his chest as my hand caresses his back tattoo. "Go kick some ass. Bring home the title."

"Done." He grabs my hand, calling Rowdy into the room. He looks over my shoulder. "No one touches her. Clear?"

"Understood," Rowdy answers with confidence, making me smile.

Gabriel nods. "She'll be there in a minute." He waits, watching. His eyes return to mine when we're alone again. "I'm gonna ask you something, and I need you to trust me and say *yes*."

I have no idea what he's up to, but I think I'd promise him anything at this point. "Okay."

"I'm going to win tonight, and when I do... You're going to marry me, tomorrow, in a chapel on the strip, not too cheesy, but still totally Vegas-style." His gaze holds me captive. His words take my breath, and his commitment brings tears to my eyes.

"Was there a question in there?" I tease, kinda wanting the girly proposal. I only intend on doing this once.

He smiles. "Not really, but if you need me to ask…" He kneels before me, my hand in his, his eyes glistening with love. "I love you, Angel. Marry me. Let me spend the rest of my life proving it to you."

I never thought I'd see the day Gabriel Stone knelt down before a woman, much less me. "Okay… Yes," I amend. "I love you too, in case you forgot."

"Didn't forget." His megawatt smile has my heart pounding and my body screaming for satisfaction. "Let's make this official." He slips a ring I didn't even see in his hulking hand on my finger.

I stare breathlessly at the large emerald-cut diamond on my finger. "Jesus, Gabriel." *It's incredible.*

Chuckling, he stands, kisses my hand. "You like it?"

"It's too much."

"You don't like it?" His frown replaces the smile he held a moment ago.

"No! I love it. It's… It's—" I grab his face. "Perfect." The light returning to his eyes is no match for my surprise and worry about the cost. He bought it. He picked it out. I'll gladly accept it and wear it like the blessed woman I am.

"Good." He fingers the band. "The rock in the middle is you." His eyes cast to mine before returning to the ring. "The… Uh… Smaller diamonds surrounding it are me—protecting you, holding you close, keeping you safe and cherished."

Oh my God. This man.

"The diamonds on the band are all our kids." His smile has my heart bursting with joy.

"It's a good thing we've already got one on the way then." I don't dare tell him there is no freaking way we're having *that* many children.

"I can't wait to get you pregnant again." His kiss is slow and lingering, only pulling away when a throat clears behind us.

"It's time."

My stomach nearly drops to my feet.

Gabriel nods to Coach, but his eyes are still on me. "I got this, Angel. No more worrying. Okay?"

"I know you do. Only, I'm not sure I can handle watching you get hit."

The tips of his fingers graze my cheek as his smiling eyes take me in. "Then I'll do my best to do the hitting."

I've seen enough fights to know it's impossible. I'll have to put on my big girl panties and be brave for him. "You got this."

"Yeah, I do."

One last kiss, and he nods to Rowdy. "Protect her like she's yours," Gabriel orders.

"With my life," Rowdy replies.

I turn on a wink, fake bravado in full bloom. I don't look back. I can't. He'd see the tears in my eyes.

"You did good, darlin'." Rowdy pulls me close as the guys flank me—Walker, Sloan, Jess, Patrick, and the new guy, Landry. Two in front, two in back, Sloan on my left with Rowdy on my right. My own person entourage, garnering stares and curious looks as we make our way backstage to our floor seats. They make me feel special, like I'm honored and cherished, and I suppose I am. These guys are my extended family.

My immediate family is growing in my womb, and I left my other half in the dressing room, getting ready to fight for our future.

Not just for a title. But for my hand in marriage.

It seems almost archaic, of times past.

But I know the truth. I'll marry him win or lose, for he's already won my heart, planted a seed inside me—literally—and promised a future I can't resist. A lifetime with him. My Big Man. My Gabriel Stone.

Loyal. Brave. True.

Let the best man win!

CHAPTER 42

"Y OU SAID YES, HUH?" ROWDY WHISPERS SO only I can hear.

"You saw? Or you knew it was coming?"

"I saw, but suspected it was coming. You two are inevitable. Soulmates." Rowdy's approval brings a smile to my lips.

I like that Rowdy sees Gabriel and me as I do now. I'm no longer afraid Gabriel will break my heart because he doubts his ability to love me. He doesn't doubt it, therefore, I don't doubt him.

"Does everyone else know?" I check out the guys as we make our way to our seats. Their expressions are stone cold and practiced to perfection. There's nothing like a death stare from a fighter who knows he can do damage. These guys mean business. Everyone else notices too as the crowded hall and walkway to the arena floor part, letting us pass without breaking formation.

Like Moses parting the Red Sea, only those who believe shall pass.

Only it's Gabriel, setting into motion all the cogs that fit into place perfectly, moving as one, revealing one revelation at a time, each building on the other, moving us to an ultimate destination. I don't know where that is, but if it means Gabriel is by my side—I'm all in.

"I don't know." Rowdy's eyes scan the crowd. His cool façade slips as the palpable excitement in the room washes over us. "This is incredible." His dimpled smile meets mine. "Thank you."

"For what?" I have nothing to do with him being here. He's earned his place.

"For everything. For giving me a spot on the Black Ops Team. For being my friend. For nearly being my wife." He winks on his wife comment with a suggestive wiggle of his brow.

Men. Total Neanderthals. "Cap gave you the chance. I just agreed with him."

"And if you hadn't?"

I shrug. He's right. Cap probably wouldn't have taken him if I didn't sign off. Cap sees something in me I don't quite understand. I study the fighters, look at their stats and medical records, and weigh their personality as a good fit or not. It's not magic—it's a gut feeling supported by facts.

"You've earned your place. Both on the team and in my life." I punch his arm to keep what could become a heavy topic light.

He doesn't even pretend to flinch. *Ass.*

His hand on my hip squeezes as he bends to whisper, "He's a lucky son of a bitch." His lips press to my temple. His next words leave in a rush as if he doesn't mean to say them out loud, "I had you for a minute, but I let you slip away."

The kiss. I remember. I seriously considered his proposal until the rush of the moment passed, replaced by panic and guilt.

My skin flushes, my eyes dart to the guys to see if they're paying us any mind. Walker's gaze locks on mine before jumping to Rowdy, then back to me and down to the ring on my finger. He gives me a quick wink and a nod before his stony demeanor falls back into place.

They don't understand the bond Rowdy and I share. The rock he's been for me when I pushed Gabriel out of my life. They've known me longer, but out of respect for Austin and Gabriel they'd never get as close as Rowdy has. He knew me first. That makes him more my friend than theirs. He helped me get on my feet again, literally helping me walk out of the hospital despite the staff's mandate I use a wheelchair. He held me when I cried over Gabriel. Then he held my hair while I puked more times than I care to remember—all because of the gift Gabriel implanted before he left. Rowdy held my hand when I wasn't strong enough to face my fears alone.

He gave me kindness without expectations.

He believed in me when I couldn't.

He offered me a future when I feared I'd have none.

No, none of these guys understand the strength of the man standing beside me. Strong enough to love me, knowing I couldn't love him back in the way he was offering. Strong enough to remain my friend as I plan to marry another.

Yeah, so much for keeping it light.

"You should watch what you say. You're getting ready to meet that son of a bitch's mother." I fight to keep my smile from wobbling for this man who's come to mean so much to me in such a short time.

Rowdy's eyes go wide. "Oh, shit."

We stop moving almost in sync when we reach a nearly empty front row section of seats. Rowdy and I gasp when we realize we have *front row* seats.

"Holy shit," I breathe out.

"You can say that again." His surprise gives him a boyish look, softening his strong features.

A few seats in sit two women I've met before, but have barely spoken to over the years—given my tumultuous relationship with Gabriel. I guess that's all about to change.

Rowdy grips my arm. "You're between me and Sloan. Say hello. Then we sit. It's almost time." His eyes apologize for the gruffness of his demeanor. He softens when he adds, "You can talk to them afterwards."

When I step between Jess and Patrick, they let me pass.

Cheryl Stone is a petite, quiet woman with dark hair and blue eyes like her son. But the resemblance ends there. It's hard to believe such a big guy came out of her. When she spots me, her face lights up. Popping to her feet, she wraps me in a hug. "It's so good to see you, Frankie." Her usually mousy nature is nowhere to be found. But she eyes Jess and Patrick cautiously as they take the seats beside her.

"It's good to see you too, Mrs. Stone." I introduce her to Jess and Patrick. Their warm smiles seem to ease her uncertainty.

"Hi, Frankie." Reese Stone's velvety voice draws my attention. Her quick hug reminds me how sweet and tentative she is. She's much taller than her mother, but still has her slender frame, dark hair and matching blue eyes. She's beautiful in an ethereal kind of way. I envy her lightness. Though her hair is dark like Gabriel's, she has an angelic quality, making her seem otherworldly.

"I'm so glad you came, Reese. It means a lot to him to have family by his side." That seems to warm something inside her. She's always looked up to her older brother by three years. But his worldly ways have skipped her. Her innocence is tangible and lies around her feet like timebombs. Innocence can only last so long. I fear her awakening will be tantamount to WWIII if Gabriel has anything to do with it.

Rowdy directs me to my seat, while he sits between Reese and me. I introduce them and watch as unexpected fireworks erupt.

Oh, Rowdy, don't fall for this one. She's off limits like you couldn't even begin to fathom.

I squeeze his hand and shake my head. He shrugs, smiling, and leans in. "Gabriel found his angel." His eyes plead with me to not take away his hope. "Maybe I just found mine."

"Oh, God." I pat his leg. *Not my battle to fight.*

Who am I to squash a man's hope in finding his own happily ever after? Not me. And not Gabriel, if I have anything to say about it. I leave him be to dig his own hole. It's up to him if it's a grave or a means to plant a seed that could flourish into something neither of them expects.

I smile at Sloan as he sits on the other side of me while Walker and Landry file in beside him. I wave at Grant and Emmy sitting on the other side of them. I assume the last two seats are for Cap and Warren, Cap's Vegas gym manager.

My attention roams around the arena as I take in its massive size in awe. It's nearly packed. Gabriel's bout is the last fight of the night. I didn't look to see how many came before his. I only know his is the main event, and I'm filled with warmth and pride knowing he's made it this far. He's worked his ass off for this and deserves every accolade bestowed upon him.

When the music changes and the spot lights go crazy shining around the arena, the audience erupts in cheers and screaming fans. They might be cheering for Killer González for all I know, but my heart is racing for one man and one man only.

As we rise to our feet, Gabriel's fight song, "Bawitdaba" by Kid Rock, blares through the sound system. Rowdy grabs my hand and nods to the silhouette of man eating up the space around him as he steps from the shadows and into the spotlight. My gaze zips to the jumbotron above our heads. Gabriel's fierce glare from under his brow as he looks up with his chin down, sends tingles down my spine. He's ready to devour, and it looks like Killer González is on the menu this evening.

As the world goes crazy around me, my focus narrows, only seeing my man making his way down the aisle to pass right by our seats. When he nears, his ferocious gaze locks on me as if he knew right where'd I'd be and that I'd be watching. Of course he did.

My pulse pounding to the beat of the music in anticipation, I bite my lower lip. His eyes drop. His nostrils flare, and then he kisses his fingers sticking out of his fingerless gloved hand, says something I can't make out, and raises his fist to the heavens. All the while, his eyes never leave mine.

When he passes, he looks back over his should, his head low. Eyes on me, he winks and mouths, "Wife." His smirk is gone as soon as it appears. Then he's all business, looking ahead, bounding up the stairs to strip down to his tight-fitting shorts, flexing and spinning for all the world to see his avenging angel tattoo on his back and a muscled body, sculpted to perfection.

The crowd goes crazy, and I nearly pass out.

CHAPTER 43

MY ANGEL IS HOT AS FUCK SITTING IN MY row with my mom and sister near and my guys surrounding them. My pack is strong. My mojo is on fire. And my destiny is in my grasp.

In the octagon, I bounce on my feet, shaking my arms to stay loose as I watch my girl out of the corner of my eye. My body responds to her heated gaze as she tracks my movements. I punch out puffs of air, calming my cock, and draw the blood to where it's needed. But damn, my woman is gonna feel me tonight.

The current champ makes his way to the octagon. I don't grant him the privilege of my eyes, or the acknowledgment of his existence as they announce our fight, calling my name, listing my stats and then his. I hope he was listening, as it's the last time they'll say he's *the current reigning and defending heavyweight champion.*

After tonight, those words belong to me.

I catch sight of my girl before the ref calls us over. She's holding her hands to keep from fidgeting. I know she's worried. I don't think for a second her worry is about my skills or ability to win. This is about the *what ifs* she has running in her head. It's not only me or her any longer. We've got a little one to consider. To look out for. To plan for. She doesn't want to do it alone. She will if she has to. She's a rock. But she'd rather not. She wants our family safe and sound as much as I do. And in the last six months, she's been in the hospital twice. She knows life can change in a split second. A fucked-up boyfriend. A fall down the stairs. A kick to the head. She knows unexpected things can happen when you least expect it.

I know it too.

But not tonight.

I'm here to claim my title.

Then grab my destiny by the balls by marrying my Angel.

The bell rings. I shake it all loose, charging before Killer even catches his breath and land the first of many blows he'll come to regret.

"Breathe, Frankie." Sloan leans over. "We made it through two rounds. He's doing great. By the numbers alone, if he doesn't knock him out, Gabriel is sure to win by a majority decision."

Rowdy joins our conversation, amped up and excited. "He's barely even gotten hit. He's taken a few on his legs and sides, but not a single punch or hit to the head or face. I've never seen anything like it."

"I told him I didn't want to see him get hit," I share as I watch Coach and Jonah work on him, feed him water, and talk strategy in the short break between rounds. I glance at Sloan and Rowdy when their excited chatter stops. "What?"

Rowdy laughs. "You asked him not to get hit?"

"No." Of course not. "He wanted to know why I was so nervous. I told him I wasn't sure I could sit here and watch him get hit." I look between them. "I've watched hundreds of fights, but tonight feels different."

"What'd he say?" Sloan asks.

"He'd do all the hitting, then."

They sit back, laughing. "I guess it's a strategy that's working for him." Sloan shakes his head in amazement. "That's near impossible, you know that, right?"

"Yeah, I know."

Rowdy squeezes my hand. "He'll be fine, Frankie. But if he does get hit, don't freak out. If you lose it, so will he, trying to get to you."

For some crazy reason, the idea loosens the knot in my gut and brings a smile to my lips. I'd love to see him climb over the fence—bypassing the gate altogether—and come to my rescue. Showing me he's just fine. I don't want him to lose. But the idea of him being safe by my side and no longer fighting is no small thing either.

I jump when the bell rings, signaling the beginning of the third round. Gabriel comes at his opponent like he's not even winded, getting him in a grappling hold and flipping him over, body slamming him like a sack of flour and leaving Killer splayed out on the mat. Gabriel bounces on his feet, giving his opponent time to get up.

Killer, on the other hand, is more than winded. He's bleeding from a cut above his eye and one on his cheek from a spinning wheel kick that nearly took him out in the last round. But it's the cut lip he received in the first seconds of the match that shocked everyone. Gabriel punched him so hard, his head fell back, and he swayed for a few beats before regaining his wits. For a moment, it seemed like Gabriel would win by KO with only one punch thrown.

Killer has been on the defensive ever since. Gabriel's offense is too superior to offset. It's only a matter of time. Gabriel is playing with him, biding his time before he goes in for the kill. I know it. The guys know it. Only I don't think it's registered in Killer's mind. He's about to lose his title.

Just when I'm starting to feel cocky, like Gabriel's got it in the bag, I catch his eye and instead of moving on, he locks on me. He doesn't see Killer moving in.

"Gabriel!" I holler as Killer lands a right hook across Gabriel's left cheek. My stomach twists, and I think I might puke. I punch out air through my mouth in quick bursts, trying to quell the nausea.

Rowdy grabs my arm. "Are you gonna be sick?"

I keep blowing air, shaking my head, trying to calm my racing thoughts and my body's base reaction. Out of nowhere, a blue emesis bag appears in my face. I glance at Emmy as she leans forward, sympathy showing all over her face. I can't believe she thought to bring a puke bag in case I needed it. *Thank you,* I mouth to her.

Rowdy rubs my back as my eyes land back on the cage.

Gabriel comes back from bouncing off the fence with a right foot push kick, knocking Killer off his feet. Gabriel shakes his head, still recovering from the blow Killer landed seconds before.

"No mercy!" I scream over the crowd. He needs to end this before he gets hurt.

The guys take up the charge and start chanting *no mercy*, getting louder each time. It's not long before our entire section raises up our call in one voice, "No Mercy!"

A wicked smile comes over Gabriel's face as he bounces on his feet, circling, and lands kick after kick, and knee strike after strike before taking Killer down with a choke hold. But Gabriel likes his power moves. He doesn't want this guy to tap out or simply pass out from lack of air. Gabriel likes his endings more dramatic.

Releasing Killer before he does pass out, Gabriel gets to his feet, circling.

Waiting.

Gabriel is winded but nowhere near tired. He could do this all night. But God, I hope he doesn't. I'm not sure I can take much more.

When Killer gets to his feet, Gabriel wastes no time.

A jab to Killer's chest throws him off balance.

Gabriel follows it up with a sweeping head-kick to Killer's jaw.

I'm on my feet screaming.

It's lights out for Killer.

He goes limp and falls back like he's gonna do snow angels—arms and legs sprawled.

Gabriel follows him down for a little ground and pound, but stops when he sees Killer isn't moving. Gabriel backs away, breathing hard, still bouncing, ready to continue.

The ref steps in. Killer rouses a few seconds later, but it's too late.

Gabriel won!

The crowd goes wild.

I can't even hear my own screams over the roar of the crowd.

Gabriel is WickedTuff's new heavyweight champion, the largest MMA organization in the US.

He wins by head-kick knockout.

Figures, my man doesn't do anything small.

CHAPTER 44

"**S**HE RIDES WITH ME." SHOWERED AND MY EYES locked on the closed door as if my Angel is gonna step through it at any second, I finish dressing.

Jonah quirks a brow. "That's a given."

"Alone."

"Nope. If you two get alone for even a minute, we won't see you for the rest of the night."

True.

"Give us an hour, then you two can sneak out." He pushes an ice-pack in my hands. "Besides, you need to ice, hydrate, and rest. You've got a big day tomorrow."

Speaking of. "Do you know where Cap is?" I press the ice to my cheek. Figures I'd have a bruised face for my wedding. I hope she doesn't mind.

"He and Emmy have everything handled. You're all set for two o'clock. Emmy will pick up Frankie at eleven."

"Noon."

He looks up, ready to argue, but decides against it. "I'll let her know."

"And, Jonah? I appreciate you being here these last few months, putting up with me, getting me to this point."

"Welcome." He grabs our bags and eyes me. "Ready?"

"Born ready."

He scoffs. "Cheesy fuck."

I shrug. "It sounded good in my head."

"It should have stayed there." He laughs.

When the door opens, my Angel comes off the wall where she's standing with my mom, sister, Rowdy and Cap. After I was declared the winner by KO, I only got to see Frankie for a second before the guys shoved me in the dressing room backstage, forcing me to shower—without her. Not my first choice.

I meet her half way. "You okay, Angel?" I saw the stress on her face after the fight. I heard her screaming for me to have *no mercy*. I lost my concentration for only a moment. But her and everyone else yelling and cheering for me got me back on track.

"Shouldn't I be asking you that?" Her hand feathers across my cheek where that numbnuts landed a blow.

"I'm good." I grip her waist and pull her closer. "Perfect now that I'm with you."

She leans into me, her breath tickling my neck. "Same."

"One hour, then we take our celebration back to our room." I link our fingers and guide her back to my family and Rowdy.

"Sounds good." Her sweet smile has me wanting to change our time clock to one minute instead.

I hug my mom and sister, leaving their safe return to the hotel in Rowdy's hands. Celebrating with a bunch of people is not their scene. I understand. Neither of them does well in crowds. I'm still shocked as hell they made it here tonight. It means more than either of them will ever know to have them see me succeed when my father told me I would never amount to shit. He was wrong about me—about all of us.

I notice the look on Rowdy's face when he eyes my sister. I pull him aside, arm around the back of his neck, maybe tighter than necessary.

Maybe. "Listen. I owe you for what you did for my Angel." I catch his eye as he pushes back, coming face to face. "I'll forgive you for kissing Frankie, but I will end you if you touch my sister."

He flinches as if my words put ideas in his head he wasn't even considering. He's a guy. I know what he's thinking. All. The. Fucking. Time. "Clear?"

"Clear." He glances over my shoulder and back to me. "This won't be the last conversation we have about this." He presses in, bold as hell. "Clear?"

My evil smirk doesn't even have him wavering. *Good for him.* "Look forward to it."

We head out, my girl under my arm, close by my side.

I feel like I can breathe again.

We stayed to celebrate with the gang for a grand total of fifteen minutes. The guys didn't seem to mind. They know what it's like after a fight. Even if I did win the biggest match of my career, I'm still one tired fuck. The only thing keeping me going is the adrenaline and the idea of burying myself deep inside my fiancée.

My fiancée. I like the sound of that. Too bad I only get tonight and a short time tomorrow to use it.

Frankie steps out of the bathroom, towel tucked in under her arms. She wanted a quick shower. I couldn't deny her. It gave me time to ice my face and the bruise on my side, and down a few anti-inflammatories.

I point to the cart. "I ordered some food, since I dragged you out of the party before we ate."

She moves toward me. "You didn't drag me. I was happy to come." She glances at the cart. "Whaddya get?"

"Steak and French fries."

Her face lights up like Christmas morning. "Oh, God. Steak sounds so good." Her hand aimlessly rubs her tummy. I don't even think she's aware of it. It's a beautiful sight, her standing there in my room, nearly naked and pregnant with my baby. It's a sight I never thought I'd see—I never dared dream. But fuck if it doesn't feel right, meant to be.

"Here." I hand her one of my t-shirts. I don't even hide my appreciation as she slips it on over her head and drops the towel to the floor. I discarded my suit the minute we stepped into our room, trading it for athletic shorts.

Settled on the edge of our bed, forgoing the dining room table for the portable table they delivered the food on, I pull her close and kiss her head, then remove the domes to reveal the steaming goodness below. "Eat, Angel. Feed our baby."

She giggles and bumps me with her shoulder. My ribs bite, but I'll never let her know. Besides, my girl giggling is a new experience. I've heard Frankie laugh through the years, but never giggle until this morning when she mentioned kneeling before me.

My cock hardens at the idea. *Down, beast, it's not time yet.*

We dig in. My girl moans around her first taste of the steak. I nearly lose it. I stifle my groan with a bite twice the size and chew more aggressively than necessary. I'm not sure I'll make it through this meal without her sitting on my cock.

Fuck. Now I'm fully hard.

"Did you notice the connection between Rowdy and Reese?"

Yep, that'll do it. My beast decides to take a nap, rest up for later.

"Yeah, I noticed," I grit through my clenched jaw. Reese is a can of worms I'm not sure Rowdy is prepared to handle. He may have the best intentions, but she's been through more than he may care for.

"And?"

"And I don't like it."

My Angel giggles again, her hand landing on my thigh, squeezing.

The beast takes notice.

She peers up at me. "I don't know the story there, and we don't have to talk about it tonight—"

"Ever."

The hurt in her eyes has me turning toward her, cupping the back of her neck. "There are things you don't know." I study the spot on her neck as I caress it with my thumb. She swallows, and I feel the effort like she's pushing down, hiding her feelings from me. That won't do. "I promise to tell you all of it… Soon."

She slips her arm between us, capturing the back of my head and pulling me down so we're face to face. Close enough to kiss. Close enough to devour. Close enough to see the compassion in her eyes. "I was going to suggest you get to know Rowdy before you dismiss what he has to offer."

Her grip tightens, and her chin wobbles, and damn if it does soften my heart to her request.

"He almost gave up his life for me. To take care of *your* baby. You *need* to give him a chance."

Unable to hold back, I take her mouth for too short a ride, but fuck if it doesn't feel like everything.

Breathing hard, I pull away. "Okay."

Her smile is endearing. "Just *okay?*"

Releasing her reluctantly, I turn to my food, determined to let her eat before I wear her out and she requires more fuel. She needs to start with a full tank. "Yeah, I'll give him a chance, but if he breaks her heart, I break him." I shove a piece of steak and few fries in my mouth, chewing, encouraging her to do the same.

She slowly moves back to eating, but not before whispering, "You broke my heart before you got it right."

Fuck. Me. A lump forms in my throat as I fight to keep my emotions in check.

She's right. I broke her heart before I figured out what I wanted. What I was capable of. The sad fact is I wouldn't change any of it, as she broke *my* heart too, and it was my heartbreak that got my head on straight.

Maybe what Rowdy needs is a road map to Reese instead of a road block.

"I hear you, Angel. I hear you."

CHAPTER 45

"ANGEL."

I open my eyes to the sight of Gabriel fresh from the shower, leaning over me. "Hey."

"Morning." He runs a hand along my face and into my hair. "Breakfast is here. You've got an hour before you need to be ready."

I blink and look around. "What time is it?" It's crazy bright in here. I must've slept in. "Ready for what?" I don't remember us making plans.

I swear his skin flushes. "To marry me."

"Oh, shit." I sit up, panic setting in. "But I don't have anything to wear."

He stills me when I try to get up. "Calm, baby. All you need to do is eat, clean up, and throw on some jeans and a t-shirt. Everything else is taken care of." He releases me and sits back. "Emerson said not to wash your hair, but to shave." He smirks. "The last part seemed a little personal to me." He pulls the covers down to reveal my breasts—I swear they look even bigger today. He's such a guy.

I direct his eyes to me. Smugly, he complies.

"She's just looking out for me." I smack his hands away as I hop out of bed, looking for his t-shirt I had on last night.

When I don't find it, I turn to see him holding it up by one finger. "Looking for this?"

"Yes." I go to grab it, but he pulls me onto his lap instead.

"I've got this fantasy of you sitting on my cock while you eat. Care to make your fiancé's fantasy a reality?"

"You said I only have an hour." It's not a *no*, but I can't be too eager. We've got a lifetime together. Besides, I haven't even peed or brushed my teeth.

He cups me between my legs and groans when he finds me ready. What can I say? I'm always ready when it comes to this man.

"It's called multi-tasking, Angel." He slips a finger inside me and nibbles my neck. "I have a feeling you'll excel at it."

I clench around him, more than willing to oblige. "Gabriel."

"Fuck, Angel. I'm not sure I can go all day without being inside you."

Yeah, he had me the minute he said *fiancé* and *fantasy* in the same sentence. "Give me two minutes." I rush to the bathroom to take care of business and text Emmy to say I may be a few minutes late.

A girl's gotta take care of her groom.

The sight of her on my lap, reverse cowgirl style, without even moving—I'm ready to blow. I swore I'd let her get at least half her breakfast in before I got serious about fucking her. We're sitting on the edge of the bed, like last night, and she's eating off the table our breakfast arrived on. Only this time, instead of her sitting next to me, she's on my cock, her legs on either side of mine. I've been playing with her tits enough to get her hips squirming. But when she leans back, her head on my shoulder, and guides my hand lower, I know my girl has had enough breakfast. She's hungry for something else.

I kiss her shoulder and up her jaw. "You done, Angel?"

"Mm-hmm," she sighs, her hand still covering mine as I start to tease her clit. Her hips shoot forward and back.

Christ. Jesus. Fuck. "You wanna ride or change positions?"

"Ride." Yet she surprises me when she stands up and pushes the tray away, flips around and reseats herself, face to face. "I want to see my fiancé when he comes."

Ah, fuck. This marriage talk is hot. I might have considered it sooner if I'd known—nah, she's the only one I could ever feel this way about. I want to get married because it's her. The only fucking reason.

"Gabriel?"

"Yeah, Angel." I grip her ass, sinking in deep.

"We gotta hurry." She caresses the stubble on my jaw. The want and adoration shimmering in her gray eyes has me hard as fuck. She kisses me softly, sucking on my bottom lip. "I want to look nice when I marry you, Big Man."

Gripping the back of her neck, I pull her down for a scorching kiss, only to give a reprieve to be sure she knows. "Francesca Angelique—soon to be Stone, you could marry me wearing my gym bag and you'd still be the hottest fucking bride ever in the history of time." I groan when her pussy contracts around me. "But I hear ya."

"You said my full name," she gasps like it's wrong, not allowed.

"I did." I try to ease her confusion. "I only called you Francesca all those years to keep a wall between us, but now there are no more walls, Angel. All the names I call you from here on out will be backed by love. Only ever love between you and me."

"Fu—" Her mouth crashes with mine before she finishes that one world response. I guess I got my message across.

I still the guilt trying to raise its wicked head for all the years I kept her at bay with nasty words. Instead, I kiss her harder, deeper. I have a lifetime to make it up to her.

We pick up the pace, my hands and hips helping her ride my cock like a rodeo champ. When she comes, I fall with her. This woman who loves me like I've never known. Who looks at me like I hung the moon just for her. Who's carrying my baby and holds my future and my heart in her hands.

My Angel.

My bride.

My soon-to-be wife.

"Holy fuck." I slam my hand over my mouth. Emmy giggles behind me. I quickly release my mouth, not wanting to mess up my makeup some nice lady spent the last twenty minutes doing. I'm in awe of this place I'm about to get married in, with its pillared, marbled terrace surrounded by flowers and lined by golden chairs.

We hear footsteps and deep voices coming around the corner.

"He can't see you." Emmy grabs my hand and drags me down the hall to the room I'm supposed to wait in until it's time. Which is now, like, in five minutes.

"Everyone is arriving." Emmy peeks out the door. "Oh, Gabriel looks so handsome." She quickly shuts the door. "No, you have to wait." She urges me back.

I fuss with my dress, not because I'm not happy with it, but because I'm nervous. "What if he doesn't like it?"

Emmy blinks at me like I'm an idiot. "You could marry him in the t-shirt I found you in a few hours ago, and he'd be a happy camper."

True. He did say he'd marry me in his old gym bag. "Thank you for this." I point to my dress, my hair, my makeup.

"Thank Gabriel and Cap. They're the ones who made a few phone calls to get the ball rolling. I only handled the finishing touches along with a handful of hotel staff."

A quick knock on the door has my heart jumping.

"It's time." Cap sticks his head in. "Damn, honey. You look beautiful."

"Thanks, Cap." I point to his black suit, black shirt, and black tie. "You look so handsome."

He smiles. "Maybe I'll get a date out of this."

"No doubt." I saw the way he looked at Gabriel's mom. I know a little about her history with her husband, Gabriel's father. He beat her. I'm not sure she could handle a tough, cantankerous guy like Cap. Except I know his heart is pure gold.

Lord help Gabriel if Cap decides to pursue her. I'm not sure Gabriel could handle both his mom and sister dating such virile men as Cap and Rowdy.

"I'm gonna go find my man." Emmy squeezes my hand. "Yours will shit a brick when he sees you. Don't forget to breathe."

"Yeah, okay." I haven't cried all day, but the closer I get to walking down the aisle, the closer I am to doing it.

Emmy slips past Cap as he steps forward. "You ready?"

I bite my lip and nod. "Cap, thanks for giving me away. It means—" The tears start. *Fuck.* I look up and fan my face.

He captures my hand. "Don't cry." He kisses my cheek. "It means the world to me too." Opening the door, he guides me out.

I slip my hand in the crook of his arm. "Let's do this."

"That's my girl."

When we step around the corner, "Falling Like The Stars" fills my ears, causing me to resume my fight to keep my tears at bay. My breath catches at the sight of Gabriel at the end of the aisle, chairs on either side filled with our friends and family. His suit and shirt match Cap's, except he's wearing a white tie to match my dress.

He waits for me at the pinnacle of the rounded terrace with a minister at his side. Each step feels like a lifetime, my nerves forgotten, my heart racing due to my excitement of making this man mine.

Forever after. Only. Ever. Him.

CHAPTER 46

WHEN SHE WALKED DOWN THE AISLE ON THE arm of Cap, I was struck at the significance of him in her life. I know he loves her like a daughter, yet him escorting her made it official. He's the only father she's ever had who gives a shit about her. It breaks my heart and heals it all at the same time, knowing Cap will serve that role for the rest of his life.

He'll be the grandfather to our children.

He said he saw me as a son. He'll have to settle for son-in-law.

Frankie and I said our vows, short and sweet, promising our devotion, faithfulness, and love eternal.

Our first kiss as husband and wife brought down the house with catcalls from our friends and blushing from my mom and sister. Yeah, PDA should be kept in check around them.

We've cut the cake. Had our first dance. And we both danced with our parents. Me with my mom. Her with Cap. We only made it a few turns before we switched partners. Neither Mom nor Cap seemed to mind.

A certain song I've been waiting for finally plays. Her eyes lock on mine within the first few notes. I hold out my hand, wanting her to come to me, but I'm not above going after her.

She slips into my arms; her hands rest on my shoulders, and I do what I've wanted to do every time she played this song—I grab her ass and pull her tight. "You've tortured me with this song for years. There's no more dancing alone, Mrs. Stone." I kiss her softly. "I'm your dance partner from here on out."

"I love the sound of that, *husband*." She smirks against my lips.

"And you, my *wife*, are sweeter than strawberry wine," I loosely quote the song, singing the rest in her ear as I hold her tight.

As the last note plays, she whispers into my neck, "Can we go now?"

"Fuck, yes." I grab her hand, turning us to face the private room we rented for a few hours. I whistle to get everyone's attention. "Thank you for coming. We love you all." I hold up our joined hands. "But the wife and I are leaving now."

Hoisting my bride in my arms, we exit to the soundtrack of their well wishes, claps, whistles, and a few dirty remarks I hope my mom didn't hear.

In our suite, after setting her on her feet, I take a second to admire my Angel in her dress. It hugs her curves and flows down her body like a waterfall of white fabric, shimmering when she moves. Her hair is pinned up with cascades of loose waves. "You look amazing."

"Thanks, you too." She fingers my tie. "But can we get naked now?"

God, I love this woman. You can dress up my Angel, but you can't take the dirty out of her. And that's just the way I like it.

"Fuck, yes."

It's a race to see who can get naked first.

She wins.

But really, don't we both win? Seeing her naked is no hardship as I lose the last of my monkey suit. And having her eyes on me as I do it, well, that's the icing on the gonna-fuck-you-all-night cake.

Once on the bed, I move to her side with plans to settle between her thighs and drill home as soon as humanly possible. But she's got other plans. Pushing me to my back, she straddles my hips, my cock nicely nestled against her pussy.

"Fuck, Angel you're so wet." I grip her hips and sit up, grinding her against me.

"I want to say something."

Fuck. Yep. Okay. I can do this. "Can I be inside you when you do? The beast needs his Angel, and my brain might just work if he's inside you."

Laughing, she pushes me back down. "You call your dick *Beast?*"

"That's what he said his name is."

Now she's rolled over in laughter. "He talks too?"

"Only about your pussy. Oh, and your mouth, your tits, and uh… Your ass. But he's discreet. I promise."

Composed, she squishes my face between her hands. "Gabriel, I think I love you more with every word leaving your mouth. You make me laugh. You touch my heart. You make me feel cherished and worshipped. I'm a lucky girl. And our baby is going to be a lucky boy or girl. Just don't talk about *Beast* with them."

My heart that used to be old and rusty has been healing the past few days. The moment she said *I do*, the last patch of dead skin sloughed off, and my heart beat like it never has before—free and hopeful. *She* did that for me. "You're killing me, Angel."

"Maybe this will help." She leans forward, reaching between us, and slides me home.

"Fuuuuck," I groan as if I've never been inside a woman before. And maybe I haven't. Not a real one. Not one like my Angel, sent from heaven to deliver me from hell.

On her knees, she rests her palms on my chest. "Something hit me today."

She rounds her hips, but I still her by gripping her thighs. "If you want me to listen, don't move." Maybe giving the beast what he wanted wasn't such a good idea.

Her knowing smile tells me she saw this coming. But whatever. I'm where I want to be. I'll listen to whatever she has to say.

"I've had a hard time getting over Austin."

Her already watering eyes have me sitting up. "Hold on." I maneuver so I can rest against the headboard. It's gonna be one of *those* kind of chats, and I need to be present for every second of it, and that means eye contact and being face to face. "Sorry. Go ahead."

Biting her lip, she gets lost in her thoughts.

I squeeze her leg. "Don't filter. Just tell me. Remember, I don't expect you not to be impacted by your time with him. I don't begrudge you that."

She rests her hands on mine, linking our fingers. "He lied so much, it's hard to know what was real about the last nine years, but here's a few facts I believe to be true."

Leaning forward, I kiss her mouth in encouragement. I'm all good with whatever she says. She's mine. Not his. I win.

"Austin promised me a happily ever after. He just never said it was with *him*."

"What—"

"He brought me to *you*. I wouldn't *know* you if it wasn't for my connection to him." She places her forehead against mine. "Secretly, unrequitedly, shamefully I've always had a thing for you. From the first moment I saw you, I felt a zing of connection. But I ignored it because of him." Her voice cracks, and I wrap her in my arms.

"I felt it too, Angel. Every fucking day. I felt it. I knew when you walked in a room. I could feel when you were hurt and when you were happy. I was such an ass to you because I felt it so deeply. I had to be sure we didn't act on it. You were his." We lock eyes. "I'm an asshole, but I'm no cheater."

"I know, Gabriel. I know. But there's something else."

Shit, there's more?

"The entire time he and I were together—nine friggin' years—we never once had a pregnancy scare. Not once." She kisses me softly before murmuring across my lips. "I'm with you one month, and I'm pregnant. *He's* with someone else and ends up knocking her up."

She places her hand over my racing heart and says, "It was always you."

"Jesus, fuck, Angel, Austin said the exact same words to me... *"Maybe it was always you."*

Her smile is blinding as a single tear skates down her cheek. "He was never my happily ever after. It was always you, Gabriel. Only. Ever. You."

Fuck. Me. "Only ever you, Angel."

As our mouths crash together and our bodies start to move—finally, our pasts and our futures click into place.

Every hardship, asshole move, and broken heart have brought us to this moment. To our joining, the merging of two souls, both broken and yet healed by the other. The baby in her womb, the outcome of our love, and proof of destiny stepping in, giving us both want we wanted but never expected.

Our one and only.

Our fucking forever after.

THE END

KB WORLDS

Want to keep up with all of the other books in K. Bromberg's Everyday Heroes World? You can visit us anytime at www.kbworlds.com.

The best way to stay up to date on all of our latest releases and sales, is to sign up for our official KB Worlds Newsletter here: smarturl.it/KBWNewsletter.

Are you interested in reading the bestselling books that inspired the Everyday Heroes World? You can find them here: www.kbromberg.com.

DID YOU ENJOY THIS BOOK?

This is a dream for me to be able to share my love of writing with you. If you liked my story, please consider leaving a review on the retailer's site where you purchased this book (and/or on Goodreads).

Personal recommendations to your friends and loved ones are a great compliment too. Please share, follow, join my newsletter, and help spread the word—let everyone know how much you loved Gabriel and Frankie's story.

AUTHOR'S NOTE

As I write this, I have to tell you my heart is breaking. I'm so sad to be closing the book on Gabriel and Frankie. I was excited to write their story. The two of them spoke to me so clearly from the beginning. Each word revealed more of their pasts, their heartache, and the obstacles they would have to overcome to find their happily ever after. I thank them for allowing me into their world and showing me their raw vulnerability of where they came from and where they ended up—together.

I'm so proud of them for making it.

For finding out a devil could, in fact, love an angel.

Here's to their… Forever. Always. Only you.

On a brighter note, I intended *No Mercy* to be a standalone, but having met the supporting cast, I can't imagine Rowdy and Cap not getting their HEAs, as well as many of the other Black Ops MMA fighters. How about you?

Subscribe to my newsletter to stay up to date on what's to come for Gabriel, Frankie and the whole gang in my new Black Ops *MMA* series.

ACKNOWLEDGMENTS

This is the first book I've written since losing my sister—my best friend—to cancer. It was a sad reality each time I realized I couldn't text her as things progressed or when I typed the last world. She would have been so happy—so supportive as she always was. Miss you every day.

Thank you to my husband and kids for your tireless support, for enduring endless nights of fast food dinners, and understanding when mommy works nights and weekends. I'm able to do what I love because of your love and support.

Thank you to my mom, her friends, and my friends who buy and read my books and try not to picture me when they read the sexy parts. *It's fiction, not a biography!*

Huge hugs and many thanks to my fellow authors (you know who you are) who support me in my writing journey, share on social media, newsletter swaps, and private freak-out sessions. Your support and generosity astound me. I am forever grateful.

To the bloggers, social media followers, reader group: Dana's Divas, and newsletter subscribers I thank you for your support, for sharing, liking, and commenting. But mostly I thank you for coming on this journey with me.

Thank you to my editor Tamara Mataya and my proofreader Krista at Mountains Wanted. You inspire me to grow as a writer, but let's face it, I'll never fully understand where the commas go. Fact. Consider it job security. Thank you for your patience and understanding of the English language—which apparently, I barely speak. Ha!

To Kristy Bromberg who probably gave me the best gift of all, the belief that I could write a story worthy of her *Everyday Heroes* series, that her readers would embrace me, and that I was welcomed into the KB Worlds fold, finding friendship and comradery within.

And lastly but definitely not least, to the readers, I thank you for buying my books, reading my stories, and coming back for more. It still amazes me I get to do this for a living, and you are the reason why. I am blessed because of you. Don't stop. Keep reading!

BOOKS BY K. BROMBERG

Driven

Fueled

Crashed

Raced

Aced

Slow Burn

Sweet Ache

Hard Beat

Down Shift

UnRaveled

Sweet Cheeks

Sweet Rivalry

The Player

The Catch

Cuffed

Combust

Cockpit

Control

Faking It

Resist

Reveal

Then You Happened

Hard to Handle

ADDITIONAL BOOKS BY
D.M. DAVIS

Until You Series
Book 1—*Until You Set Me Free*
Book 2—*Until You Are Mine*
Book 3—*Until You Say I Do*
Book 4—*Until You Believe*

Finding Grace Series
Book 1—*The Road to Redemption*
Book 2—*The Price of Atonement*

Black Ops MMA Series
Book 1—*No Mercy*
Book 2—*Rowdy*
Book 3—*Captain*

Standalones
Warm Me Softly

www.dmckdavis.com

ABOUT THE AUTHOR

D.M. Davis is a Contemporary and New Adult Romance Author.

She is a Texas native, wife, and mother. Her background is Project Management, technical writing, and application development. D.M. has been a lifelong reader and wrote poetry in her early life, but has found her true passion in writing about love and the intricate relationships between men and women.

She writes of broken hearts and second chances, of dreamers looking for more than they have and daring to reach for it.

D.M. believes it is never too late to make a change in your own life, to become the person you always wanted to be, but were afraid you were not worth the effort.

You are worth it. Take a chance on you. You never know what's possible if you don't try. Believe in yourself as you believe in others, and see what life has to offer.

Please visit her website, dmckdavis.com, for more details, and keep in touch by signing up for her newsletter, and joining her on Facebook, Twitter, and Instagram.

JOIN MY READER GROUP

www.facebook.com/groups/dmdavisreadergroup

STALK ME

Visit www.dmckdavis.com for more details about my books.

Keep in touch by signing up for my Newsletter.

Connect on social media:
Facebook: www.facebook.com/dmdavisauthor
Instagram: www.instagram.com/dmdavisauthor
Twitter: twitter.com/dmdavisauthor
Reader's Group: www.facebook.com/groups/dmdavisreadergroup

Follow me:
BookBub: www.bookbub.com/authors/d-m-davis
Goodreads: www.goodreads.com/dmckdavis

d.m. davis

SEXY WITH HEART
CONTEMPORARY & NEW ADULT ROMANCE AUTHOR

Made in the USA
Columbia, SC
26 December 2021